I0688816

Journey of a Soul

First, you must Believe.

Second, will you pass the Evaluation?

A Novel

1st in the series, The Nine Spiritual Gifts
"The Gift of Distinguishing Spirits"

Constance Santego

Published by
Editor: Ana Joldes
Interior Layout: Constance Santego
Book Layout: ©2017 BookDesignTemplates.com
Cover Design: Jennifer Louie
Soft Cover ISBN: 978-1-7772220-7-9
eBook ISBN: 978-1-7772220-8-6
Audio ISBN: 978-1-7772220-9-3
Created and published in Canada. Printed and bound in the United States of America
Ordering Information: csantego@gmail.com

Praise for Constance Santego
Journey of a Soul

"... a delightful read full of important reminders that we are not alone on our journey. Take a breath and believe you can."
–   Sage Lavine, Author of womenrockingbusiness.com

"I wish I read this before my dad passed away." – Jennifer, Toronto, Ontario.

"My God, Connie, this was a book!! I LOVED IT! I dragged it out because I didn't want it to end!! – Rosalie, Newman Lake, Washington.

"Very proud of you for wanting to make a real difference to so many people! – Colena, Lloydminster, Alberta

ALSO BY CONSTANCE SANTEGO

FICTION
(Novels based on actual events)
The Nine Spiritual Gifts Series:
   Journey of a Soul (Vol 1)

NONFICTION
The Intuitive Life, The Gift of Prophecy
Fairy Tales, Dreams and Reality…
   Where Are You On Your Path? 2nd Edition
Your Persona… The Mask You Wear
Angelic Lifestyle, A Vibrant Lifestyle
Angelic Lifestyle – 42 Day Energy Cleanse
Archangel Michael's Soul Retrieval Guide

SECRETS OF A HEALER, SERIES:
Magic of Aromatherapy (Vol I)
Magic of Reflexology (Vol II)
Magic of The Gifts (Vol III)
Magic of Muscle Testing (Vol IV)
Magic of Iridology (Vol V)
Magic of Massage (Vol VI)
Magic of Hypnotherapy (Vol VII)
Magic of Reiki (Vol VIII)
Magic of Advanced Aromatherapy (Vol IX)
Magic of Esthetics (Vol X)

Dedicated
to my Grandmother:
Thank you for teaching me
to believe in God!

The Nine Spiritual Gifts

The variety and the unity of gifts
In the New Testament my favorite story is "The Gifts."
Corinthians 1, Chapter 12, Verse 4-11
(Maybe a little differently worded depending on which Bible you have).

The variety and the unity of gifts.
There are many different gifts, but it is always the same Spirit; there are many different ways of serving, but it is always the same Lord. There are many different forms of activity, but in everybody, it is the same God who is at work in them all. The particular manifestation of the Spirit granted to each one is to be used for the general good.

To one is given from the Spirit the gift of utterance expressing **wisdom**; to another the gift of utterance expressing **knowledge**; in accordance with the same spirit to another, **faith**, from the same Spirit; and to another, the gifts of **healing**, through the same Spirit; to another, the working of **miracles**; to another **prophecy**; to another, the power of **distinguishing spirits**; to one, the gift of **different tongues** and to another, the **interpretation of tongues**. But at work in all these is one and the same Spirit, distributing them at will to each individual.
The New Jerusalem Bible

Preface

Any caring granddaughter would want to ease her grandmother's pain and fears.

Especially her fear of death.

When I started writing this, my Grandmother was turning ninety-three years old and had told me that she had a fear of dying. That each night she fears that she will not wake up in the morning, that today might be her last day here on Earth.

When I was a child, I went to church with her every Sunday. I remember her once talking to me about not being sure if she was good enough to get into Heaven, even though she knew she wasn't bad enough to go to Hell. We had talked about Purgatory and Limbo—this is where a newly passed soul waits for Judgment Day. At the time, I found this conversation very odd since she was a practicing Catholic.

My Gran is worried that she is not good enough to get into Heaven, but I believe that not knowing ahead of time if she gets to go through those Pearly Gates is her real problem. *By the way, I don't know a person more deserving to get into Heaven than my Gran.*

I believe it is time to tell my story, my encounters with the afterlife, angels, ghosts, and even demons. I believe that not knowing this information can cause unnecessary worry. Not knowing and staying in the dark is a choice, but knowing ahead of time could help your soul evolve.

I pray my story inspires you to prepare yourself while on Earth for your afterlife. Learning this essential message of crossing over and making sure you go through those Pearly Gates and into the love-light energy. Reading this may not only save yourself unnecessary grief, but you may save a loved one from an eternity of hopeless distress!

Open your eyes and Believe. . .

Journey of a Soul

Awaken to the spirit world,

for there lies your

gifts granted by Spirit.

Constance Santego

Fact:

All biblical references, science, and Tamara's (Constance's) personal ghost stories and teachings are real—*slightly changed to fit the character of Tamara.* This novel was written as a story inspired by Spirit to give you, the reader, a new perspective, a unique way to learn, and a new opportunity to empower your life. And when it is time, be assured that you will gain entry through those Pearly Gates.

All locations and characters other than Tamara are fictional, but coincidentally I had a hoot picking the New York City locations that my characters lived in. Truth be told, I haven't had the pleasure of being to the Big Apple at the time of this writing. But now that my characters are from there, I am going to have to go visit. It feels like home.

Prologue

"It's a fact that speaking about ghosts and spirits makes most people very uncomfortable. The thought that something that most of us cannot see, hear, feel, or know could exist amongst us. Ever wonder what a ghost does in the afterlife? Ever wonder what is waiting for you in the afterlife?" Tamara said as she walked onto the stage.

"Do you know that fear of death is programmed into our genetics? That we will do almost anything in our power to stay alive? Did you know that fear is formed as an automatic feeling in our reptilian brain as we are developing in our mother's womb? Fear is a natural animal instinct to stay clear of danger and harm."

Tamara slowly turned her head from one shoulder to the other, skimming over the many faces in the audience.

"Maybe we fear death because we are afraid of something evil. I am assuming that many of you were brought up with stories about the Devil. Is evil why we fear death so much? Or is evil why we fear ghosts and spirits so much?"

Tamara paused a moment for a more dramatic effect. She wanted the audience to have a moment of contemplation before she continued.

"There is physical proof painted on walls inside of many caves all around the world." She insinuated the grandness of the world by gesturing with the movement of her hand.

"Maxime Aubert, archaeologist, and geochemist used a technique he developed to date some of the paintings to at least 35,000 years old. For what reason do you think that our ancestors would paint a message on a cave wall?"

Tamara took a sip of water to give time for the audience to think. "Why did past generations think that it was so important to leave drawings of images and symbols for future generations to find? Have any of you ever wondered why?" Tamara could see some heads nodding.

"Personally, I am fascinated. I believe the drawings have been left behind for us to find so that we can receive a message, a lesson that we can benefit from, or maybe it is a warning for protection in the afterlife, such as the symbols inscribed on the walls of the Egyptian pyramids of the pharaoh's tombs."

Tamara took a long pause and closed her eyes for a brief moment. Then she asked, "Have you prepared for death? And, I do not mean your estate and finances."

With a bit of a smirk, Tamara asked, "I have a weird question for you. Does a rock fear death? I am asking because science has proven that rocks grow and change form. It's true. Many of you are wearing jewelry tonight. Go ahead and look at your diamonds, gold, and crystals.

"We are taught in school that rocks are not alive because they are not carbon-based. But coal changes over time and creates diamonds. Gold changes over time and creates different karats 10, 12, 14, 24. Even the point of a crystal in a geode will continually grow and become bigger with time. If something grows and changes form, is it not alive? And if we believe something is non-living, is it dead?" Tamara gave another pause for a few extra seconds after asking these insightful questions to the audience.

"Even though I have been told that ghosts are not real and are definitely non-living, it is in my professional belief as a medium that ghosts are real, and they do fear death. Trust me when I say it takes a lot of persuading to help a ghost move on from this world. To move away from all the human memories, experiences, and safety they had living here on Earth."

Tamara could hear quiet talking among the audience in response to what she had just said.

"I believe that one day soon, science will prove the fact that a soul emerges from 'the cocoon' of the human body and can choose to become a ghost or a spirit.

"Ask yourself this question, 'Where am I going after I die?'

"What happens to your soul if you end up somewhere you don't want to be? How are you going to get a message to your loved ones back home that you need help?"

Chapter 1

The memories appeared swiftly… as if the sun rising and setting were years passing instead of days.

A weeping mother.

Susannah Constantine gazed at her from across an aisle whose plush carpets ran red as blood. On the far side of the room, the woman stood facing her, motionless, solemn, her tear-stained face hidden by a veil. In her hands, she grasped a rosary, rubbing a bead as her lips moved silently. The stillness of death permeated the room.

"No," the woman sobbed. *"She's too young."*

Susannah heard the words as if they came from inside her head.

"Mom, why are you crying?" she called out, but her voice made no sound.

"Look for Grandpa. Say hi to him from me," the woman whispered. *Go to the light, Susannah, go into the light!"*

Susannah took a step toward her mother, but she could see the carpet twisting into a gust of wind, picking up velocity. Instantly she was caught twirling round and round as if she was in a relentless tornado tearing her away.

When Susannah opened her eyes again to see her mother, the room had become a speck in the solar system. There were wisps of energy like a cold winter's breeze, nipping at her from all directions. Her body seemed to have vanished, and in its place was a ghostly figure that flickered like a candle flame dancing with the air. Susannah could hear her name being called as if it were angelic echoes in a vast canyon of emptiness.

The darkness was getting brighter, and with every second, she could see more and more light. She was being drawn to the radiance as if she were a mesmerized moth. The luminous light was a magnet pulling her closer and closer. She could not escape.

Susannah was disoriented, and her memory was foggy. All she could remember was. . . *Try, try to remember*. As Susannah tried to focus, she noticed a faint glimmer. She tried to move closer, but her feet would not move. Looking down, she gasped, for she had no feet or hands, just a vaporous body that floated in the mystical energy.

As she looked up, the twinkle of light caught her attention again. The opulent sparkle of the gates was incredible. No mineral back home could create that shimmer. It was like imagining opalescent paint covering the pearl essence of an ocean shell under the most transparent blue water.

Now, Susannah could see the vaporous shadow of a figure standing just inside the gates. As she thought of the form, she instantly was there, lightly floating just outside the elaborately ornate gates.

The entrance was as magnificent as in any Hollywood movie. Silver and gold metal with carved designs etched into the surface. If one looked at the detail of the gate, there was an intertwined story engraved throughout the framework.

Between the spaces of the metallic bars, you could see in the distance the most luminously colored tranquil garden.

"I have never seen flowers as beautiful as those," Susannah called out. She pushed on the gates to open them, but they were locked. "Can you please open the gates? I want to come in," she asked the figure standing with its back to her.

The figure turned around and became opaque. It took the form of a man walking toward her, holding out his ancient hand as if expecting something from her.

"Who are you?" Susannah whispered.

In response, the man slowly turned his hand and brought it back to his side. He was strikingly beautiful and yet older than Susannah had imagined. Majestic, noble, ageless, like an everlasting saint. He had a stern set jaw, deep soulful eyes, and long silver-gray wavy hair that tickled his shoulders as he moved. Around his neck, he wore a thick pewter chain strung through an intricately designed vintage brass skeleton key.

Susannah sensed she knew him, trusted him. *But how? Why?*

He pointed now to a very rustic, thick padlock. Even Samson—the man with immense strength to aid him against his enemies and allow him to perform superhuman feats—even he could not break this apart.

Susannah noticed a glowing symbol carved in the lock, a burning cross with an "*S*" etched deep into the metal. *S? As in . . . Susannah?* "Is that . . . me?"

The man's face revealed nothing. *You do not believe; you may not gain entrance,* he sent the thought to her and silently walked away, disappearing into the garden as if he was never there.

"Wait, wait, please come back! How do I get into the garden?" Susannah yelled.

Without warning, she started being pulled like a particle of dust into a vacuum, deeper and deeper into the abyss. Her entire body vibrated intensely, and then, in the twinkling of an eye, she exploded into fragments of disheartened darkness.

Chapter 2

"Lexi, save me from them!"

The terror of hearing her dead sister's startling scream immobilized her. Lexi struggled to catch her breath as she tried desperately to awake from the horrific nightmare. Fear overtook her as she recalled her dead sister's voice.

She had dreamed that clawing at her sister's soul was a horde of dark and evil forms resembling giant ghostly moths, demons, and wildly dark energy-sucking creatures. They were grabbing savagely with outstretched hands—wanting to devour her as if she was their last meal. The worst horror movie could not portray the evil that was trying to steal her sister's life-force energy. Pulling the perspiration-soaked duvet aside, Lexi quickly got out of her king-size bed to escape the vivid images of those demons.

It was only a dream, she kept saying to herself as she went to get a glass of water from the fridge. *It's only a dream.* Lexi wasn't sure if that was Hell, but she knew it definitely wasn't Heaven.

It wasn't even twenty-four hours since she had last heard Susannah alive. *Why, God, why? How could you do such an unjust thing and take such a beautiful soul from this Earth, from me? She was far too young, only thirty-five. She had barely lived her life, let alone fallen in love and married the man of her dreams. She hadn't had the baby girl she always talked about having one day.*

Grabbing a blanket, Lexi curled up into the fetal position on her couch. There was no way she was going back to bed . . . with those demonic entities—real or not.

By midday, Lexi still couldn't shake the terrifying memory of the dream. Every time the nightmare and the sound of Susannah's voice crept back into her thoughts, they created an eerie feeling deep in her gut. *Oh, my god, this horrible feeling has to stop.* As the day progressed, she knew that this gut-wrenching feeling was not just because she was mourning the loss of her sister.

How was she supposed to go over to her mom's in an hour to help with the funeral arrangements? The dreadful feeling wouldn't go away. She tried to will the thoughts away by turning on the radio and playing loud music. Turning it up even louder . . . that didn't stop the terrifying voice screaming for help in her head. Not being a pill-popper, she went to the bathroom cabinet and took a couple of aspirin, for the pain was getting unbearable.

It was almost time to go to her mom's, but her head was killing her; the memory of the demons and dark entities grabbing at her sister was driving her mad. *Why? What does the dream mean? Are you trying to tell me something, Susannah?* She didn't know how she knew, but somehow, she knew that Susannah was in real trouble and needed her help.

Sitting on her couch, Lexi tilted her head forward and brought her hands up to caress her temples. *Oh, God, please help me. I beg of you to help me through this. If my sister, Susannah, is in trouble, show me a sign.*

As if by magic, a commercial came on the radio. Lexi heard the ending of it. . . "Ask and you shall"—*What did it say?*—"find." She didn't know what the commercial was really about, but it did bring an insightful thought to her mind . . . *to find someone who could help her.*

Knowing that she was supposed to be on her way to her mom's, she texted her that she would be running a bit late. *Taking care of Susannah's soul is more critical.*

Leaning back on the couch, she couldn't get the idea out of her head. *Who could help me with this dream?*

A moment later, a ridiculous idea popped into her head. She picked up her phone and googled "psychic mediums."

Scanning through the listings to see if one would jump out at her, but none did. Taking her time, Lexi started to read each person's website. It was so hard to decide. *Is this person legit? Are they just after my money? Will the person be able to help Susannah?*

Finally, she just took a breath and prayed up to God for help. *Please, help me find a person who can help Susannah.*

As she scrolled through the listings, a sentence caught her attention. ARE YOU SEEKING TO SPEAK WITH YOUR SISTER, MOTHER, OR ANOTHER LOVED ONE? *Yes, that is precisely what I want to do, talk to Susannah.*

Growing up Catholic, Lexi had never really believed in this stuff. Despite her faith, this horrible feeling of her sister's soul being tormented seemed worth the try. *What could it hurt?* She clicked on the link and called the medium.

A moment later, a lady's voice answered the other line, "Hello, this is Tamara. How may I help you?"

"Hi, I'm not exactly sure. I have this feeling that my sister is in terrible trouble, and it won't go away."

Tamara was used to these kinds of calls and asked, "When did she die?"

"Yesterday."

"I see. I am sorry for your loss," Tamara said, with sincere condolence in her voice. Tingles then started to run down her arms and legs; Tamara was getting a message from her angels that this girl's sister was really in trouble and needed her help, pronto. Deciding not to ignore or take the message lightly, she said, "Do you have time today to come in and see me? I have an opening around three if you can make that work." Tamara knew she would have to cancel her plans to go for a late lunch with her fiancé, but he was getting used to her work. Spirits came first.

"Oh yes, thank you! I can make that happen." Lexi wrote down the address Tamara gave her and said, "See you soon." She was scared to tell her mom what she was really doing, so instead, she texted her that she had a few more errands to run and would be over much later than she initially thought and would bring dinner with her for the two of them.

Her mom was the type of mother that liked to do everything anyway, so Lexi really didn't have much to do for the funeral arrangements but be supportive.

As she was still in her PJs, with only an hour to get dressed and drive over to Tamara's, she had to rush.

Chapter 3

℘ulling up to the address that Lexi had written down, she had to reread it to make sure she was at the right place. It was a brownstone, not an office building. *Yep, correct address*. Lucky for her, there was a free spot along the boulevard to park. Sitting in her car, staring at the townhouse, she had to wonder if what she was about to do was rational. Everything she was taught as a kid discredited psychics and mediums. It said in the Bible not to go to a soothsayer, augur or sorcerer, weaver of spells, consulter of ghosts or mediums, or necromancer—which is a practice of magic involving communication with the dead. *What am I doing?*

As she timidly walked up the stairs to the entrance, hesitant about knocking, lingering in the air was the most pleasantly soothing sweet and herbal fragrance. Distracting her for a moment as she looked around to see where it was coming from. She figured it was the purple flowers growing in a small container by the front door. As she looked closer to the planter, she noticed small gemstones strategically placed in and nearby the plant.

Lexi took a breath as the terrifying cry of her sister's voice crept back into her memory, *"Lexi, save me from them!"*

Just as she was about to get the courage to knock, a lovely lady in her early forties with the friendliest smile opened the door. Gesturing for Lexi to come in, Tamara said, "Hi, I'm Tamara. Come on in."

Tamara didn't look like what Lexi had expected to see. She was expecting someone dressed more like a gypsy, like what you would see in the movies. Instead, Tamara was dressed in black slacks and a beautiful blue blouse, with her dark hair curled and pulled back with sparkly barrettes. Pretty for her age.

"Hi. Thanks for meeting with me so fast. I don't know if it matters, but my real name is Alexandra, but everyone calls me Lexi."

"Good to know, but it will not matter for today," Tamara said as she led Lexi through the house to the reading room.

Entering Tamara's home, Lexi quickly glanced around, noticing that Tamara resided on the first two floors of the brownstone. It was a quaint older home in Brooklyn Heights, clean, tidy, and very tastefully decorated. Very modern for the age of the building. Starting to feel nervous and sick to her stomach, Lexi began to make small talk about how lovely Tamara's home was.

"Thank you. My grandparents on my mom's side bought it many years ago. I decided to move back to Brooklyn and look after it for them when they had to move into a retirement center."

Tamara knew how anxious and edgy her clients were the first time they came to see her. Lexi seemed even more so. Not only could she feel it in her own body, but she could also see it in her visitor's subtle body language—her heartbeat was racing, her breath was faster, her eyes seemed glossy, and she was saying trivial things to cover up her fear.

Tamara knew that these were all normal reactions when a person was about to communicate for the first time with the spirit world. It wasn't quite terror, but fear of some type.

Tamara had been doing single mediumship sessions and group seances for over ten years. She still had a hard time with the fact that when someone asked her what she did for a living, her answer was, "I speak to the dead." Growing up, her grandmother could read teacups for fun, but she knew of no one else in her family who had a biblical "spiritual gift." Tamara's gift became undeniable one day at work. It had started with a mild headache, and then the next thing she knew, there were voices in her head wanting to talk to the person she was doing a reflexology foot massage on. Bizarre how life goes. One moment everything is ordinary and mundane, and then the next, you become an outcast believed to be practicing witchcraft.

Tamara was looking at a tall and skinny woman in her mid-thirties. Lexi reminded her of a modern-day dark-haired Twiggy. She noticed that her hair was pulled back and styled in a sexy bun. And her eyelashes were so naturally dark, thick, and long that she didn't seem to need make-up. At first glance, you might think she was a lawyer with the brand-new expensive business suit that she was wearing. But the sparkly high heels didn't quite go with the lawful image.

Trying to calm Lexi's nerves, she said, "There are three suites in the building beside this one. Come, have a seat over here at the table. I made some chamomile tea. Would you like some?"

Still feeling nervous and that she might have made a mistake, Lexi said, "Yes, that would be nice. Thank you," and sat down on an antique wooden chair that matched a round table situated in the center of the small dining room. *Susannah would have loved this set,* she thought to herself. Covering the table was a bright and beautiful cobalt blue velvet fabric. Without hesitation,

Lexi caressed the soft material. She had expected a crystal globe placed in the middle like you would see in a psychic gypsy photo, but there wasn't one. Instead, to her left was a charming clear vase with a lit aromatherapy candle, giving off the same scent as the flowers outside. *Lavender.*

Tamara placed a teacup beside Lexi and sat down opposite her. "In a moment, Lexi, I am going to have you call upon your sister. It's kind of like making a phone call. She has a choice to answer you or not. We must always be respectful and courteous of the spirit world."

Disappointed, Lexi unconsciously crossed her arms. "You mean, there is a chance that we will not be able to talk to her today?" *I knew this was too good to be true. She is after my money.*

"Yes, but that rarely happens," Tamara assured her. "Let's begin. I would like you to place your hands facing down on top of mine, please." As Tamara took Lexi's hands in hers, she continued, "Take a couple of deep breaths, breathing in all the way down to your toes, and exhale. One more time. Slow deep breath . . . in and out."

Hope flashed in Lexi's eyes as she followed Tamara's instruction and took a few deep breaths. It seemed to calm her nerves even more than the scent from the candle.

Tamara had her eyes closed as she said, "Alright, Lexi, I would like you to say out loud, three times please, your sister's full name."

Coincidently, at the same moment, Lexi said her last "Susannah Grace Constantine," the flame of the candle danced wildly. Holding her breath, she knew something had just entered the room. *Oh, my God, what did I just get myself into?* It sent a spooky tingling feeling throughout her entire body. Terrified of defying God, she unknowingly squeezed Tamara's hands. Her heart started to race, and panic started to take over her body.

Tamara broke the tension by lightly but confidently squeezing back, holding onto Lexi's hands like a mother would when her child is scared. "Lexi, I am going to describe to you who has come. It is not a female. It is a man. Tall, he's about six foot one inch tall, with darker hair, with a little gray at the sideburns. Athletic build. Well-dressed, but I think he wears something different most days. Um, I think those are scrubs like a doctor would wear. And, I am getting the first letter of a name, an 'M.' Does this make sense to you?" Tamara opened her eyes to look at Lexi while she answered.

Lexi nodded in shock. Tears suddenly started to roll down her cheeks, her voice seemed to vanish for a moment, but she was able to force out, "Yes. That's my dad, Marcus, that you just described. He was a surgeon. He died four years ago. How could you know that he wore scrubs?"

Tamara was used to the shivers that ran up and down her back, arms, and legs when a spirit presented itself. This was the cool part when she knew for a fact that she had just conjured a spirit. Not answering Lexi's question, she said, "Lexi, I am confused because your dad came and not your sister. We called for your sister, so he shouldn't have come unless something is wrong. Give me a moment. I need to ask him some questions." Tamara shut her eyes as she went within to seek the answers.

Letting go of Tamara's hands, wide-eyed and very anxious, Lexi shifted to the edge of her chair and waited. *My dad, she contacted my dad. This can't be happening. But she knew things about him that there was no way she should have. I haven't even given her my last name, so she couldn't have googled anything . . . Dad. . . is it possible?*

Tamara opened her eyes and forwarded the message from Marcus. "Lexi, your dad said that you were right. Susannah never made it into Heaven. He said she is lost in a place called the Void."

Lexi took a deep breath to try to believe what she was hearing. "Wait, I don't understand. What and where is the Void?"

"I am sure you have heard about ghosts?"

"Of course, in movies."

"Yes, Hollywood does a great job of portraying them in a gas or vaporous state. I'll try to make this as simple as I can. To save your sister, I need you to believe."

"I see. You need me to believe in ghosts," Lexi said, shaking her head in disbelief.

"Yes. New science is starting to lean toward the belief that ghosts and spirits are in a state of energy made up of both matter and anti-matter. Lexi, before I can tell you what the Void is, I need you to understand the most significant difference and concern between a ghost and a spirit."

"I don't understand. Why is it so important for me to know this?" Lexi was having a hard time believing that ghosts and spirits were real.

"It is important because whatever you believe becomes your reality. If you believe they exist, then they do. If you don't, then they don't."

"Let me get this straight. What you are trying to tell me is that I have to believe in ghosts?" Lexi was staring at Tamara, dumbfounded.

"Lexi, I want you to imagine that you lost a metal ring in the garden, and you cannot find it by looking. So, you dig around in the dirt, but you cannot feel it either. And of course, a metal ring will not make a noise that you can hear, so you cannot hear it, taste it, or smell it. But you 'know' it is there, somewhere. You know that you lost it. It has to be there. You've tried finding it yourself, but with no luck, so you decide to get something that can detect it."

"Okay, that would make sense, like a metal detector." Lexi had to use one once at her mom's house to find the main water shut-off in the front yard. The cap to it was metal, and some grass had grown over, hiding it.

"Exactly. You needed to use something that could detect what you could not. This is similar to sensing or detecting a ghost or spirit. You need to use something else than your five senses to detect them."

Lexi was still trying to make sense of what Tamara was trying to say, but she understood that she needed something else to detect a ghost, which made sense.

"Lexi, you need to use your sixth sense or extrasensory perception in this case."

"Are you kidding me? Am I supposed to believe that I have a sixth sense?" Lexi was shaking her head again in disbelief.

Tamara ignored the body language and tone of voice that Lexi was using. "Now, the difference between a ghost and a spirit is that a ghost is a person who died, and for whatever reason, is now stuck to a person, place, or thing on Earth. The problem with being a ghost is that it has no freedom to move very far on its own. Whereas a spirit is free, like your dad; he can move from place to place and through many energy levels or dimensions." Tamara looked directly into Lexi's eyes and said, "Lexi, the seriousness of this is that your sister is neither a spirit nor a ghost. It was her lack of belief in the afterlife that sent her into the Void. She is considered a lost soul."

Lexi was almost in tears. "You are still not making any sense. I don't understand." She knew by the look on Tamara's face that something was seriously wrong.

"Lexi, your sister, is in the Void, and I can't contact her. I can only talk to spirits in the spirit world or ghosts stuck here on Earth. I am sorry. This has never happened to me before, where a soul went into the Void. I have had it where a soul did not want to talk, and so nobody answered when I called. I have had a dark entity pretend to be the person I was trying to contact, but this is new. If it wasn't for your dad confirming your dream and giving us this urgent message about your sister, we wouldn't ever have found her."

"So, what do we do now? We have to help her! I cannot rest knowing Susannah is in that horrible place!"

Tamara answered by saying, "Give me another moment. I need to ask my spirit guides how to help us with this situation." Taking another deep breath, Tamara shut her eyes again.

Lexi was spellbound by watching Tamara's face change as she meditated. It seemed as if Tamara almost disappeared for a split second, her face vanishing and then coming back. *Great, now I am starting to hallucinate.* Lexi tried to calm down by taking a few more deep breaths.

A few seconds later, Tamara opened her eyes, smiled, and said, "I called upon Archangel

Michael. He is an angel in Heaven that helps me when I have a client that has a lost soul or a dark entity attached to them. I help him send the soul home. And from what I can understand, it's you, Lexi. You are the only person who can save your sister and bring her back so she can ascend into Heaven."

Dumbfounded, Lexi just stared at Tamara. She may as well have said that she could ride a dragon and save the world. It all seemed overwhelming. *I am the only one who can save my sister, but how?*

Tamara stood up to end the session. "Lexi, I wish I could have magically helped you today, but your situation is going to need what some people would call a miracle. Before I can help you, you are going to need to believe. Not just in Heaven, but I need you to believe in the spirit world."

"Uh, huh." *What the. . . Spirit world. Demons, ghosts, and spirits, yep, I have officially lost my mind.* Being polite, Lexi said, "Thank you. I knew the dream meant something, but I didn't expect this. I think I am more confused now than before I came."

"Lexi, I am giving a speech this Tuesday night at seven. It will be in a hotel right here in Brooklyn. Please come. I will be speaking about the spirit world. I think it may help you to understand more about spirits." Going into her purse, Tamara pulled something out and passed it to Lexi. "Here is a ticket to get in."

Taking the ticket from Tamara, Lexi turned to leave and then stopped abruptly. "I forgot to pay you."

Tamara shook her head. "No, not this time. Not until I can receive the answers from my angels and guides about how to help you save Susannah's soul. Then you can pay me." And with that, Tamara showed Lexi to the front door.

Chapter 4

Completely forgetting to pick up dinner, Lexi drove to her mom's house. She loved this old house; it held so many happy memories. It was home to her for most of her life. Her parents had bought the house thirty-five years ago. One year after, they were married and just in time to welcome their first child into the world: a daughter named Susannah. At the time of the purchase, her dad was finishing his medical degree, becoming a general surgeon; he would start his fellowship the following year.

Lexi's family's home was in the part of Brooklyn famous for its incredible Christmas lights display, Dyker Heights. Her parents said they had bought the house because it was a rare find in New York City to have a two-car driveway and a big private backyard. But Lexi believed they bought it because it was prestigious and pleased her grandparents on both sides. A three-story home, with its ten-foot-high ceilings, parlor, library, massive kitchen with butler's pantry, grand ornamental fireplace in the living room, five bedrooms, and let's not forget the servants' quarters.

A single tear escaped and trickled down Lexi's cheek as she pulled into the driveway and put the gear shift into park. She just sat in her car, motionless. The last couple of days' emotions and memories were now coming to the surface, spilling over. As she sat there in the car, she imagined herself growing up in this house with Susannah. All the late-night laughing fits when they thought their parents were asleep. Crying on Susannah's shoulder when her first boyfriend in sixth grade moved away. What she would give even to revisit the days when they argued and fought over stupid things like secretly borrowing Susannah's shirt and returning it ruined. Who knew grass stains didn't come out?

Her heart ached for Susannah so badly that she thought it was going to break. *What am I going to do? Who is going to be there to listen to my adventures or my woes?* Lexi was sobbing uncontrollably now. *Oh, my God, Susannah, I don't want to live without you. You were my best friend.* Her lip started to tremble. *Growing up, we told each other everything.* Another great sob escaped her lips. Not being able to control her feelings, she covered her face with shaking hands.

Wiping away her tears, Lexi didn't know how much time had passed since she parked the car. *Here I am going on about poor me, boohoo. Here you are, Susannah, being tormented by demons and stuck in the Void. What if Tamara is right, and I am the only one who can save you, Susannah? How is it possible that I am the one who can help you? Why me? I don't even believe in this mumbo-jumbo.*

In a zombie-like state, Lexi got out of her car and entered her mom's house. She couldn't bring herself to tell her mom about what she did that afternoon. How do you tell a mother that her daughter didn't make it into Heaven and is stuck in a place called the Void?

So, instead, she just made small talk and listened to her mom chat about the funeral arrangements.

The evening passed quickly enough. Lexi didn't remember what her mom had quickly whipped up for them to eat, how long she was at her mom's, or driving home.

Lying there in her bed, Lexi started thinking about work. Almost a year ago, she had accepted a ridiculously insane salary as the head designer of a very famous fashion design company in the city. It had created the perfect opportunity for her to move out of her mom's house and rent a Fifth-Avenue luxury apartment. The excuse she told her mom was that she could now safely walk to work in minutes instead of trying to get through rush-hour traffic each day, which was true. The truth was that her mom kept insisting that she find a husband and start a family. At the age of thirty-four, Lexi hadn't found Mr. Right yet. She had gone on many dates, but the men who were attracted to her seemed to want a trophy wife, and her desire to become a famous fashion designer was higher on her priority list than parading around on the arm of a high-society know-it-all. Yes, many of the men were considered catches and were very successful in business and their careers, but her heart sought after a man who would encourage her to continue working and advancing in her career.

Lexi wished she were more like Susannah. Susannah knew what she wanted and didn't care what anybody thought about it, including her parents. Unlike Susannah, Lexi stayed living at the house to please her parents. They had very old-fashioned beliefs and even held a debutante ball when she was of age. A young lady doesn't leave the house until she is married was her dad's belief. And even after her dad died, Lexi felt it was her responsibility to stay and help her mom.

Reminiscing about the past brought back more memories of Susannah, who loved to come over and visit and even helped her renovate the apartment. Susannah was ecstatic when Lexi moved out and started living on her own.

Lexi smiled at the memory of the two of them. Susannah had a flare for dramatics and decided Lexi's apartment needed to reflect the brilliant creativity needed for her sister to become a famous fashion designer. They repainted the walls with bright and lively colors, different in every room—sophisticated, sexy, and breathtakingly beautiful.

Lexi loved the nights when Susannah came back from a business trip. She would come over and share her incredible stories about working for a high-end antique collector. Her adventures of traveling to faraway places and finding the most fascinating and rare pieces of furniture, paintings, ornaments, and even jewelry at auctions and estate sales from all over the world.

Lexi closed her eyes and wished that she had known to cherish every second that they shared together. *If I only knew how little time we had left together.*

Sleep came eventually.

Lexi awoke abruptly, screaming out loud, "Susannah, where are you!" She had another disturbing dream; this time, Susannah was lost, and Lexi couldn't find her. Sitting up in bed, panic-stricken, and looking around frantically for her. Susannah was nowhere to be found.

Getting out of bed, Lexi remembered that today was Friday, and tomorrow was Susannah's funeral at the Hawthorne Funeral Home.

The memory of yesterday's experience with Tamara came rushing back. *Oh my God, I have to stop the funeral! We don't know where Susannah's soul is.* Scrambling out of bed and getting dressed, Lexi knew what she had to do.

Chapter 5

Nestled in bed, Reverend Edward Julien Hawthorne slept with the blankets covering everything up but his nose. The light creeping in through the darkened early-morning clouds as he awoke abruptly from the loud and rapid pounding coming from his front doors.

Throwing the covers aside and quickly putting his arms through the sleeves of his robe, he hurried downstairs toward the entrance. "Yes, yes, I am coming!" he hollered, trying to lessen the noise as he got closer.

The funeral home stood on a hill, silhouetted against an October gray and sodden sky. This building had also been Edward's home for all his thirty-eight years. His father and grandfather before him had lived and worked here in the family business as morticians.

Banging on the big wooden doors of the building that would hold her sister's funeral service tomorrow, Lexi yelled, "Reverend Hawthorne, you must let me in."

Lexi had never been to the Hawthorne Funeral Home before today. She had driven by the cemetery over the years and heard about it from her dad when he was alive, but it was much more impressive in real life. She was looking at a large two-story building with a chapel attached to the left side of it; it even had a steeple, topped with a spire. The chapel looked like it could hold a couple of hundred people.

The surrounding funeral home grounds were more like a park than a cemetery, with thousands of trees and many ponds throughout the rolling hills. Located throughout the grounds, you could see several famous monuments, mausoleums, and wooden shelters. Lexi was impressed with the craftsmanship of the buildings. The three she loved best were one resembling an Italian villa, one in a gothic revival style, and another resembling a Swiss chalet. She was bewitched with the magnificently detailed headstones, crypts, and sculptures. There was one sculpture in particular that caught her eye. It was an impressive larger-than-life, hand-carved marble statue of Saint Michael the Archangel. His outspread wings made his form seem massive. He held in one hand a drawn sword, and in the other, he held scales. She could see that he had captured a demon whom he was standing over with one foot, keeping it at bay.

An epiphany came to her as she stared at the statue. Lexi just realized that the scales represented "virtue and sin." Weighing the outcome of a soul's life, whether good or bad, the scales decided where the Archangel would take them in the afterlife. In this case, the scales revealed the deadly fate of the demon's destiny.

Even though Reverend Hawthorne was in great shape, he almost fell on his derriere as Lexi pushed her way through the now unlocked front entrance. Regaining his balance, he looked at his watch to read what time it was. 6:00 am. "There better be a good reason, Alexandra, for you to have woken me up so early."

Barely noticing Reverend Hawthorne's dark hair, blue eyes, and height of six-foot-four inches, Lexi blurted out, "The service cannot proceed as planned. Something is wrong."

Gesturing for Lexi to follow him, Edward turned around and walked into a rather large and finely decorated office to the right. It was the same room his father and grandfather had used to meet with their clients to prepare the documents needed to have their loved ones' viewing or memorial service.

Not following in their footsteps by preparing the deceased for burial, Edward went to seminary school instead and became an ordained minister. He loved the peace of mind that he could create for a person who had lost a loved one. He had a gift to speak profound, insightful, reflective, and divine words.

"Reverend, I know this is going to sound crazy. But my sister Susannah is in serious trouble," Lexi said, with as much poise and control as she could muster through her anguish. "The dream I had the night Susannah died was more than your typical dream. It was a traumatic nightmare. Susannah is lost, confused, and being tormented in the afterlife. No, it wasn't a dream at all—it was a cry for help from Susannah! Reverend, she urgently needs help before her body is put into the ground for eternity!"

Even though Edward was only a few years older than Alexandra, he took an insightful breath. He prayed up to God for the words and wisdom needed at that moment. "Alexandra, we cannot cancel the funeral. Your mother has gone through hours of planning to have your sister's funeral be the way she envisions. I do not think what you are asking is reasonable. Think about how your mother would feel. Alexandra, you are in distress about your sister's passing, that's all. It was a terrible accident, and you two were so close."

Frustrated, Lexi started to pace back and forth in his office. "You don't understand. She is not in Heaven!"

"I see." Reverend Hawthorne felt sorry for Alexandra. He knew all deaths were traumatic for the loved ones left behind. Each person goes through a series of emotions, usually uncontrollable. The five stages of grief they call it in seminary school: denial, anger, bargaining, depression, and acceptance. He was not sure where Alexandra's outburst fell into the mix.

"Reverend, what happens to a soul that does not go to Heaven?" Lexi asked as she sat down in one of the two big wing-backed chairs on the opposite side of the Reverend's dark cherry-stained desk.

"Lexi, it is very uncommon for a soul not to enter Heaven. Alexandra, you must understand, for that to happen, the person couldn't have had any belief whatsoever in an afterlife. No belief in God, Buddha, Allah, or any other spiritual name. No belief in any religion of any kind. No belief in angels, Jesus, or saints," Reverend Hawthorne said.

"I know you think I am being emotional about losing my sister. But I know deep in my heart that Susannah is in trouble, and I need to help her." Saying it out loud, Lexi knew without a doubt that her sister was in trouble. "Let's say that Susannah didn't have any belief system before she died, that she was an atheist. If she is lost, how can I help my sister?"

"Lexi, this is not an easy task. You cannot just believe for her, and poof, she is in Heaven. It doesn't work like that. I pray that you are just having an emotional moment and that you do not believe that your sister didn't make it into

Heaven. If you still feel this way after the funeral, we can meet up next week, and I will help you deal with these emotions."

Standing up, he showed her to the front door. "See you tomorrow, Alexandra. Try to get some rest and sleep as much as possible. The worst of it will be over soon. Time heals."

Closing the door, Edward shook his head. *Oh, mighty God above, please grant me patience and understanding in times of need. Help me to help those that are not in their rational mind. Show me the way to help Alexandra believe that her sister's soul ascended into Heaven. Amen.*

Chapter 6

Susannah Grace Constantine, I remember my name. Why can't I remember what happened and where I am? Think! What was the last thing I can remember? Mom, yes, she was crying. Why was she crying, and why did she say, look for grandpa, say hi to him from me? Go to the light. Susannah, go into the light.

As Susannah remembered her mother, instantly, she was there. She could see her mother still crying, sitting on the edge of her bed, with her head bowed and her hands covering her face. Still beautiful in her early sixties, Olivia Sarah Constantine was in anguish over the horrific car accident and sudden death of her eldest daughter.

Looking around the room, Susannah felt at home. On the wall above her mother's bed was a portrait of the family, commissioned five years ago. Her distinguished-looking father was dressed in a well-tailored navy-blue suit, and her mother, born Olivia Sarah Austin, a widow now, was sitting on a stool in front of her father wearing the most elegant soft blue dress. On either side of her parents stood Lexi to her father's right and Susannah to his left.

She loved her younger sister so much. Only a year apart, they grow up more like best friends.

Noticing that her mother had stood up and started to move toward her, Susannah was shocked when she walked right through her as if she were a ghost. *How could that be? Did my mother die? I can't remember her dying.* Confused, she followed her mother into the hallway and down the stairs to the living room. There were people, family, and friends, chatting. Some were crying, and others were laughing.

Puzzled by what was going on around her, she stood there frozen in the hallway, looking around at her family and friends gathered in the living room. Coming toward her was her cousin Ted. She smiled at him. *Wow, he has grown into such a handsome young man.* Then she started to freak out as he walked right through her. Susannah started to run to her loved ones in the room, yelling at them, "This is not funny!" But nobody responded. Yelling louder, she screamed, "Stop this at once!" But nobody could hear her. Almost at the point of anger, Susannah went and shook her aunt Luciana, Ted's mom and her dad's sister. To her amazement, her

hands would flow right through her as she tried
to shake her aunt's shoulder for attention. *I must
be dreaming.*

Then she saw it—a table full of flowers and
lit candles around a picture taken of her a few
months ago. That was the moment when she
realized that it was she who was dead. It started
to make sense, the crying, and all the people.
*What? I'm not dead. I'm right here! I'm not
dead. Why can't they hear me? What do I do
now? Why can't I think?*

In the distance of her memory was the thought
of that trusting old soul saying, *"You do not
believe; you may not gain entrance."* Susannah
could now remember going toward the light and
the gates being locked. With this memory, she
was instantly teleported into a vast emptiness. It
was dark and lonely, a place between time and
space. *Believe. . .* was Susannah's last memory
as her soul drifted without direction through the
dimension of non-existence.

Chapter 7

The funeral came and went; it had been a couple of days. Lexi was happy with her mom's decisions—Susannah would have loved all the personal touches. Not quite the Catholic version Lexi was used to, but she knew in Susannah's Last Will and Testimony it stated that she wished for a nondenominational funeral. Reverend Hawthorne had done an incredible job; he completely turned grief on its head.

The ceremony became a full-blown celebration, reflecting on the highlights of Susannah's life. Anyone would have said that it was one of the most beautiful and profound services they had ever been to, starting with the funeral home. It had an impressive chapel with its beautiful stained-glass windows and wooden pews. You could hear Susannah's favorite songs being played on the piano by a lovely young lady as you walked in to find a seat. There were pink carnations and red roses in beautiful arrangements decorating the front altar. Lexi's mom, Olivia, had given everyone in the congregation a white lit candle to hold on to as Reverend Hawthorne opened the ceremony with a prayer.

"Dear Father, there is a season and time for everything in this world. Today, you have granted us a chance to celebrate the life of our loved one, and we want to say thank you. Even though we are finding it hard to accept what has happened, we know that everything works out together for good. God, give us the peace that surpasses all understanding as we start this funeral program. Give us the strength to share the beautiful moments that we shared with the departed. In Jesus's name, we pray. Amen."

Lexi watched a short presentation of Susannah's life on a big screen, from the time she was born right up until her death, revealing snippets of the beautiful soul that would be missed dearly. Photos of her smile, her first day of school, and a lost tooth. Photos from her dance class, some art she had crafted, her high-school, graduation, and university pictures. . . *Oh, my God, I am going to miss you so much, Susannah.*

After the formal ceremony, everyone had followed Reverend Hawthorne and the pallbearers outside and into the graveyard, where they watched as Susannah's body was laid into the ground. Instead of dirt, her mother tossed the first rose onto Susannah's casket to pay her final respects. Reverend Hawthorne read the Twenty-Third Psalm.

Lexi repeated the psalm to herself. *The Lord is my Shepherd; I shall not be in want. He makes me lie down in green pastures, He leads me beside quiet waters, He restores my soul. He guides me in the path of righteousness for His name's sake. Even though I walk through the valley of the shadow of death, I will fear no evil, for you are with me; Your rod and your staff, they comfort me. You prepare a table before me in the presence of my enemies. You anoint my head with oil, my cup overflows. Surely goodness and love will follow me all the days of my life, And I will dwell in the house of the Lord—forever.* It was a beautiful funeral.

Tears started to flow down her cheeks as Lexi played the ceremony over again in her mind.

Wiping her tears on her sleeve and coming back to the moment, she found herself standing at the island in her kitchen. She knew that neither good memories nor time could heal this awful feeling in her gut. No matter how hard she tried, she couldn't get rid of this sickening feeling that Susannah was not in Heaven.

As she was searching through her purse for an aspirin, a piece of paper fell onto her kitchen floor. Picking it up, she remembered the ticket Tamara had given her. Her mind was so tormented with grief, and the days seemed to pass by faster than a runway model parading down the catwalk that she had forgotten all about Tamara's lecture.

Distinguishing Spirits, Tuesday at 7:00 pm. That's tonight.

Looking at the clock and noticing the time, if she hurried, she'd make it. Without thinking, Lexi instinctively grabbed her car keys and drove to the address printed on the ticket.

Death leaves a heartache
no one can heal.
Love leaves a memory
that no one can steal.
Author Unknown

Chapter 8

Tamara was going over her notes on tonight's lecture. It amazed her that no matter how many times she gave this speech, it always seemed to come out differently. Fortunately for her, it always seemed tailored perfectly for the people listening.

Tonight's energy had a rare vibe to it. Ready for anything, she took a deep breath, smiled, and walked out onto the stage.

Men and women of all ages applauded as she said, "Thank you for coming. I want to introduce you to the spirit world with a few of my own ghost stories."

Looking into the audience, Tamara figured there were about a hundred people that came out to listen tonight.

"I was three, silently looking around I could tell it was later in the evening. It was dark and quiet, and I was lying in a hospital bed recovering from a surgery I just had. The door opened, and a nurse came in to check on me.

"I asked her, 'What does that man want?'

"Looking at me, she said, 'What, man?'

"Bringing my hand out from underneath the covers, I pointed my tiny finger in the direction of the foot of my bed. Standing in the shadows was a man slightly hidden in the darkened room.

"She turned to look where I was pointing and said, 'I don't see a man.' She turned back to me, tucked me in, and said to go back to sleep.

"Again, I turned my eyes to look at the man. I saw him standing there. Following her orders, I shut my eyes and fell back to sleep."

Tamara noticed from what she had just said a mix of responses from the audience. Some people's heads were nodding in memory of similar experiences. Some she could tell were in disbelief or defiance because they crossed their arms, and others were sitting on the edge of their seats, eagerly waiting for her to go on.

Tamara knew that this next story was usually the one that sparked the audience. "When I recall this memory, I can still smell the dust, my heart skips a beat, and I hold my breath. At the age of four, I remember climbing up onto a solid wooden chair in the middle of the hallway that my dad had just used to access the attic of the house we were renting.

"Being a curious kid, I wanted to see what was up there in that secret hideout. I asked permission from my mom, and she replied, 'No, it is not a place for little girls. It is too dirty.'

"I begged, 'Please,' over and over again.

"Luckily for me, when my dad came down, he gave his approval. He stood on the chair and lifted me through the rectangular hole in the ceiling. Next, I had to help my two-year-old sister up into the attic space. Triumphantly, I sat across from my sister, looking down at my mom and dad.

"I remember that it bothered me a bit when we had to lift our feet so my dad could close the hatch door on us, but I didn't want to go down just yet.

"We were sitting in the middle of one big open space. I could have walked it in about ten giant footsteps both in front of me and behind. And about five giant footsteps to each side.

"Past my sister, I saw light coming through a window that was in a triangular wall. Making up the floor were rows of dusty insulation, the color of dirty yellow snow, lying lengthwise between the two by fours.

"I turned my head and twisted my body toward the right and almost all the way behind me. About three feet away from the wall, in the left-hand corner of the room, was an old, worn-out wooden handrail guarding the descending stairway.

"Three figures, resembling witches, dressed in darker gray hooded robes, were starting to go down the stairs. I could see only portions of two of them, the first from her shoulders up and the second from her waist up. The third figure looked to be the size of my mom, five foot six-inch, and even though I could not see any of their faces because their hoods were drawn, she was staring at me, giving me shivers. It was as if she was probing my mind.

"I do not remember any noise. It was as if time was standing still.

"After what seemed like an eternity, she hastily turned her back, took a step forward around the handrail, and followed the others.

"Like snapping out of a bad dream, I jerked my head back toward my sister and started kicking the hatch door with my feet, screaming hysterically, 'Let us down!'

"As the hatch opened, I jumped down through the hole. My dad caught me and passed me to my mom. I still remember shakily running toward my bedroom as my mom asked me what was wrong.

"All I could stammer breathlessly was, 'Scary ladies up there. . . stairs.'

"Moments later, my mom came to me. 'You must have imagined it. Dad said there are no ladies or a stairway up there.'

"Even though both my parents could not see any ghosts, I believe what I saw that day was real."

Tamara always paid particular attention to the audience's reactions to her stories. She could hear the exhalation of breath as people were contemplating what she had just said. Their body language changed from a relaxed state to a perplexed one. She knew that when a person was rationalizing if ghosts were real and were a bit scared or nervous, they tended to rub their face and neck—which many people in the audience were doing right now.

Addressing the audience, Tamara said, "I would like all of you to take a couple of deep breaths. Some of you are here tonight because you wish to have confirmation about what you have seen, heard, felt, or thought you sensed. Wishing for proof or validation that it was a ghost or something else just as spooky and unexplainable. Or maybe you are here hoping to gain insight and knowledge. Many of you want to know that you are not alone, that there are others that think just like you and have had these mysterious experiences. Let me see a raise of hands of the brave souls that are here for this reason tonight." More than half the audience's hands went up.

"Some of you are here tonight because you think this is all bogus and want to prove that ghosts are not real. That my ghost stories are just a child's imagination gone wild. And, some of you are here tonight because your partner, family member, or friend asked you to come with them.

"I want to thank all of you for coming. I believe that most people have had a visit from a ghost at one point in their life, and like me, shut their eyes and closed their minds to the experience."

Just a few steps back from where she had been standing was a stool and a water bottle. Tamara took a seat on the stool, took a sip from the bottle, and put it on the floor beside her.

"In this next story, I was still very young, but old enough to know that this time it was real.

"I was about eight, sitting on the couch talking with my two older cousins in their unfinished basement. I can't remember what we were talking about, but I know I cut them off in their conversation with, 'What do you think she is saying?'

"They looked at me questionably, 'Who?'

"Pointing, I responded, 'The lady on the wall.'

"Both of them followed the direction of my finger.

"The image of her was like a portrait—flat and two-dimensional. I still can remember the lady's face. She was about thirty with brown eyes and a clear, smooth complexion, kind, soft lips, and wavy, brown shoulder-length hair. She was wearing a plain green T-shirt. Her lips were moving as she was talking, although I could not hear her.

"My heart went out to her. I really wanted to know what she was saying because the lost and despairing look on her face seemed to say she needed help.

"Patiently waiting for my cousins' reply, I was stunned by their reaction. As they screamed and fled the basement, it took me a moment to decide what to do.

"I was in a state of shock. I wanted to stay and find out what the lady was saying but still could not understand why my cousins fled as they didn't say that they saw anything.

"Since it was their house and they were older than me, I decided they knew what they were doing and chose not to take a chance and be left alone with this ghost. I followed them.

"As I ascended the stairs, my curiosity kept me watching the lady through the openings of the two by fours. Her eyes were following me up as she kept mouthing something. I was not afraid of this lady. I just wished I could have understood what she was saying.

"When I entered the upstairs living room, my cousins were still screaming, telling our parents that I said I saw a ghost downstairs. My mom was silent but gave me one of those disapproving looks that definitely meant, 'What did you do now?'

"I thought I was in trouble and was embarrassed to look like a fool in front of all my family, so I never did ask them what they saw. Later that evening, my mom said I should not mention the lady again because it scared my cousins, and they had to sleep down there.

"Fifteen years later, I asked my cousins if they remembered the lady on the wall. They both said they saw nothing that night, but my older cousin did tell me that sometimes she had felt like someone had walked into her room.

"I noted later that the lady on the wall was in color, not like the other story I told where those three ladies were shades of gray, as you would have seen on the old black and white TVs."

Getting up off the stool, Tamara started to walk across the stage. She took a second to look out into the audience at as many guests as she could. Observing if people in the audience needed a moment before she continued. "These stories still, to this day, give me shivers when I remember them. I really did try my best to ignore this aspect of my life. I was able to close my eyes and not see a ghost again for another twenty-three years. . . and then this happened.

"Everything started out as usual. It was close to 10:00 a.m., and I was just finishing saying goodbye to my first client when I noticed my next client was waiting for me in the lobby. I greeted her and led her into my practitioner room. I had designed my space and was able to bring a lot of my own furniture. I loved it!

"It was a cozy little room, longer in length than the width. As you walked in, to the left, there was a beautiful wood cabinet with a small corner sink and marble-like laminate countertops to both sides of it. My uncle had made it for me to store all the products, towels, and knick-knacks that I needed for my sessions.

"On the floor beside the cabinet was a three-disc stereo player. Above, on the wall, hung a large framed picture of a quaint country home with the most marvelously serene meadow and a brook gracefully wandering side to side through the tall flowing grass. The beautiful and peaceful colors matched my brand-new burgundy La-Z-Boy chair, which was placed on the left facing the entrance to the room. The recliner was so soft and comfortable that you could easily fall asleep in it. The borrowed massage table took up the rest of the right side of the room.

"I had seen my next client before, at the office. She was a regular with one of the other practitioners. She was in her mid-forties, maybe even her early fifties. Guessing, she was about five feet, six inches tall, average build, with dark-brown hair, short, cut in an English style.

"Her clothes were comfortable and casual, pants with a pullover shirt. She had very few wrinkles. Her eyes were friendly but distant, like she was here with me but not really. Without me even asking, she sat down in the recliner and readied herself for her reflexology session by removing her socks and shoes. She knew the drill, as she had been coming for years to this holistic center.

"She was starting to relax deeply in my chair and making small talk with me. I was just finishing the reflexology procedure with her right foot and about to change over onto the left foot when it happened.

"I started to feel pressure in my head. At first, it was not quite like a headache. It was just this pressure, and then it began to get worse and worse. I had maybe two headaches that I could remember in my life, and this was becoming ten times worse than either of those. It was becoming a disabling pain that was now throbbing in my head.

"I was not sure what to do. I still had another half-hour left in the session. I could not quit the session, for she had already paid. What was I going to do? The pain was getting intolerable and so much louder.

"I started to pray. I prayed for the pain to disappear and that I could finish this session. And then it happened.

"The pain turned into voices. I didn't understand it at first; it was just noise like you hear in a shopping mall. Voices, but you are not able to make out the individual words. As I tried to listen more closely, I started to hear the words being spoken more clearly. I now knew that the voices wanted to talk to the lady sitting in the chair.

"The pressure in my head was increasing, and the voices were becoming louder and more persistent. I was scared to tell her. I was so worried that I would lose my job if I did.

"I could just imagine her running out of the room, screaming. I was sure I'd be in big trouble with the girls at the front counter. They were Jehovah's Witnesses, and the practice of communicating with spirits was against their religion.

"I was trying to understand what was happening. I could have counted on one hand the number of drinks in a year that I might have had. I do not do drugs, take medication, or smoke anything. What was going on? I grew up Catholic, going to church every Sunday, catechism classes, even Catholic schools. This was neither funny nor appropriate!

"Finally, the pain in my head was unbearable.

"'I have to tell you something.' Even with just those words, her face seemed to pale. 'You have two boys who want to talk to you.' I paused, not knowing how she would respond.

"She calmly replied, 'Is that all?'

"I almost fell out of my chair. . . like this happens to me every day. *Is that all!*

"'Describe them to me, and what are they saying?'

"When I gave her the requested information, she proceeded to tell me that both of her teenage sons had passed on in tragic circumstances. I could not believe my ears. Not only did this both intrigue and trouble me, but what were the chances that I was right?

"Her husband came to visit me shortly after that, and I communicated with their sons for him as well. The couple invited me to their home and showed me pictures of the boys. I am still amazed at the accuracy of my description.

"Oh, by the way, she told me later that she thought I was going to say to her that she had cancer or something equally serious. Funny… thinking back on it, that would have been normal!

"To this day, her visit still inspires me. I am awestruck at how much healing a visit from a loved one who has passed on can bring to the family members who are left behind. The loved ones always seem to share their love, gratitude, and how they are faring in the afterlife, gifting their family members peace of mind.

"I was thirty-one when this happened—an adult. At an age when there was no mistaking what was pretend, imaginary for what was real. This memory transformed me. My life was never the same after this life-altering paradigm shift. . . knowing from that day forward that ghosts were real. This was the day I awoke from my childhood sleep and opened my eyes for good."

Tamara let the audience talk amongst themselves for a few moments to adjust to what they had just heard.

"I understand why so many people are so afraid of ghosts. Not just because they seem to appear out of nowhere, but also because there seems to be no factual proof that anything, even God, for that matter, exists in the spirit world.

"A few years back, I decided to venture out on my own quest for discovering the truth and facts about the spirit world."

Tamara bent down and took out a big blue book that was in a bag attached to the stool. "I can't say for sure that every word in the Bible is translated into English perfectly or that each story that was written had not been corrupted by the spoken soul who wrote it."

Tamara held up the book, and the cover revealed the title: *The New Jerusalem Bible*.

"In the Bible, many passages use the term 'Spirit' and 'Holy Spirit.' I find that most fascinating since the Bible is over two thousand years old. From attending church, I grew up hearing stories about the Holy Spirit, that the Holy Spirit is an entity without a body. It is a soul without a purpose of natural means, a messenger for God. And if the Bible and religions believe in a spirit, then maybe I wasn't going crazy after all. That it was okay for me to believe that I had seen spirits and ghosts." Placing her right hand on the cover of the Bible and lightly tapping it, Tamara continued, "More than two thousand years ago, they knew what a spirit was and wrote about it."

Opening the Bible, she read from *Corinthians 1, Chapter 12, Verse 4-11*, "In the New Testament, my favorite story is 'The Gifts.' It may be a little differently worded depending on which version of the Bible you read.

"'The variety and the unity of gifts.'

"'There are many different gifts, but it is always the same Spirit; there are many different ways of serving, but it is always the same Lord. There are many different forms of activity, but in everybody, it is the same God who is at work in them all. The particular manifestation of the Spirit granted to each one is to be used for the general good. To one is given from the Spirit the gift of utterance expressing **wisdom**; to another the gift of utterance expressing **knowledge**; in accordance with the same spirit to another, **faith**, from the same Spirit; and to another, the gifts of **healing**, through the same Spirit; to another, the working of **miracles**; to another **prophecy**; to another, the power of **distinguishing spirits**; to one, the gift of **different tongues** and to another, the **interpretation of tongues**. But at work in all these is one and the same Spirit, distributing them at will to each individual.'

"I find it most perplexing that not all versions of the Bible have this phrase, the power of distinguishing spirits or written as the gift of discernment. This sentence has been removed from some Bibles, but not all.

"Distinguishing spirits, what does that mean? To tell the difference between spirits."

Closing the Bible and placing it down on the stage floor, and then making herself comfortable on the stool, Tamara went on, "I was born with the gift of distinguishing spirits, but over the years, I have learned to use all of the gifts granted. Just as you can learn to walk, read, write, and speak, you can learn the techniques needed to unlock, access, and attain all the spiritual gifts."

Suddenly, Tamara took a breath and closed her eyes. Over the years, she was getting used to speaking with spirits. It wasn't a headache that she was experiencing but definitely pressure in her head. For the first time, while she was presenting, she had a spirit appear without invitation and interrupt her train of thought. It was Marcus Constantine, the deceased father of Lexi, the spirit that came instead of Lexi's sister, Susannah. He was very insistent on speaking with his daughter.

Tamara opened her eyes and looked out into the audience for Lexi. "Are you here tonight, Lexi?" she said as the pain was getting worse.

Chapter 9

Spirits were not supposed to drop in unexpectantly and uninvited. So, Tamara started to pray up for help. Trusting that her angels and guides had an excellent reason for allowing what was about to transpire, she acknowledged Marcus by thinking, *Hold onto your horses.*

Tamara stood up from the stool. "Lexi, are you in the audience?" A murmur ran through the room as a hand slowly went up. Tamara turned her head to see the person whose hand went up and saw that Lexi was indeed in the audience.

"Your dad is here insisting on sharing more information about your sister, Susannah." Tamara could sense Marcus getting even more excited, and his message came quickly, not in words that one could hear out loud, but in the celestial language of the spirit world.

Tamara was used to spirits communicating with her by using any of the four channels. She used this opportunity to introduce the "celestial languages" of the spirit world to the audience. "There are four channels of the celestial language that a ghost or spirit can use to communicate with us. In any order, one is not better than the other, just different. The four communication channels are clairvoyant, French for clear seeing. You might receive pictures like in a dream. I call this channel 'visual.' Next is a clairsentient, clear feeling. You might feel tingles running through your body. I call this one 'feeler.' claircognizance, clear knowing is another. You may be inundated with thoughts. This one I call 'knower.' And then there is clairaudience, clear hearing. I call this one 'audio.' Tonight, Marcus is talking to me. Well, in my mind, but I can hear him talk. The difference between audio and knower is that there is no noise with a knower."

It took all of Tamara's concentration to conduct the lecture while simultaneously listening to Marcus.

"When you communicate with a ghost or spirit, it all depends on his or her celestial language, their persona. It comes down to the personality traits they had when they were alive on Earth. Each of the four channels: audio, knower, feeler, and visual have unique qualities, behaviors, and mannerisms. I will be teaching a course on this in the new year."

To get back to the task at hand, Tamara repeated Marcus's message. "Lexi, your dad says that you are not stressed, crazy, or imagining all of this. The dream you had was a connection you felt because of your closeness to your sister when she was alive. He says you felt and knew things about each other growing up. Like, knowing it was Susannah calling before you picked up your phone. Or when she was having a bad day, and you called to see if she was alright, and she wasn't. Your special connection in life carried through into her death. Your dad's urgent message is, 'Don't second guess your dream. Susannah does need your help.'"

Everyone in the audience was staring at Lexi. Someone gave her a tissue, for tears were running down her face. Many people thought this was a setup and part of the show. Others were wishing Tamara would communicate with one of their loved ones who had passed on to the other side.

Once Tamara had forwarded his message, Marcus disappeared as quickly as he had appeared. Tamara ended the evening by telling everyone that their ticket was a free pass for next Tuesday's lecture, continuing the distinguishing spirits series, same place and time.

Stunned, Lexi was still sitting there in her seat after everyone had left when Tamara sat down beside her in the audience and squeezed her hand. "I am sorry for that surprise. I didn't even know it was going to happen," Tamara said sincerely.

"Leave it to my father to make a grand entrance and steal the show," Lexi replied, still bewildered from the message Tamara had shared.

"Lexi, Marcus's message was crucial. So important that he had to make sure you heard it. He feared that he might never have another chance to tell you. When a spirit has a message, and it is important, they will stop at nothing to get it across to the human world. I guess we both better listen up, for he has made damn sure we both paid attention to his message. I guess the spirit world has something important for me to learn as well."

Tamara knew that before any show, she should say a protection prayer for herself and the audience from lower energy entities who might try to cause havoc on unaware humans. Having a spirit interrupt a speech was not supposed to happen. And it wouldn't have happened, except for the fact that Tamara had ended her session with Lexi the other day by saying, "When I can think of a better and more direct question to ask. I will meditate to receive the answers that may help you."

Tamara remembered that she'd asked her angels and guides for help with Susannah's situation, and she knew that the spirit world had its own timing of when and how the answer would come back. Tonight, because Lexi was in the audience, it created the perfect opportunity for the solution to be presented.

"Lexi, can you call me tomorrow or in the next few days? We need to create a plan on how to save Susannah and help her get into Heaven."

"Umm. Oh, my God, Tamara. I think I am going crazy. All this talk about ghosts and spirits has my head spinning. I have been praying for an answer to come. I know something is wrong; something is wrong with Susannah. I can't get rid of this feeling in my stomach. I will find the time for you. I must. You seem to be the only person who believes me. Even if I think I am losing my mind."

Chapter 10

Lexi drove home from the lecture repeating the message from her deceased father. *"Don't second guess your dream. Susannah does need your help."*

In a bit of a daydream, she rubbed a thick gold band that hung on a beautiful gold chain that her dad had bought her as a birthday present when she turned sixteen. The ring she was rubbing was an heirloom. It used to be her dad's and before that her grandfather's and his father's, and now it was hers. The engraving on the inside of the band read "Fiat Lux," Latin for "Let there be light." Genesis 1:3. But to her, the ring just reminded her of love, family, and passion for life. She wore it next to her heart and hadn't taken it off since her dad died four years ago. Somehow it made her feel closer to him.

The traffic was flowing smoothly, and she made it home in good time. All she could think about was going to bed. She was exhausted. Snuggling into her comfy bed, a forgotten memory of her dad popped into her dream state.

She had just gotten home from university. As she opened the door, Lexi heard her dad yelling at Susannah.

"What do you mean you do not want to go to church anymore?"

"Dad, there is no need to raise your voice and yell at me. If you can't prove to me that there is a God, we have nothing further to discuss."

"Susannah, you have to believe that there is a God. You must believe it. Don't be ridiculous. If you do not go to church, you cannot live in this house!"

"Fine!" Susannah yelled back and stormed out of the room.

Devastated that her sister was packing her things and was seriously moving out, Lexi tried convincing her to stay, but to no avail. Susannah moved out that evening and never went to church with the family again. And worst yet, she never stepped foot into their childhood home again, even after their father died.

When Lexi awoke the next morning, it all made sense. *Oh, my God. Susannah died not believing in God.*

Lexi always thought that all you had to do was be a good person to get into Heaven. Who knew that there was even a possibility that a soul wouldn't get into Heaven if that person didn't believe in God? *Oh, my God, Susannah, what have you done to the fate of your soul?*

The next week went by faster than autumn days before winter. It was shortly after 4:00 p.m. when Lexi noticed the time. She was finishing a few final details on a new fashion design that she was drawing.

Her workstation wasn't an office like one might expect it to be since she was head of the designing division. No, her desk was a large easel that had to the one side a desk of drawers to hold her files and essential documents needed for her job. And an adjustable stool for her to sit on. The designing studio was an open loft concept, with twenty-foot ceilings. It was on the top floor of a commercial building on 5th Ave. in Manhattan. The energy of the room was always exciting, hustling, and glitzy. Models, fabric, noise, and the flashing lights of cameras was a typical day at the office for Lexi. You had to be on your game and intuitively figure out what the market will buy next. The fashion industry was incredibly fast-paced, and designs changed even before the clothes hit the stores. Lexi was in her element. She loved it!

She loved finding out which famous stars would be wearing her designs, what elaborate function they would be attending, and where in the world they would be wearing them. This bizarre world of fashion, with its skinny models and funky and fantastic runway shows, used to be all that consumed her. But when Susannah died, everything changed. Now all she could think about was her sister being lost in the Void. And how she was going to figure all this out. All she thought about nowadays was how she was going to save Susannah.

Not having a clue on how she would save her sister, Lexi decided that if she was going to make it to Tamara's next lecture by 7:00, she'd better hurry.

Chapter 11

*T*amara closed her eyes and took a few deep breaths, exhaling slowly. *God, my angels, and guides, please protect me, the room, and my audience from the influence of negative spirits while I give my speech tonight. Empower my words to be what is needed to be heard tonight. Allow my words to be your words. Sharing the imperative message that you want me to share this evening.* Taking another deep breath and any insightful inspirations with it, she wiggled her toes and fingers, opened her eyes, and walked onto the stage.

There were even more people in the audience than last Tuesday night. The room was packed. She could see the hotel staff bringing in a few more chairs to allow seating for the extra people coming in at the last minute.

Her fiancé, Greg, was at the entrance taking the people's tickets and money from the ones that were not at the previous event.

"Welcome," Tamara said as she scanned the audience. "Please, everyone, stand up and shake off the day's energy and imagine it going into a cosmic vacuum cleaner."

Many people stood up and did a little shimmy as if imaginary dirt was falling off them. Smiling and laughing as they did the little wiggle.

"Come on, shimmy your body, even if you are still sitting."

The audience got into it and shimmied. Sitting back down, many people were still smiling.

"Okay. Now take a deep breath . . . and allow all your unnecessary thoughts and concerns to be put away . . . store them for another time. For now, please give me your full attention. What I am about to share with you this evening is essential." Tamara took a deep breath with the audience to help everyone relax.

"Last week, we ended my lecture with an unusual spirit connection. It was a wake-up call for me on just how necessary believing is— having a belief in the afterlife. The intent of going into the light—let's call that Heaven. When I use the word Heaven, it means love-light energy. How many of you know the levels of the spirit world?" Tamara scanned the audience. Only a couple of hands went up.

"We live on Earth, and it is at the lowest level with the lowest vibratory rate, known as the universe. The next level is Hell. Then held, non-believers, and elementals. All five of these levels are outside of Heaven. These, including our level, are considered the underworld, under Heaven. You may know the name underworld by how Hollywood uses the term for action horror films or gangster movies. Most people connect the word with anything dark and evil. Earth could be considered that if you compared it to Heaven. Another word used is the 'nether world,' neither Earth nor Heaven, everything in between."

Tamara took a sip from her water bottle.

"Above these five underworld levels is Heaven, and inside of Heaven, there are a total of fifteen levels. Most people don't know that there are eight more levels above the seven named in the Bible. The first level of Heaven is where most people go when they die."

Someone called out from the audience, "Tell us more."

Tamara smiled and said, "That is another lecture."

The guy waved and laughed.

Tamara continued, "How many of you have seen, heard, felt, or thought about a ghost at least once in your life? Be honest."

Many hands went up in the audience.

"How many of you have lost a loved one?"

Just about every person in the audience raised a hand.

"How many of you have communicated with a ghost or spirit?"

A few hands went up in the room.

"How many of you have had dreams about your loved ones as if they were alive talking with you? Or feelings that your mother, father, or a loved one touched you somehow? Maybe a caressing feeling on your face or as if someone touched your shoulder?

"I ask you again, how many of you have communicated with a ghost or spirit?"

The room fell silent after many people put the connection together.

"Any communication with the dead, real or imaginary, is communicating with a ghost or spirit."

Tamara took another sip of water to give an extra moment for the audience to contemplate what she'd just implied.

"Did you realize that there is no difference between your partner, mom, dad, child, or best friend, God, angel, or Jesus coming to visit you and a demon doing the same?"

That caused a stir in the audience.

"Even if you pray and believe in God, how do you know that you are praying or talking to the spirit that you think you are? I am going to say that again." Tamara walked the stage, looking at as many people as she could while saying it a second time. "How do you know that you are praying or talking to the spirit that you think you are?

"DID YOU TEST IT?"

Tamara went silent for a moment.

"Do you know that low spirits can pretend to be whomever they want to be? Did you know that if you never test it, that spirit can pretend to be that person for as long as it wants to?"

Tamara stood still for another moment.

"The best way that you can tell the presence of a low-energy spirit is that the entity will always try to convince you to do something, usually with a bribe. Or talk you up, so you seem magnificent and powerful. Low-energy spirits are always trying to say something to convince you to believe them.

"So, DID YOU TEST THE SPIRIT? Even the ones you dream of, test them too."

That got the attention she was looking for; all eyes were now focused on her, attentive to every word she was saying.

"Now, high-energy spirits never need to convince you. They don't care if you listen to them or not. There are no consequences to you saying no; they will quietly move on. High-energy spirits will NEVER tell you to do anything that could hurt you or another person. They will never tell you how great you are or how if you do this, they will give you this."

Tamara clasped her hands together, "Let's try something. I want you to pretend that you are sensing a loved one's spirit. Go ahead, imagine your loved one being here right next to you."

Tamara gave the audience a few moments to summon a loved one.

"Put your hand up if you are imagining your loved one."

Most of the audience put a hand up.

"Now, how do you know if that spirit is really your loved one's soul that lived here on Earth?

"DID YOU TEST IT?"

Tamara was waiting for the facial body language of her audience.

"Can you tell if he or she has passed on to the light and is free, or a lost soul that is stuck here on Earth?

"DID YOU TEST THE SPIRIT?"

Tamara paused.

"There are laws to the spirit world. The language, the word of spirit, is extremely literal! All spiritual laws are demand and command. If you say no, then it's no. No wishy-washy maybes."

As Tamara walked to the right side of the stage, she said, "A low-energy spirit knows it can gain entrance to this world through you. Unless you test the spirit by either asking it a direct question that only your loved one would know the answer to or by radiating love-light energy to the spirit's heart and eyes. I will explain how to emanate love-light energy in just a moment.

"I am going to ask you again. DID YOU TEST THE SPIRIT? My guess is probably not. Don't worry, it's not your fault. You didn't know you were supposed to. There is a reason for the message in the Bible not to talk to spirits! I actually agree with it. Until you know the spiritual laws, trust them, and believe them, DO NOT TALK TO SPIRITS!"

Unexpectedly, Tamara said, "Lexi, please come up onto the stage." Tamara had seen that Lexi was in the audience at the start of her lecture. She signaled for Lexi to get out of her chair and join her on the stage.

Marcus, Lexi's belated father, was nagging Tamara again as she was speaking to the audience. It was extremely annoying, but this time she was ready for the spiritual encounter. Tamara pulled up a stool for Lexi to sit on. "Some of you will remember from last week that Lexi's dad, Marcus, came and had an important message to share. Well, he is here again and won't shut up. So, I am going to use this opportunity to kill two birds with one stone.

"Lexi, do you have in your possession today something that was your dad's?"

Lexi shook her head, then stopped and said, "Wait, yes, I do." Pulling out a gold chain from under the neckline of her blouse, she said, "This ring was his and my grandfather's before him."

Tamara looked relieved. She had a hunch that Lexi had something in her possession that made it so easy for Marcus to come through and talk.

"Great," she said. "This is a perfect example for me to show all of you how this spirit world works."

Tamara went on to explain, "Whatever belief a person has of the afterlife, at the moment of their death, it will manifest into reality for that soul.

"Lexi, your dad is here again tonight. We are going to test him. Here is what we are going to do to test his spirit. I want you to imagine your dad, please. Imagine sending him a combination of love and light energy from your eyes and heart to his eyes and heart and hold that for a few moments."

Taking her attention off of Lexi for a second, Tamara turned to the audience and said, "If you are unsure of how long to do this for, imagine sending the love-light energy for a minimum of five minutes. The energy of love and light is so powerful and purifying that a low or dark spirit cannot hold the illusion for more than five minutes when being tested. These spirits cannot handle the purifying power of love-light energy. The spirit will flicker and disappear in that amount of time. You can amplify the energy by ten times, and then again by one hundred times the original power."

Turning back to Lexi, she said, "Lexi, after testing your dad, is he still in your imagination?"

Lexi nodded.

"Great. Because I have met your father in spirit before, I know this is him as well. You are now connected and can answer for him. I can now start to ask him questions."

Tamara turned to the audience again and said, "If I had never met Marcus before, I would have had Lexi amplify the energy two more times."

Turning back to Lexi, Tamara said, "With your permission. I need to fill everyone in on what is going on here. I need to explain why you will be staying up here on the stage with me."

Lexi nodded to Tamara.

"Lexi's sister, Susannah, died a week or so ago, and Lexi came to me because of a horrifying dream that Susannah was not okay in the afterlife. When I went to contact her sister, I couldn't. Instead, her dad came through and confirmed Lexi's concern. Her dad, Marcus, speaks to me using the audio channel. I can hear him as if he is talking in my mind. I am about to demonstrate how you can communicate with the spirit world, and at the same time, I am going to help Lexi and her sister."

Focusing now on Lexi, Tamara started to ask some questions, "Marcus, do you know where your daughter, Susannah, is?"

Lexi could sense a negative feeling in her body and said, "No."

Tamara asked, "Can you get someone in the spirit world who does know?"

Again, Lexi sensed a negative feeling in her body and said, "No."

Taking a breath, Tamara contemplated what question to ask next. Instead, she started talking to the audience by saying, "A ghost and a spirit do not have a brain. Therefore, they cannot think on their own. They can only keep their memories from when they passed on. One of the spiritual laws is that when asked a direct question, it must be answered honestly and literally. Now, if you use slang words or words that imply another meaning, the spirit can trick you in their answering. The words must be of literal meaning. For example, my nephew is just over two, and my sister wanted to measure his height against the wall. His little feet were a few inches from the wall, and so she said, 'Put your feet on the wall.' He looked at her weird and then a few seconds later bent a leg at the knee and put a foot on the wall."

The audience laughed with the image in their head of this little guy trying to do what his mom asked.

Tamara continued, "To the spirit world, every word is literal. If a low spirit can get away with it, it will use that to its advantage."

Taking a few seconds to think of her next question, she turned to Lexi and said, "Great, thank you, Marcus. It is so nice of you to get the message through that Susannah needs Lexi's help. I will call upon you again if we need your help. For now, go back into the love-light energy and enjoy."

Turning to Lexi, Tamara said, "You and I will need to meet privately and make sure your dad is not a ghost and stuck to the ring."

She thanked Lexi for coming up on stage and allowing the audience to learn by watching her session and then gestured for Lexi to go back to her seat.

Turning back to the audience, Tamara concluded the talk by recapping what was shared that evening. "I mentioned the levels of the spirit world, how to test a spirit, and the importance of making sure you use literal words instead of slang. Most importantly, remember, test all spirits! Night, everyone, and for those that wish to come to next Tuesday's lecture, I have booked this place again, same time. The topic will be reincarnation and past lives."

Tamara finished off the evening's lecture by telling the audience the price and then had everyone bow their heads as she thanked the spirit world for allowing tonight's message to be heard.

My dear friends.
Not every spirit is to be
trusted,

but test the spirits to see
whether they are from God,
For many false prophets are
at large in the world.

New Testament
1 John 4:1

Chapter 12

Feeling better than she had in weeks, Lexi woke up with a tingling sensation in her gut. The kind of feeling you have when something good is about to happen. Not quite excitement, but a feeling that you get when you have a great idea, and your body responds with glee.

Somehow, she intuitively knew that she would be able to save Susannah's soul, that all she had to do now was figure out how.

Getting out of bed, she had a shower and got dressed. Lexi loved getting up in the morning because no one at work would even blink an eye if she dressed up as a princess or if she looked like she was going out to a New Year's Eve party. In the fashion industry, anything went, and the fancier, the better!

Walking to work, Lexi took a deep breath of the fresh, crisp morning air. She noticed that the trees in Central Park had changed colors in an array of vibrant hues from dark green to a golden brown and were losing most of their magnificent fall foliage.

Once at work, she dove right in and was bombarded with questions from her staff all morning. So, she didn't see the email from Tamara in her inbox until after her lunch break. Clicking the email, she saw it was a long note, starting with. . .

Maybe read this at home when you have a bit of time. Thinking of ya. If you need to talk, call me. Tamara.

Lexi didn't have the time right now, so she closed the message and continued with her newest fashion design drawing, secretly wishing that it would start a whole new fashion trend.

After work, Lexi went to her mom's and didn't get home until later in the evening. As she got ready for bed, she remembered Tamara's email. Bringing her iPad to bed with her, she opened the email from Tamara and read it.

Lexi, this eerie thought won't get out of my head ever since you told me the dream you had of your sister and the dark entities reaching for her. What I am about to say to you is an experience I had once, and I think you need to understand how important it is to save your sister.

The first time I listened to Reverend Weston Bailey, I was mesmerized by two humongous angels, one on each side of him that stood so big that all I could see were their wings. Their heads were through the ceiling into the next floor above us and their legs below us, massive angels with whitish-gray wings.

Every few months, back in the early 2000s, Reverend Bailey would come over from Sacramento and do evening and weekend talks about the dark side of spirits.

That next morning, he was going to share his experiences on how to deal with dark energy and needed a volunteer. Up went my hand.

That night I went to bed dreaming about those angels, awakening to the most horrible dream about my dad. Crying, I knew what I had to work on with Reverend Bailey. Without putting on make-up or doing my hair, I went to the class. Sitting in front of the class, I listened to Reverend Bailey as he talked about performing exorcisms. Then he asked me to tell them all about the dream I had last night.

I'd dreamed about my biological dad. I call him biological since Dad means love to me. At the age of ten, he had tried to assault me sexually. Failing, to my blessing, but tormenting my mind up until this day. The dream symbolically told me that I was to clear this energy of his. Through tears, I remember the look on Reverend Bailey's face that morning when I told him and the rest of the room what I had to work on. It was the look of fortitude.

Some of what I experienced that morning is a blur—most of the stuff about my dad. But I do remember Reverend Bailey speaking to a memory I had of being a black man in a past life. I was running for my life because I stole some bread to feed my family. A spear had punctured my flesh in the upper chest and killed me. Reverend Bailey supernaturally removed the weapon from my shoulder, and all my real-life pain was gone.

The next thing I remember, Reverend Bailey was talking to a spirit and asked me if it was okay to remove the spirit. A spirit in my body? Of course, I said, "YES!" Within seconds, my body started to convulse and shake in the chair as if I had an epileptic fit. The spirit was leaving my body, but not without me feeling it go.

Exhausted after the experience, I was excused from the room to go to the bathroom. Not believing what had just happened, I kept shaking my head. "How is it possible? It isn't," I kept saying to myself. "But I felt it!"

Repeating this thought over and over to myself, I went back into the room to watch what he did with the other people.

It was an incredible experience and so freeing once it was over. All this bad energy, some I knew about and some that were subconscious, being released from my body.

Lexi, when you are ready to chat, call me, and we can set up a time to help Susannah as fast as possible. The thought of dark entities going after her is disturbing as Hell.

Lexi was gobsmacked, flabbergasted, not sure if words could describe how she felt about what she had just read. She had come to trust Tamara in the days she had known her, and if these were her experiences, she believed them. *Oh my God, we have to save Susannah and fast!*

Chapter 13

Reverend Hawthorne was going through his files and making sure that he had scheduled a quick call to his clients who may need counseling. Seeing Olivia Constantine's name written on one reminded him of Alexandra and what she had said to him. He could still recall the fear in her voice while telling him about her dream.

He started thinking to himself. *Exorcism was one thing. At least you had a chance to help a soul. But being lost in the Void just because he or she did not believe in anything was another situation altogether. How do you find a soul that is nowhere? It must be like an astronaut without a spaceship, just floating for eternity through interstellar space. How would a person fix this situation? It's going to be very, very difficult.*

He couldn't get the thought of the dream out of his mind, so, without wasting any more time, he made a phone call.

"Hello?" Lexi answered.

"Hi. Is this Alexandra?"

"Yes," Lexi replied.

"Hi Alexandra, this is Reverend Hawthorne. How are you doing?"

"Better, thank you."

"I was just thinking about the dream you told me about a few weeks ago. In it, you said Susannah was in trouble. Is that still a concern of yours?"

Not knowing if she should tell him the truth or just say what she thought he wanted to hear, Lexi hesitated. She decided to tell him the truth. "I know you think I am crazy, but I know for sure that Susannah did not make it into Heaven. I have been doing research, going to lectures, and speaking with people who talk to the dead for a living. Reverend, I remember now why she moved out that night. I recently remembered a fight she had with my dad many years ago. It was about if God existed. She moved out of the house because my father could not prove to her that God existed." With tears in her eyes, Lexi said, "Reverend, Susannah didn't believe."

"Alexandra, can you come in to see me? We need to talk more about this."

"Yes, but it will have to wait until next week. I have a deadline at work, a design I am working on that must be finished before this weekend.

"How about Wednesday? Alexandra, can you pop by after work?"

"Let me check my schedule. . . I can make that work. I have nothing planned for Wednesday evening. Yes, I can come over right after work. I can be there around four-thirty or five. Is that okay?"

"That will be just fine. See you then, and in the meantime, I will pray for Susannah's soul."

"Thank you, Reverend, that would be appreciated."

Hanging up, he started to think. *If it was true that Susannah didn't make it into Heaven, we are going to need a miracle to save her soul.*

Edward pulled out his Bible and looked up a passage in the old testament, Ws - Wisdom 3:4, starting on sentence 10.

But the godless will be duly punished for their reasoning, for having neglected the upright'
and deserted the Lord. Yes, wretched are they who scorn wisdom and discipline:'
Their hope is void,
Their toil unveiling,
Their achievements were unprofitable. . .

Well, her hope is in the Void for sure. Edward jumped over to 16:13.

Yes, you are the one with power over life and death, bringing to the gates of Hades and back again. A human being out of malice may put to death, but he cannot bring the departed spirit back or free the soul that Hades has once received.

I know that the Void is different from Hades, but does the Bible mean "anywhere" in the underworld?

Edward remembered learning in seminary school that Hades was supposedly the Greek god of the dead and king of the underworld. His brother was Zeus, king of the sky, and his other brother, Poseidon, ruling over the seas.

He remembered that in the Hebrew Bible, Hades is called *She'ol* or *Sheol*. It is a place of darkness to which wicked spirits of the dead go to wait out judgment day, and under some circumstances, the spirits from Sheol could contact the living. And *paradise* was the name used for Heaven and was the place of light in which righteous spirits of the dead wait also for judgment day.

Then Edward remembered another story. Hades cared little about what happened in the sky or the sea, as his concentration was making sure that none of the souls in his care ever left the underworld. Hades strictly forbade these souls to leave his territory, and a soul would become subject to his wrath if anyone tried to leave, or if someone tried to steal the souls from his realm, or tried to cheat death.

In seminary school, Hades's domain was more like a holding district or prison for sinful souls. Whereas Hell is more of an after-life location for the worst of souls sent there to be punished and tormented for the sins they committed while living. Hell is also a place where demons and evil spirits live and travel back and forth through the realms. As Edward could recall, the primary purpose of a demon or evil spirit was to drag an unfortunate mortal back to Hell. Some religions call Hell *Kur*. Kur has seven gates that a soul needed to pass through, and its gatekeeper is the God Neti. Different beliefs have different names for the gatekeeper or guardian of Hell: the devil, Lucifer, or Satan.

As Edward was flipping through the pages of the Bible searching for answers, another passage caught his attention, Mt 18:12.

Tell me. Suppose a man has a hundred sheep, and one of them strays; will he not leave the ninety-nine on the hillside and go in search of the stray? In truth, I tell you, if he finds it, it gives him more joy than do the ninety-nine that did not stray at all. Similarly, it is never the will of your Father in heaven that one of these little ones should be lost.

Reading this passage, Edward knew he had to help find Susannah's soul and bring her back to the safety of the flock.

There are all types of sin, and even though the Void is in the nether world, it's not Hell. Susannah wasn't a bad person doing intentional evil on others. Her only problem was that before her death, she didn't have proof that God existed. She just lost her way.

Hallelujah, we can save her soul.

Chapter 14

Tamara was backstage preparing herself for another talk. As she was just to finish her prayer, an angel appeared in her mind and said that she must change the topic of tonight's lecture.

Surprised by the urgency in the angel's voice and now feeling unprepared, she took a deep breath and opened her eyes. She knew she didn't have to listen, but from past experiences, their suggestions were always in her best interest. Usually, their words came to her in a dream format, and when she was asleep, but not always. Many times, it was like tonight, when she was in a meditative state. Other times they send her messages through sensations that she could feel in her body, especially while she was driving. Urging her to turn left instead of right or to take an alternative route.

Not always did the spirit explain the reasoning for the change, and sometimes it was awkward, especially when it was right before she was about to do something, like walking onto a stage. No matter what, she was grateful for their counsel and guidance.

With the new message fresh in her mind, Tamara stood in front of the audience and decided to take the spirit's advice.

"Good evening, everyone, and thank you for coming. I told you last week that I was going to speak on reincarnation and past lives. I promise I will, but it will have to wait until our next lecture. I have received a persuasive message from a spirit to talk tonight about the removal of dark energy from a body. Not possession precisely, but a type of spirit attachment that steals a human's life-force energy."

A few people in the audience made sounds as if they were disappointed.

Tamara tried not to let the few disapproving reactions disrupt her train of thought. She continued, "I think you will be very interested in what I have to share with you tonight."

Taking a deep breath and praying that the spirit world knew what they were doing, she said, "Some of you tonight have spirits, ghosts, cords, energy vampires attached to you. You are being attacked psychically."

There were a couple of gasps from people in the audience, and the look on many people's faces was of fear, from what Tamara was insinuating.

"There are many different types of entities and dark energies that can attach to your body and your soul. But before I can help you remove them, you need to know the difference between attachment and possession.

"Spirit possession is where a second soul enters the body and can eventually take over. The original soul loses control over its body, speech, movement, how it dresses, and any other decisions or actions. The original soul becomes tiny, taking up little space in the body and eventually dies.

"Whereas in an attachment, the spirit never enters the body. It just attaches itself to you."

Tamara could see by the faces in the audience that the topic change was going to be okay.

"Did you know that if you do not say a person's name when you are talking to them, you might not be talking to the person you think you are? What if there are two or more souls in a body? Did you know the original soul can only speak if a direct question is asked by using their name? Other than that, the second soul is in total control, convincing everyone that it is the original soul."

Tamara could see by their body language that some people were thinking about what she had just said, about having to use a person's first name to make sure you are talking to the correct soul.

"You can remove the second soul, but it must be done very quickly, for the longer the possession has had control of the body, the harder it will be to remove it."

Tamara took a sip of her water.

"But there are some spirits that have possessed a body, and no one can remove it, no matter what they try to do, other than killing the person it now resides in. It is called a walk-in, also known as a soul transference. A walk-in is a contract made in the afterlife with a nearly departed soul from Earth. At the time of death, the two souls exchange places. A new soul takes over the body and continues that life. This new soul does not have to go through the years it took to get to that moment in time. It doesn't go through being a baby, learning all the things a body must know to function. Convenient if you ask me."

Tamara noticed that she would need to rent a bigger room; people were standing along the walls.

"It usually takes about four years for a complete soul exchange, but friends and family will notice a considerable change in the person's looks and personality within days. Even the person's career and family life can drastically change. The new soul may not have liked the same things the original soul did and decided to make some changes.

"What I just described are all considered possessions. Now it is true that a few of you may be possessed, but at some point, all of you have had dark energy attach itself to your body. You probably wouldn't even know it was there."

A lady screamed, and the audience's reaction was as if they had just witnessed a ghost pop up in front of them.

"It is okay. You are under my angel's protection. Take a breath," Tamara said to the lady, who started to calm down.

"Until now, you probably never thought about it. And if you don't think about something, it usually can go unnoticed for years. The attachment usually doesn't do anything to make you notice them. But they might cause you grief from time to time. The best way to know if you have an attachment is if you have unexplained pain in your body that moves."

A couple of people in the audience shivered as if they were trying to rid the feeling of dark energy being near them.

"The biggest problem is losing your life-force energy. Now with a walk-in, it is an agreement that both souls made, so the new soul is not taking anything from you. But, in the case of possession, the new soul will eventually steal all of your life-force energy, killing your soul. And even though you can live with an attachment of dark energy or even a loved one who has become a lost soul and is attached to you, it is still stealing your life-force energy, creating pain, or making you tired."

Tamara noticed a couple get out of their seats and leave the conference room.

"Tonight, I am going to help you get rid of any dark energy attached to you. I will be mostly focusing on the souls that have attached themselves to you without you knowing."

Tamara pointed to the audience. "These lost souls are stealing your life-force energy very slowly, making you feel sick or causing you physical pain. These are the spirits we are going to be concentrating on tonight. I am going to do more than talk about it. I am going to show you."

Tamara took a sip of her water and changed the seating on stage by bringing in a chair next to her stool. If anyone else was thinking of leaving, they changed their minds, for nobody else left, and the empty seats were filled by a couple that was standing.

"I need a volunteer please from the audience. I am going to let my angels decide who to pick. I am not going to tell you what we are doing until I have a person sitting here in this chair." She pointed to the chair on stage.

A few hands went up, and she picked a man in about his mid-forties to come up on stage. As he got up from his seat and walked to the stage, he looked back at his wife as if to say, *"What am I getting myself into?"*

Once he was sitting on the stool beside Tamara, she said, "Hi, what is your first name, please?"

He replied with self-renewed confidence, "Jack."

"Thank you, Jack, for volunteering."

Looking at the audience, Tamara said, "Jack is up here tonight because he has subtle negative energy attached to his body. It may be a ghost, spirit, or dark entity. We are not going to know until we are partway through the procedure."

Jack looked at his wife in the audience. With the expression on his face of *"Whoa, I hope this isn't going to hurt."*

Even the few people who initially seemed disappointed with the change in the topic were now intrigued by what was about to unfold.

Addressing the audience, Tamara went on, "Tonight's demonstration is vital for many reasons. For those of you that do not yet believe, for those of you who do this kind of work, and lastly, for those of you who can't accept that your loved one has died and don't realize that you might be the one holding them back from going into the light.

"All three reasons are significant, but I am more concerned with you having an attachment that is stealing your life-force energy. And worse yet, if you became the attachment when you die, and become the spirit stealing someone else's life-force energy."

Jack looked at Tamara and said, "What, are you saying? That if I die, I could be the one stealing a loved one's life-force energy?"

"Yes, Jack, that is what I am saying, and that person could be your wife," Tamara replied as she pointed to his wife in the audience. "You must understand what happens to a human soul when a lost soul becomes attached to it. I need you all to realize that a ghost is a lost soul."

Tamara turned from Jack to speak to the audience. "How does a person become a ghost when they die? Usually, by believing that he or she was not good enough to get into Heaven and is too scared to move on, or the ghost has some unfinished business. Another way is for those of you who can't leave your loved ones behind on Earth, and in most cases, your soul will probably become a ghost."

As Tamara turned away from the audience and gave her full attention to Jack, she said, "Usually, my client sits in a La-Z-Boy chair, but they do have a choice to lie down on a massage table. Jack, I want you to close your eyes and sense your body, starting from your head going down to your toes. Tell me if there is any pain in your body or weird feelings."

"A little pain in my neck," Jack answered.

"Which side?"

"Left."

"Anywhere else?" Tamara asked.

"Yes, in my right shoulder and my right hip."

"Anywhere else?"

Jack moved his body slightly to feel if there was anywhere else that he felt pain. "No."

"Great, let's start with the pain in your hip. Focus on the pain in your hip. Ask the pain if it has a name. In your mind's eye, literally, ask your hip, 'Do you have a name?'"

There was a pause as Jack looked at Tamara as if she had lost her marbles, but he did as she asked and went inside his head to ask if his hip had a name. Smiling back to Tamara, he said, "No."

"Great. Now do the same for your neck."

Smirking to himself for feeling like an idiot, he shut his eyes again and then said, "No."

Tamara had a hunch. "Great, now your right shoulder."

This time Jack instantly closed his eyes. "Yes. Wowzah, that is weird." Jack opened his eyes and looked at Tamara in amazement. "It is like I can actually sense a person now. His name is Fred." Quickly he stood up and shook his body as if something was on him. "Tamara, what kind of game are you playing?" Jack asked with a freaked-out emotional tone in his voice.

"Jack, sit down. With the help of the spirit world, I will help you."

Jack reluctantly sat back down.

Tamara now addressed the entity. "Fred, for how long have you been attached to Jack?"

Jack answered, "Two years." Looking at his wife, he shrugged his shoulders, his face full of disbelief.

"Fred, would you like to go home?"

"Yes." Again, looking at his wife as if to say, *"I'm not making this stuff up."*

"Excellent. Fred, in just a moment, I am going to have a loved one from Heaven come down to greet you and bring you back home. Is that okay?"

"Yes." Jack just surrendered and co-operated.

"Great. I am now asking my angels and guides in Heaven to please ask a loved one of Fred's to come and bring him home."

Ecstatic to be with a loved one, poof, just like that, Fred ascended.

"Jack, how do you feel now?"

Opening his eyes, Jack looked at Tamara again. "That was weird. I could actually feel him leave my shoulder. It was like a weight was lifted." Looking at his wife in the audience, he said, "Hun, I'm not making this shit up. I really felt something leave me."

Tamara smiled and asked, "How does your shoulder feel now?"

Jack moved his arm and shoulder a bit. "Holy crap, all the pain is gone! Can you do that for my neck and hip?"

"I wish I could, but an entity is not causing that pain. Sorry, maybe a massage or an Epsom salt bath will help that go away," Tamara suggested.

"Thank you, Jack. You can now go back to your seat."

Jack got up, and as he was leaving, he kept moving his shoulder in disbelief, thinking the pain was going to come back.

As Tamara watched Jack leave the stage, she could hear much chatter going on in the audience. Many people in the audience were watching Jack as he sat down beside his wife. He touched his shoulder, nodding, telling her that the pain was really gone.

Tamara knew listening to her guides was always beneficial. She knew that tonight's change of topic would benefit everyone in the room. "Okay, we are going to take a ten-minute break, but when we come back, I will be demonstrating another soul transportation or, as I originally called it, retrieval."

Chapter 15

Walking back on stage, Tamara said a silent prayer before she asked for another volunteer.

"Alright, who is ready to free their body from pain?" Many hands went up this time. Tamara picked a lady in her mid-thirties. She gave the girl sitting beside her a quick hug before she got up and started to move past the people in her row. Tamara noticed that as she tried to pass a man, he seemed to have said something to her and had kept her from coming up onto the stage. Coincidentally, he was sitting behind Lexi. "Please come on up," Tamara said, trying to hurry her. The girl motioned to go past again without success and decided to turn around and go the other way, shaking her head.

Trying not to give energy to whatever happened in the aisle, Tamara said, "Hi, what is your name?"

"Kalie," the lady said shyly.

"Nice to meet you, Kalie. Okay, you have seen how this works. So, have a seat and make yourself comfortable. Close your eyes and take a few deep breaths. . . now, scan your body from head to toe."

Kalie took a moment to follow Tamara's instruction. "I only have one pain, and it is in my mid-back," she said, pointing to the spot. "But Tamara, this pain has been here for about five years. I have gone to doctors, and they say that nothing is wrong. I've been to see many acupuncturists and massage therapists, and nobody can get rid of it for me or figure out why I have this pain. I have tried everything."

Tamara nodded and asked, "Kalie, does the pain ever move?"

"Actually, yes. Sometimes it is here." Kalie pointed again to a lower point on her back about three inches away.

"Uh-huh. How often does it move?"

"Every few days or so." Kalie looked at Tamara with surprise and hope. No one had ever asked her that question before.

"Interesting. Now, just relax and take another breath. Does it have a name?"

Shutting her eyes, Kalie took another breath and then said, "No."

"Kalie, I am going to talk directly to your pain. Just answer whatever comes to mind."

Kalie nodded. She understood.

Talking now to the pain, Tamara asked, "Did you know that you are held to this body?"

"No," Kalie said.

"That you are not free to leave it?"

"No," Kalie said.

"That you are stuck to it and can only move a few inches? Do you want to be stuck to this body forever?"

"No," Kalie said, with a tear slipping away from her eye.

"Most attachments don't know this information, but now that you do, I can help you leave. Would you like that?"

"Yes." Kalie had a few tears slowly moving down her cheeks.

"Great. I am going to have Archangel Michael come down to help take you home. Is that okay?"

"Maybe." Kalie shrugged.

"No problem," Tamara closed her eyes and took a moment. She was calling Archangel Michael to come to her aid and help this soul, who was attached to Kalie, to go home. Opening her eyes, she said, "Archangel Michael is here to help guide you home. Would you like me to come along to make sure you are okay?"

"Yes." Kalie nodded.

"Great, take my spiritual hand, and I will go with you and Archangel Michael to your home."

The instant Tamara said home, Kalie trembled as if something had left her body. Many people in the audience gasped. Tamara took a deep breath and opened her eyes. "Thank you, Archangel Michael, for assisting me." Turning to Kalie, she asked, "How do you feel?"

Tears were free-flowing from Kalie's eyes and running down her cheeks. She used her sleeve to wipe them away. "That was incredible. I can't explain the feeling. It was so sad. The energy was hiding and was afraid. Man, that was just incredible."

"How does your back feel?" Tamara asked as she pointed to Kalie's back.

Kalie stood up and bent over, and then she tried twisting in both directions. "Amazing! The pain is gone. I mean really gone. No more pain." Crying, she hugged Tamara and thanked her. Smiling, she wiped more tears away and left the stage.

Most people in the audience, including Lexi, looked astonished by Kalie's miracle healing. *It's bad enough that Susannah is in the Void, but thank God she is not attached to me.* Lexi's body shivered from the thought. *That would be creepy, and I would have to be in pain because she would need my life-force energy to survive. Let's pray it never has to come to that.*

Tamara was used to the emotions a person has when they experience this type of healing. Some people are stunned, shocked, astounded, and even dumbfounded. Until you feel it for yourself, it is hard to imagine what actually transpired.

Tamara took a sip of water then addressed the audience again. "When Archangel Michael comes, he is so sweet, patient, and polite. Archangel Michael's job is to guide souls back home, wherever home is. Home is not what you think it is. Usually, it is in the level of love and light, a place that I call Heaven. But sometimes, it is not. I have experienced other localities he has taken a soul to a few times, and it was to another planet. He doesn't take pleasure or have any remorse. To be honest, he doesn't have any emotions. He diligently does his job.

"My job is to find out if it is an entity and then if it needs assistance in bringing it home. Most of the time, all I need to ask is a loved one from Heaven to come and show themselves to us to help guide the attached soul home. Sometimes it is an animal that the soul recognizes and instantly departs. If I do require Archangel Michael's help, he usually comes alone, but sometimes he comes with whom I call the Bronze Master.

"Occasionally, the entity is extremely stubborn. And we need the help of the Bronze Master and his net to retrieve a soul. The Bronze Master has the skin color of beautiful bronze, muscles that would put any bodybuilder to shame. He seems to be from a time when loincloths were worn. He has a sash that he wears across his torso and carries with him what resembles a fisherman's net. The fibers of the net's mesh are made from something that an energy spirit cannot escape.

"I have had the honor of having many spirits present themselves in my life, for the purpose of healing, knowledge, wisdom, prophecy, tongues, miracles, faith, and distinguishing spirits. People come to me, and others like me, to seek spiritual guidance, direction, confirmation, protection, ascension, inspiration, motivation, and transformation. All of which can only be guided through the help of the spirit world.

"Traditional medicine may help cure the pain. BUT there are people with spiritual pain in their body, **AND YOU WILL ALWAYS KNOW IF IT IS A SPIRITUAL ISSUE BECAUSE THE PAIN WILL MOVE!**" Tamara said with extra intonation in her voice. "The pain can move a few inches or to the other end of your body. And I do not mean in a simple case like you hurt yourself, and as you heal, the pain is sore in the one area for a few days and then changes and moves up or down a little bit. I mean that in the same day, even within the same few moments, the pain travels and changes places dramatically."

Tamara stood in the middle of the stage. With outstretched arms, she gestured for the entire audience to rise. "Please stand. We are going to do this next part together." Waiting a moment for those who would stand to get up from their seats. "Take a deep breath and sense your body. Where is the pain located in your body?

"Take another deep breath, sense it again. Did any of the pain move from one location to another?

"Now, ask each spot of pain individually if it has a name." Tamara waited for the audience to get an answer.

"If the answer to both questions is no, then please have a seat." Many of the people in the audience sat back down.

"Great. Now for everyone sitting or for those of you that came and do not have a seat but answered 'no' to the questions, please help me by thinking the thought of love-light energy. Just by saying the words in your mind, you are generating the energy I need to help these lost souls. The more people thinking love-light energy, the more love-light energy we'll create."

Tamara smiled as she noticed a few people in the audience, including Lexi, who closed their eyes while they mouthed the words "love-light energy."

"Archangel Michael, please come down into this room and help guide these beautiful souls attached to the people in this room. It may be a loved one who has not moved on, a spirit or ghost that is scared and does not know where to go, or a dark soul that doesn't know any better. Archangel Michael, please, allow your troop of angels to guide these lost souls back to their home, wherever that may be."

With that said, Tamara took a deep breath. She imagined that the angels were taking the "stuck and lost souls" home, detaching themselves from the humans in the audience.

In the split second that Tamara had taken the breath, many of the people standing in the audience moved. They jolted, flinched, inhaled, or shook. Many people collapsed onto their chairs.

"Please, rescan your body. Any pain left? If not, please sit down if you are not already. And if you are sitting but the answer is yes, please stand back up.

"If yes, ask it if it has a name or notice if it moves." Only a few people were left standing.

"Archangel Michael, please protect these people from any more harm from the souls that are still attached. Lost souls, let me help guide you to your home. Archangel Michael, please allow part of my spirit to go with you and these souls to show them where they will be going."

Tamara closed her eyes and took another deep breath. In her mind's eye, with the guidance of Archangel Michael, Tamara could see loved ones that had passed on coming down to greet their lost family member. For some of the souls, it was a beloved animal that met them, and again, poof, the soul detached.

Again, many of the remaining people's bodies flinched or shook as the soul separated from them.

"As the lost soul leaves your body, please have a seat."

There were only two people left standing.

"For the two of you left standing, there will be a reason that the spirit did not leave. It may be because you do not believe any of this is possible, and it is you that won't let the spirit leave, or it may be because the spirit needs more help and has unfinished business left to do before it can leave.

"Let's offer the spirit, that beautiful extra soul attached to you, a view of a few places it can go. Archangel Michael, please show these spirits a few choices of where they can go." Luckily for Tamara, both people standing wobbled, and she knew the entities had left their bodies.

In her mind, Tamara thanked Archangel Michael and then said, "Thank you, everyone, for participating. Take a deep breath. Sit if you are standing, even on the floor, and take a few more deep breaths."

It only took a few moments for the audience to readjust to the new energy in their body.

"Good job, everyone." Tamara clapped her hands. After taking a few more deep breaths herself, Tamara continued, "I am going to finish tonight's lecture with a story about my first experience meeting an Archangel.

"It was many years ago when I was working in a natural health and healing school. I was practicing the art of meditation. In my meditation, I was visited by a man who seemed to be in his early thirties who had a cobalt blue energy field. He never spoke to me, but I remember how he looked:; strong, fit, good-looking, and trustworthy.

"Once I had finished the meditation, I remember asking up to the heavens, 'Who is this man, and what does the meditation mean?' I remember a thought popping into my head. . . proof that an important message comes in threes.

"Over the next few days, I kept hearing about Archangel Michael, even from strangers. A customer came into my place of business. By coincidence, she told me about a painting she was creating of Archangel Michael, dressed in blue.

"Next, I decided to go to a metaphysical bookstore and asked the owner if she knew about Archangel Michael. She brought me over to the section about angels and pulled a book down from the shelf on Archangels. Sure enough, a darker haired clean-shaven Michael was dressed in the most amazing blue Roman-like garment revealing his powerful features. He wore a cape that swirled around him like it had an energy of its own. He was just as I had envisioned him in my meditation.

"My third message of proof came to me when a client had come in and was having a reiki healing session with me. While I was performing the hands-on-healing energy technique, suddenly, for the first time during a session with a client, Archangel Michael appeared in my mind. It all happened so fast. He appeared, said nothing, removed a negative energy form from the room and disappeared just as quickly as he had come.

"You must understand that I have one of those minds that needs answers and proof—lots and lots of evidence. I didn't remember anything about Archangel Michael from my childhood catechism classes, other than his name. For many weeks I researched everything about Archangel Michael that I could. Anything about what I had seen in my meditation and felt in my reiki session.

"Was it really Archangel Michael or just my crazy imagination gone wild?

"Michael is mentioned in the Bible; Dn 10:13, 21; 12:1; Jude 9: and Rv 12:7.

"Even though I have grown up believing in God, Jesus, and all the angels and saints, I can only speak from my own experiences. I have come to count on the powerful energy of Archangel Michael, coming to the aid of my clients in need, for the purpose of removing a soul that is attached and draining their life-force energy."

With that said, Tamara asked everyone to bow their heads and give thanks to the spirit world for their help and guidance.

"My next lecture will be held on Tuesday, Dec 2nd, but you will have to check my website for where it will be held. I am going to have to find a much bigger location," Tamara said as the audience chuckled and nodded in agreement.

"Everyone, take a few deep breaths and ground yourself, bring yourself back to the awareness needed for driving. Drive safe and thank your angels before you go to bed. They do a great job protecting you." Tamara clapped her hands in appreciation to the angels and walked off the stage.

Tamara was watching as Lexi was leaving the lecture. The man behind her seemed to have left before Tamara could get a good look at him.

Chapter 16

It was a beautiful Wednesday afternoon as Lexi drove over to Reverend Hawthorne's. The sun was shining. It had been a warm fall with daytime temperatures nearing 60 degrees Fahrenheit.

The Thanksgiving weekend was coming up in a couple of weeks, and Lexi was so grateful because her new fashion design got accepted. It would to be showcased in the next big fashion show. She loved to envision famous and influential people wearing her design to their next extravagant event or gala. Imagining that their picture would be taken, and her exceptional creation would be on the front cover of *People Magazine*, or even better yet, a fashion magazine like *Vanity Fair*.

She was still daydreaming as she pulled into the parking lot of the funeral home. During business hours, the funeral home's doors were unlocked and open to the public.

When Reverend Hawthorne was too busy, he had staff that could help the grieving people purchase a casket or make the necessary preparations, for either a funeral service, if the body was present, or memorial service, if the body was not present.

Having a scheduled meeting, Lexi was escorted into Reverend Hawthorne's office. Standing up, he greeted her and gestured for her to take a seat. "Alexandra, I am so happy you found the time to come in and speak with me. How is your mom doing?"

"She's doing as well as can be expected. Thank you for caring enough to call. I do wish to speak with you." Lexi didn't know where to start, but remembered to take a deep breath. Which she now loved to do, thanks to Tamara. Taking a deep breath always seemed to calm her nerves and mind, giving her that extra split second to focus her thoughts before she spoke. "Reverend—"

Reverend Hawthorne interrupted her. "Please, call me Edward. We've known each other for a long time now." Most of his clients were well into their seventies and eighties. He had been so busy the last few years that he never seemed to meet people his age. It was refreshing to have such a beautiful woman in his office.

He was in love once, but she could not come to terms with the life he led; he knew the thought of dead bodies made her skin crawl. He had a feeling Alexandra was different.

Lexi took a breath as she looked into Edward's eyes and pleaded for understanding and help. "Edward, I know I am the key to helping my sister, Susannah, get into Heaven. I don't understand or even, for that matter, believe everything, but we must find her and bring her home. I stumbled upon an article written by Edgar Cayce, the famed psychic." Pulling a piece of paper out of her purse and unfolding it, she passed it to Edward to read.

The Void:

After death, we may enter a region that is Void of love, life, and light, Void of everything. For some, this region is apparently where their wish can come true. Here they are truly alone with themselves. For some souls, this is a pain that is unbearable. In the absence of truth, love, gentleness, and kindness, some souls fill the Void with an irrational and unbelievable amount of pain and fear. It is so dark in the realm of outer darkness that the darkness hurts, and panic grips them without knowing why. There are various degrees of darkness to this realm, and it is darker and denser at the center than at its outer fringes. The closer we are to the outer edges, the more interaction there is with others in the realm. The closer to the center, the darker and more painful the solitude is. Those who find themselves in outer darkness cannot travel across this dimension. They must grow through the levels of this realm. After death, one may find themselves in a particular degree of darkness that most closely corresponds to the degree of the absence of love in one's life. Outer darkness is not a punishment. It is a region that operates lawfully for the benefit of those who are there. This region is not a realm that was created for any soul to experience but one that came about as a consequence of the negative activity of souls in creation. So great has been the desire for self, so monumental across time and space has been the selfishness of some of God's creatures that this realm is the creation or manifestation of their own collective activities. Outer darkness and the reality with which it is associated were created and are held in place by collective self-interest.

After reading the description, Edward nodded. "I remember in seminary school that we did a brief review of the belief of the Void. It is supposed to be a space that amplifies thought and emotion. It is believed by researching the stories of people with near-death experiences.

This nothingness can be agony and torture for some souls, a void of all love, life, and light—the ultimate experience of aloneness. But there are also articles written that it can be a temporary stop-over for the soul. If the soul can embrace love and forgiveness, it can ascend into Heaven."

Edward looked deep into Alexandra's eyes as he passed the paper back to her. *Was she ready for the task of bringing a soul out of the Void?* "Alexandra, your sister was not an evil person. Her soul can be retrieved if you believe it can."

"Reverend— I mean Edward. I fear that she is being tortured by the dark entities grabbing for her soul. My sister may have been going through a time in her life when she questioned the existence of God. But her soul does not deserve the penalty of being stuck in the Void. We need to help her. And I will not stop until I know for sure that her soul rests in Heaven."

That was all Edward needed to hear. He was in, and with his heart not following too far behind him.

Chapter 17

From the depths of Hell, Adramelech was hungry and thirsty for the never-filling life-force energy of a human. Picking up on the scent of Susannah's recently departed soul as it entered through the realms, Adramelech and his demonic troops had almost scooped Susannah's soul up. He had touched her light energy just as she was whisked away in the cosmic tornado, taking her out of his reach.

Adramelech knew the laws of the spirit world, and once Susannah soul was stuck in the Void, nothing but love could get her out. But there was no law saying that he couldn't try for the next best thing. Which was when a person is in a dream state, their mind is slightly manipulatable. The underworld, full of dark entities, can try and sway a person while they are dreaming, creating the illusion of reality. And Susannah's sister,

Lexi, was in the perfect state of mind for the spirit world to prey on her grief and unhappiness. So, he decided to give Lexi a visit.

Frustrated with having to defend her sanity and urgency to save Susannah's soul, Lexi was brushing her teeth in the bathroom when she broke down and started to cry. Rinsing her mouth, she grabbed a couple of tissues to wipe her nose and went to bed. *Lord, how am I supposed to believe in all this ghost stuff? God, honestly, I am having second thoughts. I don't think I can pull this off. I love my sister dearly, and it kills me to think that she may be out there, lost, but how can a person so sweet as Susannah not be in Heaven? It makes no sense.* Pulling up the covers, she snuggled deeper into her bed and closed her eyes.

In her dream state, Lexi started to call out Susannah's name. *"Susannah! Susannah, where are you? Stop playing hide and seek. We are too old for this game."*

Lexi was dreaming that she was looking for Susannah. She looked everywhere but couldn't find her. *"Susannah, this game is getting boring. Where are you?"*

"I'm here, Lexi. Just come look a little longer. You are so close," Adramelech said, pretending to be Susannah.

"Susannah, keep talking so I can find you. When did you get so good at hiding? I was the one that used to hide, not you."

Coxing Lexi's soul closer to him, Adramelech said, "Lexi, I am over here. Come and find me."

Chapter 18

Adramelech, the King of Fire, knew the only way he could keep his title was to become stronger and more powerful by feeding off living beings' emotions, such as fear, anger, and greed, or the ultimate conquest, to receive a full soul. He knew that winning an entire soul would grant him a new demon to join his command. The more demons in his control equaled a higher rank. A higher position gave him more power. More power granted him the opportunity of a new position, Archdemon, and all the entitlements that go with it.

In today's world, most humans don't believe that we even exist, let alone that we have any power over them. The fools, if they only knew that all we need to do is tempt them into any of the seven sins.

The Seven Governing Royalty Leaders of Hell were each controlling a sin. Lucifer, the

Archdemon who controls the dark entities that feed off pride. Beelzebub, the Archdemon who controls the dark entities that feed off gluttony. Satan, the son of Lucifer, is the Archdemon who controls the dark entities that feed off wrath. Leviathan, the Archdemon who controls the dark entities that feed off envy. Mammon is the son of Satan and also an Archdemon. He controls the dark entities that feed off greed. Belphegor, the Archdemon who controls the dark entities that feed off sloth. And Asmodeus, the Archdemon who controls the dark entities that feed off lust.

Each dark entity is associated with specific acts and sins, and each of the seven Archdemons has countless dark subjects that do their bidding.

Adramelech had pledged his allegiance to Satan in the Kingdom of Wrath. Adramelech had died eons ago, and his soul was not granted access into Heaven due to the sins he had committed on Earth. These were not the deadly sins of gluttony or lust. No, his sins were of the evilest kind: murder, violence, and destruction.

Over time, he had worked his way up the ranks and now helped to govern Wrath's malevolent beings, demons, fallen angels, ghosts, goblins, evil spirits, hybrid creatures, the daevas of Zoroastrianism, creatures of hell, and the oni who were the attendants of the gods of the underworld.

Each full soul that his soldiers brought back granted Adramelech more power, abilities, and, eventually, a promotion. But to survive, a *shedim* (demon) or *ruhot* (dark spirit) must tempt a soul of the light into committing a sin. It was Adramelech's job to make sure that all the newly fallen angels, demons, or darkened human souls, learn the techniques of temptation.

The laws of the spirit world are extremely strict. A soul must give in willingly or be out of control of their body. Then and only then can a demon or dark entity feed off their life-force energy, and only while they are committing the sin.

Even though there are many souls of the light in Heaven, it is forbidden to enter, and a demon will be incinerated if it tries to gain access. The only sustainable nourishment is found from a weaker, clueless human's soul.

It is so easy in today's time compared to the past to feed. The humans don't believe as they used to in the protection of charms, amulets, and talismans that are inscribed with efficacious formulas.

Humans are so easy to prey upon. Their minds are weak; they are so easily tempted. Speak nice things to them and boost their egos. Show them their favorite or forbidden foods. Tell them little stories to make them believe the worst of their foes. Dangle jewels and riches and tell them that it is theirs. All they have to do is... We hardly have to do anything for those that cherish more.

Negative thoughts, such as the information the media broadcasts, do most of the mind-altering for us. All we have to do is be near.

Their minds are so pathetic that it is easy to convince them that they are sick and tired. And the easiest of all is tempting them with each other. Humans' downfall is their emotions, and this is where we demons can feed for all eternity. As long as there are humans, we will be fed.

Adramelech was summoned to a devilish meeting with the other kings of the underworld.

Lucifer, the son of Aurora, the morning-light-bringer, and the father of all the devils, boomed over all that was in his court, "The time is now. Humans are ripe for the picking. War, disaster, disease, they are killing themselves. All we have to do is wait for them to come to us. Don't worry. You can still send your troops out to scavenge the land and tempt the souls to commit sinful acts. Which one of you created the pandemic? That was brilliant!"

Berith popped his shadowy figure out of the crowded room and said, "That was mine and Mammon's idea. We combined the ability to murder with the sin of greed." He chuckled. "There always seems to be a human that we can tempt to do our bidding."

"Well done, that added many souls to our list. I can't believe what those humans will do just to get toilet paper. Greed is greed in any proportion. Won't they be surprised when they go up to the pearly gates and can't gain entry? They don't seem to understand the consequences of their actions. How doing such a little thing adds up to many little things, which is enough to weigh the scale in our favor."

Lucifer looked into his globe that emanated an eerie glow around it, showing him all the souls on Earth.

Adramelech was seated next to Satan, the worst devil of them all, who was sitting next to Lucifer. Being so close to Lucifer's globe, Adramelech could see what they were seeing. He was surprised to see that Lucifer's globe was different from his own. Lucifer's revealed the souls that shone the brightest. Adramelech knew that the brighter the light, the more life-force energy the soul possessed. *No wonder he is so powerful. He has an advantage over us.* Before Lucifer noticed his prying eyes, Adramelech had time to notice one soul in particular whose flame was incredibly illuminating, Susannah Grace Constantine's. *If I could only get that soul, I would become an Archdemon. Just to outsmart Azrael.* Adramelech's archrival was Archangel Azrael, Ruler of the Heavenly Kingdom of Patience. Each Archdemon is connected to an Archangel in heaven whose actions could override those of the demons.

Chapter 19

Adramelech was still fixated on the one enlightened soul that he saw in Lucifer's globe. He could not get the image out of his thoughts. *I must find a way to get that soul before any other demon does.*

Asking around, he had found out that Mammon's minions were busy working their magic through the corrupted gang members, creating the type of chaos needed to bring down the greed of the many.

This was his chance to become even more powerful than Satan. All he had to do was figure out how to get to this soul.

I need a plan, one that can grant me access to that marvelously tantalizing morsel. I need her soul!

Deciding to take a chance and tell another demon of his plan, he chose Archdemon Pythius, the God of Lies.

"Pythius, how would you like to gain even more power than you already have?"

"Adramelech, I have more power than you. Why should I listen to your lies? That is my ability?"

"Yes, great master, you are powerful but not as powerful as Lucifer. Did you know that his globe reveals souls that ours do not?"

"That is impossible. All our globes are the same."

"Yes, mine and yours are the same, but no, his is special." With the amount of devilish energy coming out of Adramelech, it attracted the attention of Archdemon Leviathan, the God of Envy.

"What is going on here? It must be evil because you two are emanating the stench that only goes with devious thoughts."

"Leviathan, this has nothing to do with you. Get out of here," Adramelech said.

"He has a plan to take over Lucifer," Pythius bellowed.

Adramelech hotly replied to Pythius's snide remark by saying, *"I knew better than to ask for your help. Don't worry, I can do this on my own,"* and vanished from the other two before they could belittle him.

Adramelech was not sure how he would pull this dark mission off, but he was sure he would come up with something. He stared at his globe, feeling burning greed for Susannah's soul.

Chapter 20

December was coming up so fast, and Tamara had been so busy since giving her lectures, with all the extra phone calls, e-mails, and private sessions, people grieving or for other spiritual reasons that she had hardly noticed Christmas was just around the corner.

She knew without a doubt that sharing this information about the spirit world was essential. She prayed that people understood from her previous lectures that communicating with spirits was important, but testing them first was even more critical.

She prayed that her audience had learned that only a human soul could become a ghost by attaching itself to a person, place, or object. And when that soul chooses to attach itself to a person, they are stealing that person's life-force energy.

She prayed that the audience understood why it was so important not to become a ghost and even more important to believe in an afterlife.

And for tonight's lecture, she prayed that her audience would be open to a life-changing experience.

"Good evening, everyone. Thank you for finding your way to this new bigger conference room." Tamara was happy that she could find a space big enough on such short notice.

Tamara took a moment to look at who was in the audience, then said, "Tonight's topic is a bit controversial, and to be honest, a little scary for some people to imagine as being real."

She took a sip of her water.

"How many of you have heard of the word 'metempsychosis'?"

A few hands in the audience went up. "The word 'metempsychosis' means that a soul can move from one physical body to another."

Tamara walked over to a small table beside her stool and picked up a paper she had lying on top. Glancing at it, she read, "Another common name for metempsychosis is reincarnation. Did you know the word reincarnation derives from Latin, literally meaning, 'entering the flesh again?' As promised, tonight I will be speaking on the topic of reincarnation."

Tamara continued, "Reincarnation is the concept that a soul from Heaven comes back down to Earth and starts a new life in a different body. Some people call reincarnation rebirth or transmigration."

She put the paper down on the table.

"I find it fascinating that even though the word reincarnation is not in the Bible, statistics show that over eighty-four million Christians. . . plus if you add up all the other religions combined that believe in reincarnation, it is over two point three billion people in the world.

"Reincarnation means that you have a choice to come back down here to Earth and experience a different life as a different person, or you could choose to be an animal, or many people believe that you could choose to be born on another planet somewhere else in the universe."

After hearing the words, "other planets," some chuckles in the audience could be heard. Tamara could tell their reaction that not everybody in the audience believed in reincarnation.

"How many of you know what muscle testing is?" Tamara raised her hand for the audience to put their hand up if they knew. Many people in the audience knew what it was. "Muscle testing is a way to program your subconscious mind to give you a yes or no answer. My test revealed that I had reincarnated many, many times. I have lived one day in some lives and moments in others. I have lived prosperous lives and impoverished lives. Lives where I am obese and others where I am anorexic. Lifetimes where I had addictions and many in sobriety. I have been a bad person and have lived like a saint. Sometimes I was a male, and sometimes a female. Other times, I was an animal. I've been all different ages, nationalities, and races. I have spoken many different languages. Some lifetimes I lived alone and some with more people than any one person could ever need. Some I died young, and some I died at a very old age. So many different lifetimes."

Tamara sat down on her stool and slowly scanned the audience, then took a deep breath and said, "Why?" Then paused for a moment to let the word sink in. "Think about it. Why are you living here on Earth?"

She paused again.

"My best guess for living that many lifetimes is so that I could experience every emotion one could sense."

"I once had a teacher who told me her theory about the choices a soul could make in the afterlife before reincarnating. She said, 'I want you to imagine that there are two souls that are up in Heaven, and the one soul says to the other soul, "I have never experienced being an aborted baby." And the second soul replies, "I have never experienced being a mother who aborted a baby." They both say to each other, "let's try that this next lifetime." And both souls agree on the experience to help each other evolve.' My teacher also agreed that only as a human can we feel emotions and evolve.

"Part of my job as an Earth Angel is to help a person's soul to evolve. There is a technique I call 'story mode.' Some people call it past life regression. I love to use this technique for a couple of reasons."

The words past life regression caught the interest of a few more people in the audience.

"I do a lot of holistic counseling, and story mode has an infinite number of lifetime possibilities. The imagination your subconscious mind has is incredible. The story one can create, real or not, while doing a past life regression is absolutely brilliant. The information the person tells me can be interpreted, and the symbolism or dream life parallels the issues that are going on in this lifetime.

"Another reason I love this technique is to find a person's life purpose and life lessons."

Tamara was happy with the reaction from the audience. Some people were sitting on the edge of their seats waiting for what was going to come out of her mouth next. Some were nodding their heads in agreement with what she was saying, and even though some would never believe in reincarnation, they were going to be interested in what she had to share.

"What if I told you that there is a way to help you fix an emotional, physical, mental, or spiritual life issue? Fix a disabling problem that is limiting your full potential just by using the 'story mode method?'"

Tamara took a sip of her water, then brought a chair closer to her stool for someone to sit on, and said, "Sometimes, words are not enough. I need a volunteer, please."

Looking at all the hands that went up, Tamara chose a lady in her early thirties to come up on stage with her.

The young lady walked up to her with an outstretched hand.

Shaking her hand, Tamara asked, "Hi, what is your first name?"

"Hi, Tamara. I am so happy to meet you. My name is Rebecca."

As Tamara pointed to the chair, she said, "Thank you for volunteering, Rebecca. Please have a seat and make yourself comfortable. Have you ever had a past life memory or experience?"

"No, I don't think so."

"No problem. In a moment, I am going to have you imagine a train station. But first, I would like to know if you have a fear or problem in your life, one that you wish would disappear?"

"Yes, actually I do."

"Tell me about it, please," Tamara said with a slight smile to make the lady feel comfortable.

"I have been having this dream about my husband dying. It gives me panic attacks. It feels so real."

"How long has this been going on?" Tamara asked.

"A couple of years now."

"Is your husband sick?"

"No."

"Okay, does he have a dangerous job?"

"No."

"Okay, anything else you can tell me about this feeling?"

"No, not really. It is just there, and it seems to be getting worse."

"Thank you. Okay, Rebecca, I would like you to take a couple of deep breaths, and I am going to start the first part of the meditation. . . I want you to imagine a train. . ." Tamara continued for a few moments talking about the train ride. "Now, I want you to step off the train and move to the side, not blocking anyone else's way. Look down to your feet. What are you wearing?"

"Nothing," Rebecca replied honestly. She could not imagine her feet.

"No problem, now scan the rest of your body. What are you wearing? Just imagine it like a dream or a really good B.S. story."

People in the audience laughed at the thought of a B.S. story.

Tamara smiled at the audience and said, "There is nothing you could say that could be wrong, and even 'nothing' is an answer."
Tamara was very used to the replies that a client would say and never paid much attention to

when they couldn't answer. They usually could with the next couple of questions.

Taking a moment, Rebecca replied, "I'm wearing a long dress like in the wild, wild west days on a farm. I am a little grubby from the chores."

"Thank you. Now, look around. What do you see?"

Quickly answering this time, she said, "I have three children, and they are playing outside, not too far from where I am working."

"How long have you lived there?"

"Many years, all three of my children were born here." Rebecca's eyes were shut now as she was imagining the story.

"Are you married?"

"Yes."

"Where is your husband?"

"Umm, I don't see him."

"Can you hear him?"

"No."

"Is he there on the farm with you?"

"Umm, I think so."

"That is okay, take your time. Is he in the house?"

"I am not sure."

"Go in and look."

"Okay. . . Yes, he is in bed, and he is very ill. I think he is dying."

"Okay, thank you for sharing that information. I want you to imagine now that you have a remote control in your hand. Please, fast-forward this life to another important moment for us to know about."

Tamara paused and waited until Rebecca answered her a moment later.

"I am dancing in a saloon. I think I do even more than just dance." Rebecca started to cry on stage. "Oh no, I love him so much, and he is dying. The farm is in shambles because he cannot work it. We have no money because of the doctor bills." She started to sob, and instead of asking for a tissue, she rubbed her nose on her sleeve.

"Rebecca, take a breath, use the remote control, and go a bit further into that story. What happens to your husband?"

Tears started to pour down her face. "He died. And now I am an outcast in the town. I have wrecked not only my life but my children's by working in the saloon." Tears were streaming. "But I loved him. I needed the money."

"Rebecca, I need you now to take a deep breath. Is there anything else about that life that you need to tell me that could help you in your real life?"

"Yes, that I am not going to make that mistake again."

"Rebecca, take another deep breath and imagine that you are getting back on the train. This time the train comes back to this very moment in time." Tamara finished the meditation by saying, "Wiggle your toes and come back to the moment. You can now open your eyes." Tamara gave Rebecca a moment to focus on the now. "How are you feeling, Rebecca?"

"That was incredible, so insightful."

"Do you understand the meaning of that lifetime? Does it make sense comparing it to your life right now?"

"Yes, actually, it is dead on. I fear my husband is dying and is going to leave me and our two children alone."

"And now how do you feel after knowing he died in another lifetime?"

"To heck with that, I am not wrecking my children's life for a man that is going to die anyway. There was nothing I could do to help him."

"True, another person's fate is their responsibility, not yours. So, what can you do in this lifetime to make a difference and not get panic attacks about something you cannot control?"

"Tamara, I am not going ever to feel that embarrassed again. The people in that lifetime respected my husband and didn't say a word about what I was doing until he died. And then they turned on me like I was a bad person and banished me and my children from society. That is not going to happen in this lifetime. I promise you that."

Rebecca got up off her chair and gave Tamara the biggest hug, took a couple of tissues from the box Tamara had on the floor, wiped her nose, and left the stage.

Many people in the audience clapped and cheered for Rebecca's ah-ha moment.

Tamara turned to the audience and said, "In a meditative state, it is remarkable that the mind has a way to create a story in such specific and vivid detail. The information you are imagining is as if you were being inundated with a lifetime of memories, and every second that you are in the story-mode meditation is mind-blowing. The answers and solutions that come to you during a session can be astounding.

"Usually, I ask the person to imagine how they die in that lifetime and to go to Heaven and look back down on that life, asking them what their life lesson and their life's purpose was.

"Also, I never give them a tissue when they are crying. It tells them to shut up, and in counseling, that is the last thing I want them to do. I always have tissue within their reach.

"I can't prove to you if reincarnation or past lives are real, and maybe it's a really good story that a person makes up in their imagination. A dream, or perhaps it is an excellent Sant B.S. story. But what I do know and can prove to be true is the stories that people come up with are life-changing, and the healing that comes from the story they just told me is astonishing, as if they had lived the life."

Tamara paused for a moment.

"I was never afraid of dying. Having lived so many lifetimes, I knew I could come back and experience a new life. But not too long ago, I found out that this was my last lifetime living here on Earth. My last lifetime watching a sunset, smelling a flower, tasting chocolate ice-cream, the sensual feeling of making love, or hearing the enchanting sound of children's laughter."

Tamara took a breath and looked out over the audience.

"In the afterlife, everything is blissful, but the thought of never living on Earth again makes me cherish every moment I have even more."

A tear fell from her eye as she took a deep breath and put her hands into a prayer formation, bowing her head saying, "Namaste." As she stood, she said, "For those of you who are not accustomed to this word, it means my soul acknowledges the light in your soul."

Ending the evening, Tamara said, "Thank you all for coming. Please check my website for the next lecture I will be giving. With Christmas coming up soon, it won't be until the new year. Night everyone, and remember to create awesome memories!"

Chapter 21

Reverend Hawthorne was in the audience,
listening to Tamara talk about reincarnation. The
school he went to did not teach the belief of a
soul coming back to Earth in another body. As a
Minister, though, working at a funeral home, he
had probably heard every story you could
imagine coming from the families of his clients.
Stories of their father, mother, sister, grandpa, or
friend visiting them, right up to stories about
scary hauntings and missing items.

Standing up to leave, he saw Alexandra and
hurried through the crowd so that he could catch
up to her. He accidentally bumped into a couple
of people as he made his way through the
crowded foyer of the hotel. Not wearing his
clerical Roman collar, he fit right into the rest of
the crowd and didn't have to stay and apologize.
He quickly said, "excuse me," and moved
through the people.

Lightly grabbing Alexandra's elbow, he said, "Alexandra, how did you enjoy Tamara's topic tonight?"

Startled, Lexi turned her head to look at who was touching her. "Rev— I mean, Edward. Hi." Very surprised to see him here, she didn't answer his question. Instead, she said, "What are you doing here?"

"You got me intrigued, so I decided to come and find out for myself if I believe in what Tamara is talking about."

"And what did you decide?"

"Do you have time right now for a coffee? I would love to chat about it."

"Sure."

Edward put a hand on Alexandra's lower back, guiding her through the crowd to the hotel's lounge, and asked for a table. He made sure she was comfortable before he sat down across from her. Answering her question as he sat, he said, "I am not sure what I was expecting. She made some fascinating points and shared interesting concepts. She had some new ideas about reincarnation and past lives that I hadn't heard before. How about you, what did you think?"

Lexi took a moment to rethink what Tamara had talked about that night. "Edward, what if . . . It could be a crazy idea, but what if all we need to do is get Susannah's soul back to Earth and have her become a ghost? Maybe that way we could help her believe so she could get to the light?"

"That is an interesting thought."

The waiter interrupted them to get their drink order.

Edward continued, "Since you are not going to move on from this notion, here is my take on the matter. I grew up around the dead. My father and grandfather were morticians. Their job was to prepare the corpses for a funeral or to be cremated. When I was young, I helped them many times with the process. I was taught that a dead body is just that. Dead."

The waiter interrupted them again by putting their drinks on the table.

"Ever since I was born, my bedroom has been above a morgue. Alexandra, I have imagined seeing, hearing, feeling, and talking to ghosts all my life. The afterlife has intrigued me for as long as I can remember. Trust me when I say I didn't become a minister for any old reason."

The look on Lexi's face showed she was relieved. It meant a lot to hear him say that he believes, not just in God and religion but also in spirits and ghosts. "Oh, thank God. I knew there was a reason I was supposed to come to see you that day. Okay, you couldn't stop the funeral, but I know there is a very good reason that you are part of this odd predicament." Lexi was grateful to have a familiar face to help her with this situation.

Edward shook his head. "Maybe I am a small part of the answer, but I am not sure of how to bring Susannah's spirit back now that she is dead. If we could do that, the rest is easy. Truth be told, I can sense them and prepare them for ascension into the light, but I cannot summon them. My job is to pray for a soul to go to Heaven, not to create a ghost."

Lexi was not really listening to what Edward was saying because she was too caught up in her own thoughts. It was like a light bulb went off in her head. She had a brilliant idea. Tamara and Edward, together the three of them could accomplish this feat. She got shivers running up and down her arms and legs just thinking about it. Yep, this was going to work. Excited now, she sat on the edge of her seat closer to Edward. "Edward, please say yes. I know how to make this happen. Well, maybe not how, but who. I need you and Tamara to help me. Please, say yes, you'll help me get my sister to Heaven?"

Edward stared at Alexandra. She was so beautiful. Her dark hair cascading down her back. Her bright eyes gleamed with enthusiasm and confidence in saving her sister from eternal damnation. So fragile, yet so powerful. How could he say no? "I'm in. I am always up for a new challenge. I might even learn something."

"Yes, oh my God, yes. You don't know how happy you just made me! Okay, I'll get hold of Tamara and find out times that may work. I will call you after to set up a group meeting. I think what we are about to do is called a séance."

"Please, let's call it a prayer group. I don't think my religious upbringing can handle the term séance. I may believe in spirits and ghosts, but I am still a Reverend."

"Sure, you say tomato, I say 'tomaeto.' No matter how you say it or what you call it, it's the same thing. I will call Tamara tomorrow. I can't wait to find out her ideas on this matter."

They both got up, and Edward paid their bill on the way out. "Alexandra, I promise I will be open-minded and as helpful as I can be. This step is essential in the grieving process. The faster you can find peace, the better it is for your well-being. Not to mention the well-being of Susannah's soul."

"Thank you, Edward, that means a lot to me. It is like having an angel with me in the flesh. See you soon." Giving him a quick hug of gratitude, she left.

Edward could still smell her perfume lingering in the air. He could not believe the romantic feelings he had when Alexandra was around him. *I think she is oblivious to my feelings for her. Once this ordeal is over… Edward, remember, keep this professional.*

Chapter 22

Tamara had been on the phone again all morning. Her lectures triggered so many of the attendees to make sure their loved ones were safely in Heaven. *Oh, there it goes again. I need an assistant.* Picking up the phone with a smile, she said, "Good morning, this is Tamara. How can I help you?"

"Oh, I am glad I caught you. It's Lexi. Hey, by the way, excellent lecture yesterday. I find your lectures so informative and fascinating."

"Hi, Lexi. Thanks. How are you doing?"

"Actually, awesome. You wouldn't believe who was in your audience this time. Reverend Hawthorne. And, get this, we went out for a drink after in the hotel, and he said he would help us get Susannah back. Oh my God, Tamara, I am so excited!"

"I can hear that in your voice. That is great news. I actually have some ideas for us. I have been asking up for any ideas or dreams to come to me. I have also been researching online on how to do this soul retrieval."

"Awesome. Tamara, I want to thank you so much for believing my story. You don't know how happy I am that we are going to save Susannah. And I want to tell you that I believe! I believe that there is a possibility that ghosts and spirits are amongst us. Well, almost a hundred percent believe; there is still a tiny part of me that is skeptical. I am scared that I would be doing a sinful act."

"It's okay if you have a slight doubt, as long as you believe it is possible. There is nothing sinful in what we will be doing. We are not hurting anyone or breaking any laws, real or spiritual. In fact, we are saving a soul, and God is pleased when one of his flock comes back to him. Imagine that you are a shepherd, and you are on a journey to find a lost soul."

"That makes it easier, Tamara, thanks."

"I will be right there with you. You are not doing this on your own. And remember, somehow, you even convinced a minister to come and help you. You will be well protected."

"Right. There is nothing to be afraid of, is there?" Lexi said with a hesitant voice.

"Lexi, I can't promise for sure to get your sister out, but my intuition says that it is going to be a success. There is nothing that can happen to you while you are in my care. I promise."

"You can actually promise me that there is nothing that can happen to me?"

"Yes."

"That makes me feel better. And for sure, I am not breaking any spiritual laws? Or that what I am about to do won't somehow stop me from getting past the pearly gates?"

"In the Bible, it says to not talk to a spirit only because it can trick you. Lexi, they can't trick me. I have been doing this for a long time now. I know the rules to the game, so to speak, inside out and backward. You are in safe hands, I promise."

"I believe that I have no choice. Susannah's soul needs saving, and it is my job to save her."

"You always have a choice, Lexi, but in your case, you have done your homework. You didn't just believe me, you have come to see me, you have had prophetic dreams, you have brought in the power of a man whose sole role in life is to help the dead ascend into Heaven. You have come to how many of my lectures now, two, three?"

"Four, I think."

"You are not going into this blind or unprepared. You have done your homework and have two extra people with knowledge in this matter. Your soul is safe, and it probably counts as a virtue."

"You are right. I am not going into this blindly. I do trust both you and Edward. I guess my upbringing is giving me doubts."

"You were taught well. Don't second guess what you have been taught in the past; just know there is always more to the story."

"Thanks, Tamara, that helped."

"We will save Susannah, but Lexi, I have been so busy with all my new clients that we're going to have to wait a couple of weeks before I can help you. I am so sorry."

"Oh." Disappointedly, Lexi said, "All right. No problem. Can you give me your ideas on how you're going to get Susannah back?"

"I wish I could, but I don't have all the details yet. I do know it's going to be successful, especially now that you've said Reverend Hawthorne is going to help us. Not sure how you pulled that one off, but we are going to need God on our side. I gotta go now, Lexi, but let's plan for two Monday nights from now. After work, around seven. I'll call the Reverend myself and set it up and see if we can meet at his place. That way, I can tell him what I will need. I'll call if it won't work. Otherwise, see you there."

Hanging up the phone, Tamara jotted down in her calendar the time, place, and what they were doing, smiling to herself. *This is going to be fun.*

Chapter 23

Edward picked up the phone. "Hi, this is Reverend Hawthorne. How may I help you?"

"Hi, this is Tamara Reeves, Lexi's friend."

Edward had to think a moment, "Oh yes, Alexandra's friend, the medium. Hi, Tamara. I am glad you called. Alexandra has spoken very highly of you, and your lecture the other night was very interesting. I enjoyed the topic. You are an excellent speaker."

"Thank you, Reverend, that is very kind of you to say. I am hoping you have a couple of minutes to talk right now?"

Putting the papers in his hand down, he said, "Sure, how can I help?"

"First, do you have time, two Mondays from now, at 7:00 p.m. for Lexi and me to come over and try a soul retrieval session?"

"Let me see." Flipping through his calendar, he said, "You're in luck. That date will work. Any later, though, I'll be quite busy with the holiday season coming up. Unfortunately, Christmas seems to be a time when the elderly have more health issues and more emotional stress. The death rate seems to go up around this season."

"Same in my business, it increases. People miss their loved ones and want to communicate with them." Getting to the point, Tamara said, "Reverend, I will need a few things for you to have on hand when we do this soul retrieval. I am assuming it is okay if we come there to your place?"

"Yes, that will be fine. What do you need?"

"Holy water, white candles, and oil. Do you have these, or should I bring some?"

Subconsciously, Edward knew why Tamara needed these items. There was only one reason. "Yes, not a problem. I have the items you are requesting; they're always here on hand. Anything else?"

"Nope, other than your spiritual talent of prayer and a strong connection to God. That will be all that I need. Pulling someone out of the Void is not going to be an easy undertaking. I am praying that Lexi will be strong enough in her faith and belief to carry this through. Actually, I am so grateful that she has a strong Christian upbringing. It helps me."

"Really? How does that help you, Tamara?" Edward was intrigued to find out her answer. He didn't think that someone who dealt with the occult would care about a religious upbringing.

"I know that a lot of religions do not approve of what I do. But I am on the same side as they are. My sole purpose is to help souls go into the light, no matter if they call it Heaven or not. I need a person to have a belief system of a power greater than ourselves that is holy. Especially if a person starts to dabble in the spirit world and has no belief set in place, it can cause a huge problem if they ever find themselves in a tricky situation. Whereas a person who has a solid belief in a higher power can call on to it to help if ever there is a need."

"That is reassuring to know. Thanks, Tamara, for explaining that."

"Reverend Hawthorne, we are going to need all the spiritual help we can get to pull this task off. And I am looking forward to saving a deserving soul. It makes my heart sing. See you in a couple of weeks." Tamara hung up the phone and emailed Lexi to confirm the date and time.

Interesting. It should be a very enlightening experience, Edward was thinking to himself as he hung up the phone.

"*Angel of God, my
guardian dear,
to whom God's love
commits me here, ever this
day be at my side
to light and guard, to rule
and guide. Amen.* "

Chapter 24

Standing by her station in the huge designing gallery, Lexi was talking with one of the other fashion designers about an up-and-coming fashion show.

"Mmm, mmm, he's a tall drink of iced tea." When she turned to look at who the girl was referring to, Lexi saw a well-dressed man in his early forties, with short straight blond hair, fit, and clean-shaven coming toward her.

"Miss Constantine, I am Detective Redington with the New York Police Department. I was wondering if I may have a word with you about your sister Susannah's death." He moved his suit jacket to the side to reveal his badge as proof.

"Thank you, Sherie. I will talk more with you a little later about this design."

Known for coming from money, the high-society and beautiful young lady from S'vanah gave her best smile, saying, "Yes, mama," and with the most elegant strut, and flirtatiously batting her eyelids, she walked away from Lexi and the plain-clothed police officer. Quickly looking back as she left.

"This is strange of you to be here, Officer Redington. Is there a problem?"

Not paying any attention to the young lady who just walked away, he said, "It's Detective Redington. I am following up on the investigation, and I need to ask you a few questions."

"There is an investigation into my sister's death? I thought she died in an automobile accident."

"She did, but I am wondering if you have seen this man before." He showed her a picture of a man in about his late thirties, shorter, about five foot six, husky build, with dark hair and a large mustache. He looked a little rough, with a day or two growth on his beard.

"I don't believe so. Why are you asking?" Lexi was now very concerned. *Was it not an accident? It must not have been if he is still looking into the cause of death. Oh, my God, Susannah, what did you get yourself into?*

"Miss Constantine, if you see this man or anything suspicious, or if you receive a package, please call me at this number. It is my direct line." He gave her a business card with his information printed on it: *Detective Ferguson Redington, Homicide Investigator, Manhattan Bureau – Midtown South Precinct, Shield number 1323*, and the contact number to call him.

As he turned around and disappeared as quickly as he had shown up, Lexi said, being a little cheeky, "I will, Officer."

As Detective Redington was walking away, he thought to himself, *I hate this part of my job. A family thinks that it is over. They buried their loved one, only to find out many weeks later, sometimes months, that it isn't. The look on Alexandra's face was one of shock. She doesn't even know what I am talking about. I am pretty sure she doesn't know that her sister was involved in trafficking drugs.*

Back at his precinct, Detective Redington stared at a whiteboard that he had hanging on the wall in his office. For almost sixteen years, he has been with the Midtown South Precinct, one of the twenty-two Manhattan bureaus. Ever since he became a detective, his primary job was to investigate homicides relating to the Midtown Business District.

What do I know so far? Susannah had worked for one of the top antique dealers in the city, Aryeh Jacob Kofman. His Jewish ancestors had been in the business of buying and selling people's estate items since the Renaissance period. Redington knew that his retail gallery *was in the Manhattan Antique and Design Center on 40th St. and 6th Ave. He also knew that Kofman had a few warehouses where he stored his precious antiques, vintage, and collectibles. One was located on Staten Island, and the other was in DUMBO, where Susannah's loft was located.*

Detective Redington had been on this case for almost a year. It started by investigating the homicide of a gang member, Andy Barkley, who was associated with the criminal mastermind, Italian American Mafia member Marko Calponi, unacknowledged grandson of a famous gang member.

Marko had been importing stolen goods out of New York Harbor from all over the world. Many of his shipments contained items packed with secret compartments that could conceal drugs. He was so good at his job that even the best K9 could not sniff out any evidence.

And he knew that the night Susannah was killed, the man, Maxwell Shrewder, driving the other vehicle, worked for Marko. The police had found enough evidence in his truck to prove that her accident was, in fact, a murder. Under the seat, they found the guy's phone, and once they unlocked the screen, a photo of Susannah appeared.

Chapter 25

Twirling a strand of her dark brown curly hair, Sherie came back over to Lexi's easel once the detective had left. "Oh, my golly, he's rather peng, isn't he?" she said with a distinctive Southern drawl, as she pretended to fan her face and faint. "I don't know about you, but I love a detective all gussied up in a suit. Even better yet is imagining what he is concealing underneath."

"Sherie! Honestly, someone would think that with your Southern belle upbringing, you would have a purer mind." Lexi laughed as she smiled in agreement with how the detective looked. He did look "as pretty as a peach," as Sherie would say it, in his Stefano Ricci copycat suit. She was sure he had it custom-tailored to conceal his weapon, handcuffs, cell phone, ammunition, business cards, and a notepad. Oh, and any good detective would be carrying with him a stain remover stick, in case he had to chase a suspect down and his suit got dirty. Hey, a girl in the fashion world needed to know these things; it's taught in first-year Basic 101 Style Design Class.

"What do you reckon he was here for?" Sherie's curiosity was getting the better of her.

"It was weird, actually. The detective asked me about a man," Lexi said as she raised an eyebrow.

"Oh, foot! Lexi, I know that look. I reckon there is more to this story. What has it got to do with you?"

"Not me. Susannah."

"Susannah, bless her soul, but I thought it was an accident."

"So did I."

"Who was the man y'all was asking about?"

"I don't know. I have never seen him before."

"Did the detective say anything else?" Sherie was getting right into this investigation thing.

"Umm, what did he say? Oh yeah, he said to tell him if I receive an anonymous package. I wonder what he meant by that."

"A package? That is strange. Why would you be getting a package? And from who?" Sherie was in her head, thinking of what kind of package Lexi would be sent, just as their boss came over.

"Sherie, get back to work," Sebastian said, pointing in the direction of her easel.

"Don't pitch a hissy fit with a tail on it, Sebastian. I'm going," Sherie said as she curtsied for a dramatic effect before she left.

Shaking his head at Sherie's drama and then turning back to Lexi, he said, "Lexi, I need to see you in my office."

Following him into his office, Lexi said, "Is there a problem, Sebastian?"

Shutting the door so no one else could hear, he said, "I was going to ask you that same question. Why was the detective here?"

"To be honest, I am not sure. Detective Redington showed me a photo of a man and asked me if I had seen the fellow before. I guess the guy who hit my sister's car worked for a mobster."

"And did you?"

"No. I have never seen him before today's photo."

"Lexi, I can't have the police coming here to the design center. You will have to make sure in the future you talk somewhere else. We can't have our prestigious clients think we are running an undercover business."

"No problem, Sebastian. It won't happen again," Lexi said as he opened the door to let her out of his office.

What in blazes is going on? Lexi thought to herself as she went back to her easel, sat down, and stared at her design.

Chapter 26

From his precinct on the fringes of Hell's Kitchen, Detective Ferguson Redington with his already impressive resumé of wrestling a murderer into handcuffs in a back alley, cracking the case of a corpse in an art museum, and chasing suspects through the Empire State Building, Grand Central Terminal, Rockefeller Center, as well as Times Square, can add… *How the hell am I going to close this case?*

The Midtown South Precinct, also known as the Manhattan squat brick station house on 35th Street, has a long reputation as a station house with a swagger. The reputation comes from its officers being assigned to the precarious task of policing some of the city's most iconic buildings and districts—the garment and theater districts, to be precise.

Not caring about the reputation of his station house, Redington was staring at his whiteboard. He was frustrated that he hadn't solved the case and was still trying to figure out the missing pieces of this homicide. *I have followed one of Marko Calponi's guys, the one they call "Little Eddy." And on two accounts, I can connect him to Alexandra Constantine. The first time was at a lecture in Brooklyn on October 29th, and the second time was at the same location on November 5th. The weird part is, both times, he sat directly behind her but did nothing. What does she have to do with all of this?*

Officer Blaine Davidson walked into his office, interrupting his train of thought. "Red, we have a problem. The court order you asked for to search Miss Alexandra Constantine's apartment has been denied." Davidson, shorter in height for a cop, with fire red hair and sideburns, had been a good friend and stuck around when Redington was going through his divorce. It had been two years since Laura left.

"What? They can't do that," Redington roared, banging his fist on his desk. "What excuse did they give?"

"They said that you have no proof that she has any connection, other than being her sister. They said you could bring her in for questioning, but that is all."

"There has to be a connection! Why else would Little Eddy be following her? We have to find a connection."

"What do you want me to do?" Davidson asked with concern for his friend's obsession with this case.

"There has to be a connection."

"If you say so, Red, but if you ask me, we have a closed case. Both people are dead."

"I know, but I can feel it in my gut that there is more to this," Redington said, rubbing his chin while he was thinking. "We have two of Marko's guys dead. Andy Barkley a year ago, and the guy in the other vehicle who killed Susannah, Maxwell Shrewder. Both guys have a connection to Calponi's smuggling of drugs into the country." Redington stood up and stared again at his whiteboard. "We suspect Kofman for how the drugs are being brought in, but we can't prove how they are being brought in or how they are transferring the drugs. We know that Susannah Constantine worked for Kofman and looked after most of the estate and antique shipments." Redington shook his head and crossed one arm at his chest and the other resting on it, rubbing his bottom lip.

Trying to help, Davidson said, "Don't forget, Red, that you also have the not-so-accidental death of Susannah. There is no way that she ran a red light, there was a car in front of her, and your investigation team found a vehicle tracking device planted underneath her car. Somebody knew where she was heading."

"True, but why would they want her dead if she was working with them to bring the drugs in? It doesn't make sense."

"You'll crack this case. You always do, Red."

"Yeah, hopefully, sooner than later, and I pray that Miss Alexandra Constantine is not the next name on the list."

"You'll figure it out," Davidson said, as he was called away on another task.

Redington contemplated to himself, *How come Little Eddy was following you, Alexandra?"*

Chapter 27

"So, have you heard anything new? What are you fix'n to do?" Sherie asked as she took a seat across from Lexi, and placed her elbows down onto the table and propped her chin up with her pretty little hands.

The lunchroom was full of people, and Lexi nervously said, "Shhhh, someone might hear you."

Sherie looked around the room and said, "Nobody is even noticing us. So, have you?"

"No."

"Aren't you going crazy with not knowing? What did your mom say?"

"Oh, my God. I didn't tell my mom. That would be the last thing I would do. She is heartbroken by Susannah's death. The thought that one of her babies could have committed a crime and was murdered would break her," Lexi said as she thought about how her mom would react to the news.

"I am dying to hear the details," Sherie beamed. "Our own version of unsolved mysteries like they have on TV."

"Really, Sherie? Honestly, I can't believe what comes out of your mouth sometimes." Just as Lexi was going to add to what she was saying, Sherie pointed behind her.

Turning her head to where Sherie was pointing was one very dreamy detective making his way to the lunchroom.

"Oh, my God. Sebastian freaked out last time he was here." Quickly getting up from her lunch, she rushed over to the detective and grabbed his arm. "Detective, you can't be here," Lexi said as she tried ushering him back from where he had come.

"Miss Constantine, let go of me. You are not allowed to push an officer around. It is against the law." Detective Redington was trying to loosen her grip on his arm as he was being turned in the opposite direction.

"I got in trouble last time you were here. My boss reprimanded me and said that if he saw you in here again, I could lose my job."

"He said he would fire you?"

"Well, not exactly, but he was adamant that you do not show your face in here again."

"Really?" Redington started looking around for her boss. "Miss Constantine, where can we go to talk? It's important."

"There is a coffee shop next door. Let's go there." Lexi let go of the officer's suit jacket and led the way.

She's a feisty little thing. I'll give her that much, Redington was thinking to himself as they entered the coffee shop.

"Detective, this better be important, as you disturb me at work, again."

"I came at your lunch hour," he said with a smile.

"Funny, how conscientious of you." Lexi smirked back. "So, what is so important? And how am I involved?"

"I can't tell you everything, but the gang who killed your sister is now following you."

"What!!!"

"For some reason, the guy I have been tailing has been sitting behind you at two lectures that you have been at."

"Oh, my God. Behind me?"

"Yes. I haven't seen him around you since November 5th, but there must be a reason that he is stalking you. You haven't seen anything suspicious?"

"No."

"Why are you going to Miss Tamara Reeves's lectures?"

Lexi felt foolish now. "She is helping me with a spiritual issue."

"Really?"

"Yes. She is a medium, and I have been going to her to learn more about the journey of a soul."

"I see. And don't tell me, this soul happens to be your sister?"

"Why yes, who else would it be?" Lexi said, realizing how crazy that sounded. Feeling stupid, but at that moment, an epiphany came to her. "You said he followed me up until November 5th."

"Yes. That is correct."

"That was the night that Tamara did a soul retrieval on the whole audience."

"I don't see the connection," Redington said as he shifted his eyebrows in a questioning motion.

"The guy was possessed. That has to be the explanation."

"What? Really? You believe that a guy following you is possessed? You mean by a demon?"

"Yes."

"Wow. I might have heard everything now."

"Detective, it is very impolite to judge others, especially when they are sitting in front of you."

"Sorry, but really, a demon?" Redington was shaking his head in disbelief.

"Think about it. Has he followed me since that night?"

"No."

"That is because Tamara cast out all dark entities and attachments. Wow, am I lucky I was there that night."

"Miss Constantine, I fear for your safety. I need to know everything that you know about why the mob murdered your sister."

"As I have told you before, I don't have any idea. Susannah was a beautiful person; she wouldn't have hurt a fly."

"How about drugs? Did she do drugs?"

"What! No."

"Are you sure about that?"

"Positive."

"Why are you so focused on Susannah? What evidence do you have that she was connected to the mob?"

"I am not at liberty to divulge that information."

"Well, isn't that convenient? Am I under arrest, Detective?"

"No."

"Then we are through here." Lexi stood up and walked out of the coffee shop.

Dang, it! I need to find the clues to solve this case. Somehow both sisters are connected. I need to find out how. Detective Redington paid for their coffees and left the shop.

Chapter 28

$\mathcal{L}$exi kept getting the creepy feeling that she was being watched. *Great, now I am imagining things just because Detective Redington freaked me out. Wonderful, all I ever wanted was to be a top designer. I never asked to save my sister from the Void or having to watch out for demons and the mafia. Where did I go wrong?*

To Lexi's unaware knowledge, the demon Adramelech was looking into his globe, watching her every move. He had been focused on her ever since he found out that her sister Susannah's boss had been coerced into working with Marko.

Adramelech had come up with a brilliant plan that would guarantee him what he wanted most, to become an Archdemon. All he had to do to get to Susannah was to go through Lexi.

His new idea was to tempt the same man that had been following Lexi around to do his malicious bidding for him. But instead of attaching to him, he was going to enter the man's body and possess the man. That way, he would have total control over his actions.

Waiting for the perfect opportunity, Adramelech entered Little Eddy's body while he was drunk and high on adrenaline from another engaging illegal and violent gangster crime. *It is so easy to enter a body this way when every virtuous moral is vacant of a man's mind. I didn't even have to tempt him with my fire ability of creating a flame in the image of a provocative dancer to insinuate that he will gain the affection of his lusting heart.*

Now having complete control over Little Eddy's body, Adramelech snuck away from the gang and set upon completing his plan before anyone noticed he had left Hell.

Lexi was working on another design at her easel when the fire alarm went off. Quickly grabbing her design and purse from a drawer in the easel, she headed toward the exit. Following behind her co-workers to go outdoors, she covered her mouth as the smoke made her choke.

Once outside, Sherie found Lexi. Coughing she said, "That was close. I heard it started in the lunchroom. Some guy left a bag in the garbage can, and it exploded."

"What, is everyone okay?" Lexi said with concern in her voice.

"I think so."

"Some guy? They don't know who the guy was?"

"No. I guess it was some stranger, but nobody thought twice because lots of times boyfriends or detectives come looking for one of us," she said to lighten the mood.

"Funny. Did they say what the guy looked like?"

"I didn't hear if they did," Sherie said. Now she was curious about what the man looked like. "I will go and find out if anybody knows more."

Detective Redington found his way over to Alexandra. "Miss Constantine, I see you are alright."

"Sure, if you call coughing up a lung, alright."

"Miss Constantine, I am going to ask you to willingly come with me to the station house."

"What? Why?"

"I can tell you on the way," Redington said as he took hold of her elbow to guide her in the direction that he wanted.

Lexi moved her arm away from him, teasingly saying, "Detective, it is against my law for you to touch me."

"Touché, Miss Constantine, touché." Once in his vehicle, he said to Alexandra, "I have been doing a facial recognition computer search since I noticed Little Eddy following you."

"And?"

"We have confirmation that he was seen leaving your building moments before the fire alarm went off."

"Oh, my God. I had this creepy feeling that someone was watching me today."

"I am putting you into witness protection."

"But I haven't witnessed anything," Lexi argued. "I can't afford to not go to work."

"Don't worry. It will be weeks before the police and fire department let you guys back into your building."

"Wonderful, that is all I need right now. It isn't like I don't have enough on my plate. Now I have to add going into hiding on it," Lexi said as she sat back into the seat and crossed her arms in defiance.

"Alexandra, are you sure there is nothing you want to tell me?"

"You wouldn't believe me anyway."

"Try me."

"Fine. My sister's soul is in trouble, and I need to save her."

"Really. And you have proof?"

"I have a dream, and that is enough for me!"

"I see," Redington said as he drove the rest of the way to the station house in silence.

Adramelech knew that part one of his scheme had successfully connected Alexandra Constantine to Susannah's crime. Now all he had to do was move to part two.

Chapter 29

Lexi was directed by Detective Redington to phone her mom, Sherie, and the staff at her apartment and let them know about her intended absence. She told her mom that she would be away on a business trip; she should only be a week or so. She told Sherie and the apartment staff that she was getting away for a family affair, and Redington made sure she told the staff to call her if any packages came for her.

She had been held in a safe house with guards for a couple of days now, and Redington was using this time to figure out how Alexandra was connected to all of this. Deciding to go and ask Alexandra some more questions, he headed to the safe house where she was being held.

He knew the guards well and brought them both a fresh coffee. The aroma of the coffee followed him as he found her sitting in a bedroom reading a book. "How do you think you are connected to all of this, Alexandra?" Redington asked her.

Deeply absorbed into reading her book and oblivious to the outside world, Lexi was startled when the detective walked in. Quickly gaining her composure, she looked up and said, "I told you, I'm not. But if I was, it has to be the demons that want my sister's soul. They are now after mine."

"We are on that again." Redington shook his head. "You seem like an educated person who wouldn't believe in the nonsense of the occult."

"I am, and I didn't until my sister died. Now I am open to believing that there is a possibility of the spirit world and all that it entails, good or bad."

"So, how would you like me to prove your innocence to my captain? With a cross and holy water?"

"Funny. I thought I wasn't a suspect?"

"Alexandra, when it comes to murder, everyone's a suspect. Your sister was murdered for some reason. We just need to find out what that reason is."

Lexi got that creepy feeling again, and it gave her shivers. The sound of gunfire and shouting made her feel like she jumped out of her skin.

Peeking out the door, Redington could see Little Eddy. He had found her safe house, and a gang of Marko's guys was firing at the two guards, killing them. Detective Redington's quick thinking had him and Alexandra safely out the window, running for his car, swiftly driving off as gunshots whizzed past his head.

"Oh, my God. They found me. How could they find me? I thought it was a safe house."

"It is. There is no way that they could have found you unless someone is working on the inside."

"You mean a cop?" Lexi said as she sat low into the seat so that her head was not seen.

"You have any other ideas?" Redington said as he sped through the streets, trying to lose Little Eddy.

Lexi thought for a moment and then said, "Yes, I do. A demon could find me if I was its target. Tamara had sent me an email describing all kinds of horrid things that can attach to us."

Redington wasn't sure where to take Alexandra. He couldn't take a chance and call it into the station if there was a dirty cop involved.

"Where are you taking me?" Lexi asked.

"I am not sure yet. I don't know how this got out of control. But I knew it in my gut you were involved, and now I have proof. They're after you."

"Why? I don't know anything."

"Somebody believes otherwise."

"Detective, we can go to my apartment if you think we have lost them."

"Your apartment, why?"

"Do you have a better plan?"

"No. I guess not. Alexandra, give me your cell phone."

Holding onto her phone with dear life, she said, "What, why?" but gave it to him anyway.

He broke the phone and then dumped it out the window.

"Hey! It had all my pictures on it." She was now looking behind her out the back window at the pieces bouncing as her phone broke on the pavement. "Plus, that is littering."

"We can't have anything that can track us." He pulled out his own phone and did the same. "Okay, we will go to your apartment."

"Don't you need my address?"

"No. I know where you live."

"Really?"

"I have been investigating you for weeks now."

"That is creepy."

Redington pulled up to Alexandra's apartment, and a nicely dressed young man at the valet counter, Sam, came around and greeted them by opening the passenger side door, saying, "Welcome home, Miss Constantine. Nice to see you."

"You too, Sam," Lexi said as nonchalantly as she could muster.

Redington passed Sam a twenty-dollar bill. "Please park the car where you can easily get it."

"Will do, Sir. Oh, by the way, Miss Constantine, a package arrived for you today." Quickly Sam unlocked a door to the side of the valet counter and retrieved the package, presenting it to Lexi.

Redington took the package from Lexi as they entered the elevator.

"Hey, it's my package!"

"It's police evidence. Cute kid, he seems to have the hots for you."

"Who is it from?" Lexi was trying to get a peek at the return address. "And he does not. Sam is being polite. It's his job. He's like that to everyone."

"We'll find out once we get into your apartment. We don't want any prying eyes to see what's inside."

"Oh, that makes sense." Lexi was thankful that the purse she had worn the day Redington took her was a small over-the-shoulder kind. She had it on now. Getting her key out of the purse, she unlocked the door and entered her apartment. It had been ransacked.

"Oh, my God. Detective, someone has broken into my place."

Redington pulled out his gun and cased out the rooms making sure no one was still there. "They must have picked your lock since there was no sign of breaking in. It's all secure. Nobody is here." He shut the entrance door saying, "Alexandra, it is not safe to stay here. Get a few things, and let's go."

"How long do you think we will be gone?"

"I don't know."

Too scared to argue, Lexi got a small bag and threw in a few clothes and her toothbrush and make-up.

Back down in the lobby, Redington asked Sam to fetch his car.

Without asking any questions, Sam ran. The man's face looked like he meant business. Coming back with the car, as he hopped out, he said to Lexi, "Miss, are you alright? I can get the police if you need help."

"It's okay Sam. He is the police."

"Oh," Sam said, as the two hopped into the car and sped away.

Chapter 30

Part two of his plan had failed. Adramelech didn't get Alexandra. He didn't have his globe to look into while he was in this body, so he didn't know a third person was in the safe house with her. He, as Little Eddy, was told there were only two guards.

After his failed attempt to get Alexandra, he went back to Marko Calponi's headquarters. It was in the back of a brothel. Adramelech walked past an illegal gaming hall with people gambling and through the hotel-looking brothel into a big room that resembled a private bar.

"What the hell were yuh thinking?" Marko shouted in his thick Italian accent at Little Eddy. Even though it killed him to be in this pathetic human body, he had to play along and be Little Eddy. Adramelech, not used to existing as a low-life thug taking orders, answered, "What the fuck is it to you?"

"What did yuh just say?"

"I was doing as you wanted, bringing in Alexandra Constantine."

"You killed two cops. I never said to bring the heat down on us. You idiot!"

"What did you just call me?" Adramelech roared, moving toward Marko about to kill him with his bare hands as three of Marko's guys pulled him back.

"What the fuck has gotten into yuh? It's like there is a demon inside of yuh. You're lucky I need yuh, or I'd have your head for this."

Lucky, I need him, or I'd have his soul for calling me an idiot, Adramelech thought to himself.

"We have a shipment coming in tonight, and it's the mother load. It's gonna make us filthy rich. You guys know the routine. Giovanni and Lorenzo, you two are going to do the bidding again. Little Eddy, you and Enzo will guard the gallery. The rest of you know your role. Meet me at Kofman's Auction by six-thirty sharp!"

Adramelech needed to figure out another way to get Alexandra's soul, and this might get him closer, so he went along with Marko's plan.

Six-thirty came quickly, and Marko's guys were all in place. Marko's idea to hide the drugs in the items to be auctioned had been working for months now, and Marko was getting more powerful with each new shipment.

Adramelech watched as twenty or so high-profile elites walked into the room and sat down. It was a private auction that Kofman set up for his most prestigious clients to get the first opportunity at buying the items up for bid. Two of Marko's men were sitting amongst the other buyers. The agreement was that Marko's men would bid whatever was necessary to outbid the others on the specific items that contained the drugs. It was brilliant, a legal auction.

It didn't matter how much Marko's guys paid for the item they bid on. Kofman never took their money. The deal was that he got a kickback when the drugs were sold and to stay alive. As Marko saw it, it was a win-win.

Kofman suspected that Susannah's death was no accident. She had walked in one day while he and Marko were doing a transaction. Even though she played it cool, Kofman knew she knew. And that meant so did Marko. Marko hated having loose ends that could come back and bite him, so in the past, he just got rid of them.

Being able to still hear the human's thoughts, Adramelech found this auction very interesting. *I can use this to my advantage.* Waiting for the perfect opportunity to present itself, he followed Marko's orders.

Chapter 31

Redington drove upstate to a cabin that Officer Davidson's parents owned. He had been there a few times over the years with Blaine. "Breaking in," not really. He knew where the family's key was kept.

Waiting for the door to open, Lexi asked, "Whose place is this?"

Opening the door, he said, "It doesn't matter. You should be safe here." Going back out and opening the trunk of his car, he pulled out two bags and the package.

"Don't tell me. You have a bag packed with your essentials in your trunk for days like today?" Lexi said as she pointed to his bag. The other bag was hers.

"Yes. Any good detective is always ready for anything."

"Handy."

"It is." Redington set the bags down and went over to the fireplace to heat the place up.

Lexi was looking at a beautiful log cabin with a high vaulted ceiling and a loft. It looked out onto a fishing lake, which was well hidden from civilization. "This is a cozy little cabin they have," Lexi said sarcastically.

Looking around, Redington said, "I guess it is pretty impressive."

"Do they have any food in this place? I am starving."

"Make yourself at home." Redington pointed to the kitchen.

Snooping through the kitchen pantry, Lexi found some canned beans. "Good enough for camping," she said as she found the can opener and a pot.

"Aren't you curious to see what is inside your sister's package?"

"How do you know it's from my sister? It could be from anybody. There is no name on it."

"It's from your sister. I can feel it."

"You question me about saving her soul, yet you know it is her because your gut feels it? An oxymoron if you ask me."

"I'm opening it."

"Hey, that is a federal offense to open someone else's mail, Detective."

"Then hurry up and get over here. I want to know what is inside."

Lexi brought over two bowls of warmed beans with a spoon in each and set them down on the handsome wood living-room table.

"Patience is a virtue, you know?" Lexi said as she sat down on the rug in front of the warm fire. The smoke from the fire carried with it the aroma of a freshly cut spruce tree from the forest.

"I've heard. Just open the damn thing."

Lexi took the package and shook it. It didn't rattle, and it was quite light. Opening it up like a savored moment at Christmas, she unwrapped the parcel. Inside was a letter. She emptied the parcel by turning it upside down and shaking it in case there was anything else inside.

Dear Lexi,

If you receive this package, then I am dead. I am so sorry for any pain that my death may have caused you and mom. I am soooo sorry.

No matter what the police say, if I am dead, then I was murdered. It wasn't an accident.

"I knew it! She was murdered," Redington piped up as Lexi was reading the letter.

Lexi, you have to go to the police and tell them everything. Kofman is working with Marko Calponi. He is bringing in his drugs with our shipments. The bastards! I didn't know until yesterday. I swear!!!

I had walked in on them as Marko was paying Kofman, not the other way around.

I had started to get suspicious when two men would take turns outbidding Kofman's prestigious clients. It didn't matter what anyone bid. On certain items, Marko's guys would bid crazy amounts of money to win.

Lexi, tell the police that I am innocent and that they need to check out Kofman's auction.

Love you, little sister, you are my shining star! With all my heart and soul, Susannah.

"I knew she was innocent. I told you so." Tears were coming down Lexi's face as the detective took the letter from her.

"Maybe, but now we have to prove it."

"We?"

"Well, no. I have to." Redington sat back on the couch, staring at the fire. *How am I going to pull this one off when I don't know who to trust in my unit?*

Chapter 32

"Davidson, it's Red. I need your help."

"Red, everyone is looking for you. What the hell happened? The safe house looks like an old-fashioned Tommy gun shot up the place, killing two of our men. Where are you? They're looking for you."

"Alexandra and I are safe at the moment, but I don't know for how long. Listen, I know how they are doing it."

"Who are you talking about? Doing what?"

"Marko and his goons, I know how they are getting the drugs into the city."

Davidson took a breath. He was hoping this day was never going to come. *Shit! He knows.* "That's great, Red. I told you that you would figure it out. Where are you? I can come and get you."

Redington's hair on his arms stood up. Something was amiss. "I'll call you back." And he hung up before anyone could trace the call.

"Fuck!"

"Watch your language!" Lexi said as she was finally eating her beans.

"He's in on it. He's the dirty cop."

"Who?"

"One of my best friends."

"No. Are you sure?"

"You know how I get gut instincts. Well, I also get hair that stands up on end when something dark is happening."

"Oxymoron is all I'm going to say." Lexi smirked at what she'd just said. "Now, what do we do?"

"I don't know. But we are not safe here. We have to move."

"Again, it is getting so late. Aren't you tired?"

"Get your things. We're leaving," Redington ordered.

Lexi grabbed her purse, the letter, her bag, and followed Redington to the car and got in.

"Tamara could help us," Lexi blurted out as they were driving in the dark.

"Who?"

"Tamara, the lady who has been helping me."

"The one who speaks about ghosts?"

"Don't say it like that. She is very professional."

"Uh-huh, sure she is," Redington said as he turned onto the highway.

"She is. I bet she would know what demon is following me."

"Not that again," Redington said as he gripped the steering wheel firmer.

"Hey, how do you explain the dude not following me after that lecture?"

"He is following you. He shot up a place that you were hiding in."

Lexi said the first thing that popped into her mind, "It's probably a new demon."

"Right, demons. That is the answer to all the crazies and gangsters out there. Demons possess their bodies."

"Or attach to them," Lexi added.

"Do you have any magic that gets rid of demons, Alexandra?" Redington took his eyes off the road for a second to look at her. *Shit, I think she really believes this stuff.*

"Tamara would."

"Go to sleep, Alexandra. I think you are delirious. You need to rest."

"She would," Lexi said as she laid her head back on the headrest and closed her eyes.

The sun was just rising as Redington pulled into a rest stop off the highway. He stopped the car to get out to go to the restroom.

Lexi woke with a startle, as she forgot where she was for a moment. Noticing her surroundings, she got out to go to the ladies' room.

"Lock the door," Redington called with his back to her.

When they both returned to the car, Redington said, "We'll rest here for a couple of hours, and then we will continue."

"This is ludicrous. Don't you think we should go to the cops?"

"Not if you want to stay alive."

"Great, do you have a plan? Where are we going to go now?"

Redington leaned his head back onto the headrest and shut his eyes. "Go back to sleep, Alexandra."

Wide awake, Lexi started to think back onto what she had learned from Tamara. *Demons, what did she say about demons? I wasn't really paying attention. Why would I? I didn't believe they existed. Crap, I wish I could remember what she said.* Lexi's mind was searching for answers, answers about the underworld, in both contexts—the mob and demons.

Chapter 33

The underworld was in an uproar over

Adramelech's disappearance. He went rogue and
left his command, breaking the Demons' Creed.

I dedicate my death to Lucifer, the father of
devils, the gatekeeper of Hell,
and the underworld.
I believe in his son, Satan,
his greatest achievement.
He was conceived by the power of the Dawn
and born of Aurora.
He suffered under God's authority,
was disempowered, fell, and abandoned.
He descended to the dead.
On the third day, he rose again.
He ascended his minions onto the earth,
and is seated at the throne of Sin.
He will come again to judge the dead.
I believe in the power of dark Spirits,
the temptation of human souls,

the communion of the dark,
the consequence of sins,
the damnation of the soul,
and the death everlasting.
All Hail Lucifer.

"Satan, he was in your control and was one of your best officers. FIND HIM, before they do," Lucifer commanded his son. Lucifer knew that if Adramelech wasn't found quickly, it could start a war with the Archangels. He knew the consequences of breaking the law of the spirit world; his father in Heaven had thrown him out for far less.

If Adramelech broke the demons' law of command, Lucifer's heavenly brothers would be looking for him, and if they catch him before he can, there will be hell to pay, literally. Lucifer would lose control over Hell.

He was trying to figure out why Adramelech would leave Satan's kingdom—he was the King of Fire, he had a league of thousands in his command, he was second of command to Wrath. *Why would he risk losing everything and being incinerated? What had tempted a demon to go rogue?*

Lucifer looked into his globe to find Adramelech's darkness. Each dark entity has a "signature" darkness, just as each soul has a signature light.

Lucifer could see that Adramelech had possessed a human body. *"Damn him, he will be found by Archangel Azrael and be incinerated."*

Lucifer's pride was still his downfall, and to this day, he was secretly seeking his father's approval. He never forgave his almighty father for casting him out of Heaven.

Remembering back to when he was young, growing up in the celestial hierarchy. He's the son of Dawn; her name is Aurora. She would greet him each morning as their light would fill the sky. His light was the first light that humans could see. His light was so bright it would reflect off the planet Venus.

As he grew older, he became more beautiful, intelligent, and powerful. He started to enjoy the position he held, so much so that he started to brag and strut around like a peacock.

It got to the point where his father, God, could not reason with him. He was acting worse than an adolescent who thought that no one knew better than he did. Lucifer's pride became brighter than his light. Needing to show off his brilliance, he started to perform sinful acts. At first, God had Aurora try to deal with him, but she too could not get Lucifer to obey the rules of the celestial world.

Finally, one day God had no other choice than to teach Lucifer a lesson and cast him out of Heaven, taking away his light. Lucifer was imprisoned in Hell and was given the task of Ruler.

Lucifer's pride became so sinful that he rebelled and married Lilith, sealing his fate to Hell forever. Lucifer never forgave his father in Heaven for casting him out. And even though he could not get his revenge, he taught his sons how to do it for him.

His firstborn, Satan, became the best and darkest devil that possessed the ability to torment and tempt God's precious human souls on Earth.

The spiritual laws were strictly enforced, and even though he found loopholes, he knew the consequences of breaking any of God's rules. He had to stop Adramelech before it was too late.

Chapter 34

"**Men**, we have to find Redington," Captain Mike Sawyer said to the officers standing there listening to his speech and direction. "I pray he has a good explanation for the kidnapping of Miss Constantine. Take him alive. He is still one of ours."

"Captain, I know he was my best friend, but a cop killing two of our officers is madness," Officer Davison said. *If Red knows about the auction, then my life will be terminated. Marko doesn't take chances, and he will think that I told Redington. I have to direct the blame on him and take the heat off of me.* "He called me."

"He called you, and you didn't say anything?"

"Well, Sir, I was about to, but you called this meeting, and I wanted to know what you were going to say before I put in my two bits."

"So, where is he?"

"I don't know. He hung up before I could get the trace on the call."

"What do you know?"

"He has Miss Constantine with him."

"Anything else, smart ass?"

"No, Sir," Davidson said, trying not to give away too much information. He had to make this look like Redington was in on Marko's plan.

"Davidson, just get out there and find him." Captain Sawyer couldn't believe that Redington would kill two officers; it didn't make any sense. He knew Redington was following the leads on the connection to Susannah Constantine's death with the mob. The captain watched as Davidson and the other officers left the room.

Davidson had been an officer of the law for the same amount of time as Redington. They met at the police academy. They had been partners before Redington became a detective. He was Red's best man at his wedding, and Red was his oldest son's godfather.

Davidson was thinking about the call Redington made to him last night. Red knew that Marko was smuggling in the drugs through the estate dealer, Kofman. It wouldn't take him long to start putting all the pieces together and connect himself to Marko. *Where did it all go south?*

Davidson remembered back when he was on duty, and some kids had broken into a house and stole some valuables. The kids were young and didn't think about the consequences of whom they might be robbing. They were caught in the act, but not by the cops. They had broken into one of Marko Calponi's hideouts, trying to prove that they were worthy of joining a rival gang. The boys were beaten almost to death when Marko found out who they were. Davidson got a text on his cell phone of the boy's whereabouts. When he and his partner got to the location, they found the boys near death and a letter.

Davidson, meet me at midnight on the docks... alone! I know where you live.

One of the boys beaten was Davidson's second-oldest son, Bradly.

Davidson had gone to the docks as the note had said, and Marko met him with his goons. "Davidson, you have two choices, join me, or your son dies."

Davidson knew he couldn't take Marko down, so he was forced to turn a blind eye to Marko's drug business. That was three years ago.

He had sent his children away to boarding school to get them out of harm's way. To pay for their schooling, he started to do some of Marko's dirty work. One thing led to another, and now he was so far deep into the shit that he didn't know how to get himself out of it.

It's not like Redington has any family. He wouldn't understand. I have to protect my family at all costs.

Chapter 35

"Have you decided where we are going?"
Lexi asked Redington. "We have to stop soon.
We can't get money out of the bank, or use our
credit cards, or stay in a motel. This is like some
cruel joke."

"I know, all you wanted was to be a top
designer, and you never signed up for any of this
other stuff."

"This is not a joke, Detective, and I do not
find your humor funny." Lexi was starting to
lose her mind. This was getting to be too much.

"We're almost there. It is just around the
block," Redington pointed in the direction.

"Whose place is this?" Lexi asked as
Redington was pulling to the side of the road.
He had parked in front of a modest house with a
big oak tree planted outside. There was an
American flag blowing in the wind, attached to a
pole on the house.

"An old friend and mentor."

"Mentor. From your station?"

"No. He was an instructor at the academy."

"Oh. And you think he can help us?"

"He is a retired cop, and he is my only hope of getting out of this with my badge."

They got out of the car and walked up to the front door. Redington knocked. A man with gray hair and a potbelly in his late sixties came to the door. "Red, is that you? What did you get yourself into this time? Come in and hurry. I don't need the nosy neighbors to be wagging their tongues."

"Bob, this is Miss Alexandra Constantine. Alexandra, Bob." He introduced the two and then said, "Bob, it's a long story. Do you have a beer?"

"It's eleven in the morning."

"Don't give me a lecture. It's been a hectic few days."

Retired Sergeant Bob MacFalen went and got three beers and brought them into the living room. "I'm listening."

"Alexandra's sister Susannah worked for a man who owns an antique business, Jacob Kofman. You know who Marko Calponi is?"

MacFalen nodded.

"Well, he has his filthy hooks into him. Kofman is bringing in the drugs with his estate items and selling them back to Marko during his private auctions. Brilliant actually, I don't know of a police officer out there that knew how Marko was bringing in the drugs."

"Have you told your captain?" MacFalen asked.

"No. I don't know who to trust. Alexandra was in a safe house when Marko's goons overtook it. We lost two good men. I barely escaped with Alexandra. Thank the Lord I was there. Who knows what would have happened to her."

"I see. And you have proof?"

"Yes."

Lexi pulled out Susannah's letter and gave it to him.

Reading it, Bob said, "Why are you getting me involved?"

"Bob, I don't know where to go, and I am running out of money and ideas."

"Hmm," the retired sergeant said as he leaned back into the couch.

"Sir, you have to believe Detective Redington. My sister is innocent. We all are," Lexi pleaded.

MacFalen rubbed the top of his head as he was thinking about what to do. Crossing his arms, he said, "We need a plan. The only way you are going to get out of this mess is if you catch Marko."

"How are we going to that?" Lexi asked.

Redington just sat back and listened.

"You say the drugs are transferred at the auction."

"Yep. That is what her letter says." Redington nodded.

"Okay, you will wear a disguise and go undercover and break this case open and put those goons away for a very long time."

"Oh, my God. You want me to do what?" Lexi went white as a ghost and almost fainted.

"What are you thinking, Sarge?" Redington was sitting on the edge of his seat, waiting for the plan.

"Here is what we will do. You will dress up as an Arabian ambassador and his wife. I have the costumes in the attic. One Halloween, Margaret and I, bless her soul, won the first prize."

Redington chuckled. "That's your plan? Have us dress up and go to the auction?"

"Do you have a better idea? You need proof."

"Sarge, Alexandra is a civilian. We can't have her getting involved in this."

"She is already involved, and you need someone who can help you get into that auction."

"Fine. We need to know when the next auction will be, and hopefully, it is before Davidson tells Marko that I know."

Reluctantly, Lexi piped up, "If you have a computer, I can look up the next auction."

Sergeant MacFalen got up and showed them into his office and typed his password in and unlocked the screen.

It only took Lexi a few moments to find the information. Susannah had many times talked about how exciting the bidding wars got. "Tomorrow night, at 6:30 p.m."

"Good. Now, Red, all we have to do is pull your car into the garage, so nobody sees it. I don't need the cops or robbers on my doorstep."

"Good idea," Redington said.

As MacFalen tossed his car keys to Redington to swap out the cars, he said, "I'll put some steaks on the barbecue."

Chapter 36

Adramelech was getting antsy. He was getting tired of Marko's leadership. To waste some time while he waited, he journeyed to Hell's Kitchen in Manhattan and tempted the atheist Satan worshippers with the power of gaining immense magic. He knew they craved the ability to bend an individual or situation to one's will or have the enchanted emotional energy to focus on a specific purpose to attain their heart's desire. *Such easy prey.* He knew that Lucifer fed off of their primary belief, pride.

Adramelech needed to find Alexandra's soul fast and before it was noticed that he had left his kingdom. *When I have her soul, I will have her sister's, and then I will be the ruler of Wrath. Satan can't be in the power of Inferno forever. I will overrule him.*

While Adramelech was out scavenging the sinners, Marko was having a meeting with Officer Davidson.

"He knows. Redington knows about your arrangement with Kofman."

"And where is Redington now?" Marko took a bite of his lunch. A dribble of spaghetti sauce ran down his chin.

"I don't know. We can't find him. He took off with that Constantine girl."

"He has Susannah's sister?"

"Yes."

Marko pulled out his gun and shot Officer Davidson in the chest, killing him. "Get him out of here. He is of no use to me anymore."

As his goons were removing the body, Marko called out, "Little Eddy, I need you to—" Looking around, he couldn't see Eddy. "Find Little Eddy and bring him to see me!" *What the fuck has gotten into him? It's not like him to take off without my say-so.*

Just as three of Marko's men were about to go and find Adramelech, he walked in.

"Where do you get off thinking that you have the authority to get up and leave without my say-so?" Marko wiped his chin with his napkin, got up, and came over to Little Eddy, punching him in the gut. His hand nearly broke as Little Eddy's stomach didn't even flinch.

Adramelech was now fuming that Marko had tried to hurt him. *These imbeciles cannot hurt a demon.* "What is your bloody problem now?" Adramelech roared. As he did, the items on the table, and the pictures on the walls started to shake.

Marko motioned to have his men attack Little Eddy, only to have them dead within seconds after being tossed onto the floor.

"Marko, you have far greater problems than trying to kill me. Your empire is about to crumble, and if you don't get that drug shipment, you're finished. You may need my help, so stop messing around," Adramelech said as he took Marko's bread from his plate, took a bite, and walked out the door.

Marko was in shock that Little Eddy had that much power. As he put his hand on ice and motioned to the remainder of his men for the dead bodies to be taken out of his place, he thought to himself, *Something weird is going on here. Little Eddy didn't have that kind of personality or strength a few days ago.*

Adramelech was gaining more and more power as his spiritual troops were devouring these souls. He only needed a few more, and he would have enough power to overtake Archangel Azrael. Adramelech knew that the Angel of Patience would be there shortly. He was just hoping that Lucifer hadn't sent Satan to come and stop his plan.

Chapter 37

On the way to the auction, Lexi cried, "Stop the car!"

Redington pulled over as fast as he could. "What's the problem?"

Lexi didn't answer. Instead, she opened the door and went running toward the building, climbing the stairs as fast as she could and opened the big wooden doors at the top.

Redington jumped out and followed her into the church. "What in God's name are you doing?" He was watching her dip her hands into one of the containers that held the holy water that parishioners blessed themselves with before entering the assembly. She was washing her arms with it.

"Protecting myself from demons."

"What the—? You got to be kidding me!"

She pulled her sleeve back down and walked past Redington and out the door, down the steps, and got back into the car.

Once Redington was back behind the wheel, she said, "Hey, I know that you don't believe me, but I know there is some kind of demonic hunt being done. And I believe it is me that they are hunting."

"Don't do that again. You almost gave me a heart attack. I thought something was really wrong."

Redington started to laugh.

"What is so funny?"

"Look at you. Do you know how many weird looks you got in there?"

Lexi looked down and then at the church. "Ah. I didn't think about that."

"I can just imagine what those Catholics were thinking. . . what are two Arabs doing with our holy water?" He started to laugh even harder as he remembered their facial expressions.

"Well, I needed protection." Lexi made the sign of the cross to ask God for her forgiveness in case she caused any harm by putting on the holy water.

"You crack me up, Miss Constantine."

"That's Amani to you. If I must dress up as an Arabic wife, then my name is going to be Amani."

"Well, if you have a name, then my name will be Al-Muthanna ibn Rawahah."

"Where did you come up with that name? Can't you pick an easier name? I don't think I can pronounce that one."

"I like watching TV. If you don't like that one, then you can call me Majstir."

"Does that mean what I think it means?"

"What do you think it means?" Redington was just pulling up to the auction house.

"I am not calling you master."

"How about Alsyd?"

"What does that mean?"

"Lord." He got out of the car as the valet opened Lexi's side of the door.

She made sure that she stayed a few feet behind Redington to play the role of an obedient wife.

They were escorted into the auction galley and were given a numbered paddle and their seats. As she passed one of the guards, she got shivers. *How did I get myself caught up in all this?*

Lexi had never met Kofman in person. She only knew what he looked like from the pictures that Susannah showed her. He was standing at the podium as the auction began. The auctioneer was very good, and you could hear the bids being called as the paddles kept going up to acknowledge each person's bid.

Lexi observed as incredible antiques were being auctioned off. Susannah was right; the bidding wars were incredible. Some items were being sold for millions of dollars.

"Something is fishy about those two," Redington said as he pointed in two opposite directions and careful not to catch the attention of the auctioneer. God forbid someone thought he was bidding on something, and he won the bidding war.

Lexi noticed the two well-dressed men in suits that Redington was talking about. And even though they were on different sides of the room, with every item they bid on, they seemed to drive the price up and won. "You think they are Marko's guys?" Lexi asked.

"Yep."

Just as another item was coming up for bid, Lexi noticed the man from the picture. "Detective, isn't that Little Eddy?"

Just as Lexi said the mobster's name, the guy turned around and looked directly at her.

"Oh shit!" Redington said as Little Eddy was making his way toward Alexandra. Red could see that he had pulled out his gun, and it was now aimed at Alexandra's head.

People panicked at the sight of a gun. Noticing the commotion and seeing one of Marko's guys draw a gun, Kofman screamed from the podium, "What are you doing?"

A shot went off, and Redington grabbed Alexandra out of the way just in time.

Lexi remembered what Tamara had said—ask and Archangel Michael will come and remove the dark spirit. *God in Heaven, please bring me the protection of Archangel Michael's army. Amen.* At the moment her prayer ended, Little Eddy was almost on her. The next thing she knew, a smoke bomb went off, and the lights went out.

It was as if time stood still. Everything happened in slow motion. As Redington tried to get her out of Little Eddy's path, somehow, she was torn away from him. Not knowing what happened to the detective, she crouched down low. A moment later, she could see a SWAT team storm into the room wearing their night vision masks with rifles leading their way.

As Little Eddy was about to pull the trigger to kill Lexi, a shot hit him in the back, killing him. She saw his body collapse onto the floor. It was Redington who shot him. Before she could react, a man seated in front of her pulled her up and helped her run toward the doors. As he did, his hand slipped off of her outfit and touched her skin. He drew his hand back as if he had been burned. Lexi saw his eyes glow red as he looked down at his hand in bewilderment. That was the moment that she knew a demon was seducing her into believing he was saving her.

Lexi pulled out of her pocket a piece of holy wood. She had stolen it from the door of the church. The wood had splintered at the edge by the hinge, and she broke it off as she was leaving. Without thinking, she stabbed the wood into the man's hand, and he screeched like he was possessed by the devil. She ran blindly.

Chapter 38

Adramelech's energy was draining quickly. He had used it all up to transfer bodies from Little Eddy to the man sitting in front of Alexandra. He was about to go after her when an Archangel from Heaven showed up and intervened. An uncontrollable eerie screech came out of Adramelech's mouth when Archangel Azrael touched his dark energy, incinerating him instantly. The human body Adramelech had been controlling collapsed unconsciously to the ground.

Satan was looking on from the side of the street as the people came running out of the building. The police surrounded the building. No one escaped.

Archangel Azrael's angelic body came floating toward Satan, "*Nephew, you'd better leave with all your minions, or there is going to be a war like no other.*"

Oblivious and invisible to the humans, behind Azrael, the other Archangels started to appear: Michael, Cassiel, Ramiel, Uriel, Raphael, and Gabriel.

"Uncle, I was only coming to get him. I do not know why he left his position within my kingdom. I take full responsibility. It will not happen again," Satan said as he vanished from the earthly realm.

Once back in Hell, Satan sought out Lucifer. *"Father, I was too late. Azrael found him first."*

Archangel Raphael appeared in Lucifer's court. Raphael is the Archangel who empowers souls with humility and is Lucifer's archrival. *"Brother, Father has sent me down here to give you one warning, and only one. The next time one of your demons disobeys the spiritual laws, you will lose your place as ruler of Hell."*

Raphael's light was so bright and pure that it was burning holes into the demon's wings.

Flinching as the light was burning through his once angelic flesh, Lucifer replied, *"Tell Father that I received his message. And Raphael, the next time that you come into my kingdom, expect a war."*

Raphael smiled and vanished.

"Satan!" Lucifer bellowed.

"Yes, Father?"

"Call in Maalik. I need to change the locks on our gates."

Lucifer called an emergency meeting with all the kings from the realm of Hell. *"My demonic followers, go forth onto Earth and tempt the souls, I have a war to prepare for and I need as many demons as we can create. For the prophecy is about to come to light. . . when the fifth trumpet is blown, the 'abyss' will open, and demonic locusts will be released to torture those who have not received God's seal. And you, Abaddon, will be their leader."*

Chapter 39

Redington found Alexandra outside; she was standing with the retired sergeant.

"MacFalen, how did you pull this one off?" Redington asked as he moved his shoulder to insinuate that he had hurt it.

"Quite elementary, my dear Watson. A good cop always has a mentor, mine just happens to be the brother of the mayor. Once he found out what was happening, he made a few phone calls and voila, SWAT team at your service."

"Thanks, MacFalen. I owe you one." He shook the retired cop's hand and said to Alexandra, "May I take you home, Miss?"

"I would love to go home and take a nice long hot bath."

Once they were at her apartment Lexi said goodbye to Redington. "I hope we never have to meet again, Detective."

"Hey, I thought we were having fun."

"Your kind of fun and mine are very different," Lexi said as she smiled. Lexi gave Redington a very sincere thank you, by saying, "I am in your debt for clearing my sister's name. Good night, Officer."

Noticing that she called him officer instead of detective, Red teased back, "It is all in a day's work as a detective. It was my pleasure."

Lexi got out of his car and went inside. There was a different valet on tonight that she didn't know too well, so just smiled at him as she went in.

Once in her apartment, she went about cleaning up the mess that the robbers had left behind. She found nothing stolen, but she did find a black feather. *Weird.*

As she had finished cleaning up, she started a bath and poured herself a glass of wine.

Her home landline rang, and she picked up the remote phone. "Hello."

"Alexandra, it's Edward. How are you?"

"Edward, you wouldn't believe me if I told you."

"Are you alright?" Edward could hear the stress in her voice.

"I am now."

"Is there anything I can do?"

Getting into the tub she said, "Actually, I am interested in the hierarchy of angels."

"Sure. What you want to know?"

"Everything. Do you have time, Edward?"

"For you, Lexi, I can find the time."

Lexi settled into the bath and put the phone on speaker.

"Let's see, where should I start? The old Christian religions believed that there is a place called the Inferno, also known as Hell. A place called *Purgatorio*, known as Purgatory, and a place called *Paradiso*, also known as Paradise or Heaven.

"In the 1st Hierarchy of Angels are the Seraphims, who are closest to God, then Cherubims, known for their wisdom and understanding. And Thrones, where it is believed that God resides."

"That's interesting," Lexi said, feeling calmer just hearing his voice.

"In the 2nd Hierarchy of Angels are the Powers, who are agents of God. Dominions, who dominate the rest of the angels, and Principalities, who have direct power over the other angels."

"What is in the third hierarchy?" Lexi asked wondering where Archangel Michael fell into the mix.

"In the 3rd and last Hierarchy of Angels are the Virtues, who work miracles. And in this hierarchy is where the Archangels, bearers of good news are. And there are also the Guardian Angels, who have the lowest rank of all the angels but are the closest to man."

"Thanks, Edward. Oh, how rude of me. Was there a reason you called?" Lexi said almost spilling her wine as she remembered he called her.

"No, not really. I guess I am a bit nervous about tomorrow's soul retrieval is all."

"Oh, my God. I almost forgot about it. Thanks for reminding me."

"You almost forgot about your sister's soul retrieval? You have been asking for this day for months."

"I know. I have had a really stressful two weeks. I guess time slipped by without me noticing."

Not understanding what she could have been doing for the last couple of weeks that she could forget something as important as her sister's soul retrieval, he said, "I heard that your design center will be open in a few days. That should take one stress off of you, Alexandra."

"Yes. I am looking forward to some normality in my life."

"Well, you might have to wait another day, I don't think tomorrow goes under the category of normal."

"Yes, I suppose you are right. But it will be worth it to save Susannah's soul. Thanks, Edward, for chatting with me. I am awfully tired. I'll see you tomorrow night."

"Night Alexandra."

Lexi added more hot water to the tub and lay back in for a little bit longer. *Oh, Susannah. How I miss you.*

Chapter 40

Tamara was extremely excited that the day had finally come. She had all the goodies she needed for tonight's soul retrieval packed in a special box to bring with her, quickly double-checking her list for anything that she might have missed. *Dang, I forgot the incense.* Going over to the cabinet in her office, she pulled out a couple of Satya Sai Baba – Nag Champa incense sticks. Tamara put her coat and boots on, and with everything in hand, she left for Reverend Hawthorne's place.

As Tamara was getting out of her car, she could see Lexi drive up to the funeral home and park beside her. She waited patiently for Lexi so that they could walk in together. "Good evening, Lexi. Wow, this place never ceases to amaze me. How are you doing?"

Lexi was so nervous for tonight's event to proceed. "Hi, Tamara. I know, right? I am okay." She was still exhausted from the last two weeks' ordeal, but she was determined not to let it show. "I am so excited for tonight." Changing the subject, she said, "Wow, that's a pretty box." She was looking at a beautiful wood carved box that Tamara was holding, with embedded gems that sparkled in the night as the light from the lamp post shone brightly on them.

"Thanks, I love sparkly things. Greg, my fiancé, loves to joke around. He tells people that I have A.D.D.O.S.—attention deficit disorder oh, shiny. And he even moves his head as if something else caught his attention. He thinks he's funny."

"Cute. It's nice that you have someone who loves you enough that he finds your quirks adorable."

"It is." She knew Lexi meant what she said in a nice way. "Isn't it incredible that the Reverend is offering his spiritual knowledge to help us? The power of three, well the power of three plus the angels and God, is just what we need if we are going to get Susannah out of the Void." Chatting, they walked together up to the front entrance.

Edward was there opening the doors even before they knocked. He was a bit anxious for tonight's soul retrieval. He had never tried to summon a spirit before and was not even sure if this was sacrilege or heresy. Probably both. "Welcome, ladies, please come in."

He led them into a counseling room just to the left of the entrance. Inside was a burgundy crushed velvet semicircle couch facing the opposite wall, taking up most of the space with a few small pillows thrown randomly on it. The walls were oak wood, from floor to ceiling, stained in dark cherry color. Beautifully carved wood columns, one on each side of the door, stood as if they were protecting the entrance from the inside.

Incredible art hung on all four walls. Three of the walls held paintings. As you looked closer, you could see the signatures on each. They were all by famous artists: Leonardo da Vinci, Michelangelo, and Rembrandt.

Not believing her eyes, Tamara stood transfixed, staring at the fourth wall. She had seen it in the Vatican, in Italy. A replica of "The Resurrection of Christ," the most magnificent tapestry she had ever seen. Two disciples, one on either side of a table, with Jesus at its head. Their eyes and the table followed you as you walked past the tapestry. She remembered walking back and forth many times, being mesmerized by Jesus's piercing gaze, watching you as you walked by. Such a fantastic miracle of artistic ability and illusionism, especially for that era.

Edward walked over to Tamara and said, "My great, great grandfather was fascinated by the European Old Masters. Beautiful, isn't it?" Taking a moment to enjoy the work of art, he turned from the tapestry and said, "Come, have a seat over here."

As if coming out of an enchanted spell, Tamara came back to the moment, "Yes… yes, right." Taking a seat next to Lexi, she said, "Thank you, Reverend, for having us here."

"Please, call me Edward."

"Thank you, Edward. Do you have the items I asked for?"

"Yes." Edward got up and went over to a small table. Picking the table up with everything on it, he brought it closer to them. Sitting on top was a beautiful white candle standing in an ornate silver base that could burn for a full 24 hours and two matching small glass pitchers. One contained holy water and the other blessed oil. He lit the candle and had a seat beside Tamara.

"Lexi, did you bring the item I asked for?" Earlier, Tamara had sent an email to Lexi asking her to bring an item that was very dear to her sister, Susannah.

"Yes. I did." She pulled a well-loved stuffed animal out of her bag. It was her sister's toy lamb. "Susannah carried this toy everywhere when she was young. She loved it."

"Perfect," Tamara said. "I am going to begin tonight by honoring as many religious beliefs as possible. First, I am going to believe that we are on sacred ground. With Reverend Hawthorne's prayers and guidance, like his family before him, many blessed souls have departed with the washing of the flesh as a ritual for spiritual ascension. Many religions have rituals of the washing of the body before the burial takes place. Some religions use prayer and imagine the soul being cleansed. Some use natural rainwater to wash the body, and others have added essential oils to the water for the soul's purification and rites of passage into death."

Tamara closed her eyes and said a silent prayer, asking Archangel Michael to be her main guide, helping her with tonight's soul retrieval.

Next, she asked the aboriginal spirit helpers to hold the positive love-light energy for her. Reaching into her box, she brought out a small bound bundle of dried sage, a lighter, half of a glistening green abalone shell the size of her palm, and a remarkable eagle's feather and placed them on the table.

Lighting the sage, she let the fire burn for a few seconds before blowing it out. Silently in prayer again, she turned to face all four cardinal directions. North, south, east, and west. One by one, feathering the smoke from the sage in that direction. Finishing the ritual, she butted out the sage by using the seashell and leaving it inside, then placed the feather upon the table.

Her next request was asking for help with tonight's soul retrieval from the Indigenous and Tibetan angels and guides in the spirit world. As an offering to them, she retrieved from the box a sliced orange piece and placed it into the seashell next to the sage and its ashes. She then brought out a container made of tin. Opening the lid, she grabbed a pinch of loose tobacco and sprinkled it beside the orange slice.

Then, she took out a small packet. It was a small piece of folded light gray paper. Unfolding it, inside was the holy ash Vibhuti, which Sathya Sai Baba had produced from his fingertips when he was alive.

Tamara placed the pad of her ring fingertip into the substance. She then proceeded to rub Lexi's forehead, and with dignity, she pulled aside her shirt at the neckline to reveal a small portion of her upper chest, just above her heart. She rubbed a little there too. Then, asking Lexi to open her mouth, Tamara lightly rubbed her thumb and ring finger together for any remaining Vibhuti to go internally, blessing her both inside and out.

Next, Tamara brought out a golden metal bell and dorje. She said to Lexi and Edward, "In the Sanskrit writings, this is known as a Ghanta and Vajra. Some teachings indicate the bell represents wisdom and the dorje compassion. The dorje resembles an intricately hollowed four-sided infinity sign."

Tamara brought her finger up and traced the shape. "It reminds me of an unshelled peanut." Showing them the piece, she continued by saying, "I am amazed at the intricate designs on both the bell and dorje. The art is symbolic and represents a multitude of insightful meanings."

Both Edward and Lexi were in awe of the many ways that a person could do a blessing and ask for spiritual help.

"We can begin now. Lexi, make yourself comfortable. If it's okay with Edward, even lie down." Tamara looked at Edward for his approval.

"Yes, no problem. Here, you can use this pillow for your head." He placed one of the pillows from the couch under her head.

Nervous about what she may encounter in the underworld but very keen on saving her sister, Lexi made herself comfortable on the couch by lying down. Whatever they needed, she was game. She trusted them both with hers and her sister's soul. She said a silent prayer, *God, Lord of the light. Please bless my soul. Know that whatever happens, I am at your mercy, and I am expecting you to help protect me from any dark spirits that may be lurking in the shadows. Please, help us save Susannah's soul. She was innocent and deserves better than being stuck in the Void. Thank you and Amen.* She did a quick sign of the cross on her forehead, lips, and heart.

As Tamara looked at Edward, she said, "Edward, for now, all I need for you to do is pray to God to protect us all during this ceremony. If everything goes well, I will also need your assistance at the end."

Edward nodded and took note of Alexandra's sign of the cross. He bowed his head and said a silent prayer for all their protection. *Dear Lord, forgive us for our ignorance in this matter. Help us bring back Susannah Grace Constantine's soul so that she can ascend into your light. Please, protect Alexandra. She is brave and willing to help her sister, even though it could cost her her own soul. Protect them both. Amen.*

"Lexi, take a few deep breaths and relax. Know that you are safe here. I am calling down my angels and any spirit helpers that I can that will help me in performing this soul retrieval." Tamara closed her eyes and took a deep breath. "Blessed angels, please guide me in this request to save Susannah Grace Constantine's soul, who passed on October 20th of this year, in the city of New York, USA." The room became very still. It was as if time was moving in slow motion. As if you could notice each grain of sand falling one by one in an hourglass.

"Lexi, in a moment, I am going to have you imagine a safe place. It can be anywhere in the world, indoors or outside. This place is where you and your soul are protected. Nothing can harm you in any way from this point forward.

Tell me about this place, please." Tamara took a deep breath and waited for Lexi to answer.

"It is outside in a beautiful field, somewhere in the mountains. I can hear the sounds of a creek nearby, and it smells so fresh and clean. There are tall trees and wildflowers everywhere." Lexi took a deep breath and relaxed even further into her meditative state.

"Wonderful. Relax there for a bit. I am going to tell you what is going to happen next. In a few moments, you are going to teleport to a train station. You can imagine it looking any way you want. It's okay that different people may have different versions, a unique illusion of how they think a train station looks. It does not matter what Edward or I think a train station should look like. It only matters what you think it should look like. And because you are in the realm of the spirit world, anything is possible. Lexi, go there now, imagine a train station, and tell me what you see or sense about this train station."

"It's the historical version of Penn Station—Pennsylvania Station in Midtown Manhattan, close to the Empire State Building. Oh my God, this is so much better than any picture I have ever seen. It's like I am there, walking through it. It's so majestic. The entrance to the station is so grand with all the massively impressive columns and archways. It's like walking into a building inspired by the Roman Baths of

Caracalla. Pink granite everywhere. Enormous pillars and stairways. The main waiting area is a block and a half long with vaulted glass windows as a ceiling. The space is incredible. The top looks to be one-hundred and fifty feet above me. Oh my, it's beautiful even where the trains emerge. That area resembles a fairy-tale greenhouse with an incredible arched glass and steel roof. It's so sad that it had to be demolished in 1965, but I love that I get to use this old train station to help Susannah." Lexi's meditative facial expression was that of a child in a candy store for the first time.

"Great. Okay, Lexi. I want you now to imagine that you just bought your ticket to go to your destination stop, the Void. Once you have bought your ticket, then go ahead and make your way over to your train and get on it, please.

Make yourself comfortable by imagining that you are sitting anywhere where there is an empty seat. You can sit on the bench in either direction. Facing forward or backward to the motion of the train, you choose."

Tamara paused a moment to give Lexi time to do what she asked.

"Now, imagine that the train conductor comes and checks your ticket, punching a hole in the upper right corner. He is marking that you have now used your ticket. You can hear the sound of the engine and the ringing of the bell, with the conductor yelling the last call, 'All aboard!' The doors close, and the train slowly starts to move out of the station.

"Please take note that this is an unusual but very special train that ordinary humans could never ride. Most people do not even know of its existence, even though there is one at every train station in the world. It is only known to souls, spirits, or people in an astral state as you are now. You would even have access to the ones that have been shut down, have been renovated into something else, or have been torn down altogether."

Tamara paused again for Lexi.

"In a moment, Lexi, the train will slow down and come to a halt at the stop you are getting off at. Your father, Marcus, will be meeting you at the door of this train.

"Give me a moment. I am going to call Archangel Michael to bring his steed, a Pegasus, one of his mythical winged divine pure white horses, to come and help us.

"Archangel Michael will be tethering you and your father around the waist with a mystical Aka cord, a secret Huna invisible rope named by Max Freedom Long. It has also been called the 'silver cord' in other esoteric teachings. The threads connect our subconscious, conscious, and superconscious mind. As well as the belief that the cord can also attach us from person to person through interaction with each other. These threads can turn into thick cords when we have a strong connection to that person. It is a very special cord that cannot be broken or removed from your body without your consent. These cords are the only way I can think of for us to pull you back out of the Void," Tamara explained.

Edward was intrigued by the creativity of this concept. It sounded logical.

"Alright, Lexi, take another deep breath. Relax and follow my guidance on what to do. See it in your mind's eye as if you are doing it."

Tamara closed her eyes again. "I call upon the spirit of Marcus Constantine, Susannah and Alexandra Constantine's birth father in this lifetime. Please, come and assist Lexi in her dream state to retrieve Susannah's soul from the Void. Lexi, when the doors open, he will be waiting for you.

"I can see Archangel Michael wrapping a single Aka cord and attaching one end around your father's waist now as I speak.

"Lexi, I want you to notice now that the doors have opened, and Archangel Michael is coming onto the train and tethering an Aka cord around your waist before you get off the train.

"The opposite ends will be tied and secured to Archangel Michael's waist, for both your and your father's safe travel into the Void.

"Archangel Michael's winged horse, Phantachus, is ready for you both to mount him. Please, get off the train and get on him now."

Lexi imagined her father, Marcus, just on the outside of the train doors. He was being tied around his waist with a silvery opalescent rope. The other end was securely fastened to a man who radiated the most vivid purple-blue aura she had ever seen. The same man tied a cord around her waist as well and then helped her onto the most magnificent creature she had ever laid eyes upon.

In horse measurements, he was over twenty hands high. The steed had the body of a thoroughbred racehorse, with a long mane and tail that flowed even though there was no breeze. His wings were magnificent. As large as an ancient pterosaur, with a wingspan of over thirty-five feet. The size of this creature gave her peace of mind that the three of them, Marcus, Susannah, and herself, would effortlessly be carried back through the Void.

As she seated herself onto Phantachus, her body seemed to become one with the winged animal. She knew there was no way she could fall off.

Tamara continued the meditation. "Wonderful. In a moment, Phantachus will be flying you and your father into the Void. I will lose the ability to talk to you while you are in the Void. So, here are the rules you MUST follow to the letter.

"Do not talk to any other spirit other than Susannah and your father. I do not care who you think they are. Remember, low-energy spirits can pretend to be anything and anybody they want to be. Your father, Marcus, will know that it is Susannah's soul. Trust him only!

"Lexi, you will notice a third Aka cord tied to Archangel Michael, which Marcus will use to tie around Susannah's waist.

"When all three of you are back on Phantachus, just click your heels lightly three times into his torso, signaling for him to fly back to this room.

"I am giving you a maximum of twenty minutes. If you are not back here on your own, I will be getting Archangel Michael to pull you back to your body in this room, no matter who is with you.

"When you enter this room and before any of you get off Phantachus, tell me that you are all here in the room, and then I will proceed with what is needed next.

"Periodically, you will hear the sound of this bell." With the bell facing down toward the floor, Tamara was holding the Ghanta between her left hand and thumb and the middle of the dorje between her right hand and thumb. She rang the bell as an example.

"I will use this to help guide you into the Void and summon all four of your souls back to this room: yours, Marcus's, Susannah's, and Phantachus's. When I ring it once, it is so you can hear our direction. When I ring it twice, it means that there are five minutes before you all need to be on Phantachus's back, returning to this room.

"I want you to imagine the bell as if it were a lighthouse shining its light for safe travel. Do you understand, Lexi? Just nod your head if you do." Tamara watched Lexi for an answer.

Lexi nodded.

"Okay, then. Lexi, when you are ready, click your heels once to give permission to Phantachus to fly all of you into the Void."

A few seconds later, Tamara and Edward both noticed that Lexi's heels clicked lightly together in real life. Looking at each other, they both looked up as if to say, *"It is all in your hands now, God."*

Tamara rang the bell once.

Chapter 41

The last time Lexi could remember riding a horse, she was eleven. It was on a family vacation in Finger Lakes National Forest, New York. They were staying at a stable, whose riding trails were amidst breathless lake views, cascading waterfalls, and rolling glacier-carved hills.

Riding Phantachus reminded her of the blissfulness she felt of her family being all together.

Marcus hugged Lexi from behind her. Without any words spoken out loud, she heard her father say, *"That was such a pleasant memory. I so enjoyed that vacation. Thank you for thinking about it."*

Startled that her father could hug her, let alone communicate with her directly, Lexi thought back to him. *"Dad, can you hear my thoughts?"*

"Yes."

"Wow, this is a surprise." Tears rolled down Lexi's face with the realization that after all these years, she was with her father. It felt so real, and he sounded so real in her mind.

She remembered him holding her like this when she was a young girl sitting and watching TV with him. She leaned back into him even deeper. Lexi was enjoying the memory of what it felt like to feel his love and protection. *"Dad, does it hurt being dead?"*

"No. It is blissful. But I have to say, being here with you brings back memories of feelings I had of the joy my family brought me."

"Do you understand what we have to do today?"

"Yes. I am here to help Susannah get out of the Void."

"Yes, Dad, that is correct. Are you nervous?"

"No. I don't feel feelings anymore. All I have is the ability to remember memories when you ask me a question, or if you think something, then I can sense it through you. Should I be?"

"No. I guess not. It wouldn't be beneficial for us, anyways."

Just at that moment, she heard the bell ring once. It brought her attention back to what they were supposed to be doing here.

In case it worked on the Pegasus, she sent a thought to Phantachus, asking how long before they would find Susannah. In return, she had a vision of being lost in the pitch dark. No matter which way she turned, she couldn't see a thing.

"Dad, I think we are in trouble. Phantachus cannot locate Susannah. What can we do to help him?"

"Lexi, I do not have a brain to think, so you will have to do the thinking."

Closing her eyes, Lexi prayed to God for guidance. *God, please help me find Susannah.*

A moment later, Lexi imagined a light shining. It was the memory she had of Susannah playing with a Christmas ornament that lit up. Both girls revealed how beautifully delightful it was, and many times during the holiday season, they would sit together and stare at it.

The love she felt for her sister at that moment was intense. She could feel the love vibrating out of her like a beacon. The waves of this love radiated out in a wave of energy in all directions.

Phantachus sent her another vision. Turning her head, she could see the waves hitting an object in the far distance. It was Susannah. It was her love for her sister that had radiated a beam of energy that found her sister's soul.

Phantachus flew even faster now that he knew where he was going.

Her heart felt like it was going to explode with the amount of love she felt as they came closer to Susannah. She felt Marcus's body going rigid behind her. *"Dad, are you okay?"*

He had disappeared from behind Lexi. She could now see him bringing the third cord to

Susannah. Lexi could still understand him as he communicated with Susannah.

"Susannah, I am so sorry. Will you ever forgive me?" he said to Susannah as he got closer to her.

"For what?" Susannah thought back.

"I was so wrong for kicking you out of the house all because you didn't want to go to church. I was so inflexible in my belief that a person had to go to church to be a godly person. This false truth lost me so many good years with you. I lost all the pure joy and love that you brought into my life.

"I punished myself with the grief I felt from that day forward, and not until I died did I realize that to be holy, all a person had to do was believe and lead a virtuous life. That no matter what you believe in or call it, any person can be holy and accepted into the light. All they need to do is believe in love and light before they die. And, for those that call it Heaven, that is all they need as the key to unlock the gates.

"The key to open the gates is so simple that even a newborn baby can do it. If a person feels that they did not lead a virtuous life, all a person needs is the ability to forgive their earthly sins.

"Once they forgive themselves, they can then emanate pure love energy into the lock. The ancient key that the Saint wears around his neck is a symbol of love. The weight of the key touches his heart, and his heart is an extension

*of God's immeasurable love. The 'S' symbol
stands for supernal, which means—heavenly,
ethereal.*

"Can you forgive me?"

Tears of joy ran down Susannah's cheeks. A
spark of love entered her heart, and an aura
started to glow around her form. This glow
started to heat an opening around her in the
Void.

At that very instant, Marcus tied the cord
around Susannah, and Phantachus backed up,
pulling her out of the spot she was stuck in.

At the same moment, Marcus's mom
appeared. Lexi couldn't believe her eyes.
"Grand-mère, is that you?"

"Yes, my child."

Lexi hopped off Phantachus and went running
over to her grandmother when Phantachus
neighed as a warning.

Looking back at Phantachus, Lexi
remembered what Tamara had taught her, TEST
ALL SPIRITS. Lexi sent love-light energy from
her eyes to her grandmother's and from her heart
to her grandmother's and waited.

Marcus grabbed his lost daughter and hugged
her so tightly. The joy he felt from having her in
his arms was more than words could describe.
Looking back at Lexi, he saw the devil, and fear
ran through his spirit. *"Lexi!"* he yelled. Not
being able to let go of Susannah, he could not go
and save his other daughter.

Lexi sent ten times the love-light energy toward her grandmother. Her grandmother's ghostly figure flickered.

"Lexi, my dear child, it is me, your Grand-mère. It is okay. I am here to help you. Come over here, child, and let me give you a hug."

Lexi stood her ground and increased the love-light energy one thousand times to her grandmother.

"Lexi, don't you love me? Don't you want to give me a hug?"

Lexi ignored her grandmother's words and held her ground. *"In God, I trust, if this is my real grandmother, she will be happy I tested her."*

Marcus could see that Satan was impersonating his mother and knew that the spiritual law held firm. He could not help his daughter unless she asked for help, and she had not.

Lexi was almost certain that this was her grandmother's soul coming to help. She was about to let go of the love-light energy and run to her when she remembered Tamara's lecture. It reminded her that demons could be very tricky and to look into their eyes—what color were they? Lexi looked into her grandmother's eyes. First, she saw blue, which was weird because her grandmother had brown eyes. Taking a deep breath, Lexi increased the love-light energy one million times. Her grandmother's eyes turned red.

"Child, you do not know what you have done. You will pay for this! You little brat, how dare you!" Satan's true appearance shimmered through his illusion just before he vanished.

Lexi heard the ringing of the bell. It rang twice. Remembering that they only had five minutes left, she sent a thought to her dad. *"We have to hurry, Dad!"*

Lexi ran back to Phantachus and jumped on him, holding out her hand to help her sister up.

With no time to spare, Marcus flung Susannah up onto Phantachus behind Lexi. He then jumped up just in time, as Lexi clicked her heels three times and Phantachus bolted like a bat out of hell.

Chapter 42

In the Void, there was nothing. She had forgotten everything but the feeling of being alone. Susannah didn't realize until this very moment how much she had missed her younger sister.

When she sat behind Lexi and wrapped her arms around her, she was able to tap into her thoughts. And in a split second, Susannah was flooded with a lifetime of memories that they had shared.

Susannah remembered everything as if it were yesterday. The memory of all the love they had for each other flowed to her as if it had the force of a dam that just broke loose. Susannah was relishing in the memories of all this love.

Faster and faster, they sped through time and space toward this warm glow. The sound of the bell rang continuously, getting louder and louder as they got closer to a warm glow of light.

Phantachus was flying as fast as he could. The shadows were filled with demonic entities waiting to pounce.

Susannah noticed that Phantachus was vibrating and looked around her. From her peripheral vision, she could see the dark forces were back. The same ones that were nipping at her soul as she entered the Void. She gave Lexi a hug, and the love she felt, shone a light, and the demons had to back off.

Phantachus flew even faster.

As the glow became larger and clearer, Susannah could make out three forms in the room. She could see a lady lying down on a couch and two other people. A lady sitting and a man down on his knees beside the person lying on the couch, with his head bowed and hands in a prayer formation. The other lady was frantically ringing a bell.

The ringing was so loud that the noise started echoing in her head. She was wishing that the lady who was ringing the bell would stop. Miraculously, at the same moment she wished it to stop, it did.

Susannah noticed that it was Reverend Hawthorne, a son of one of her father's friends, who was kneeling beside th— *Oh goodness, that's Lexi lying there on the couch.*

That was the moment that Susannah realized the gathering was for her, that these three people had come together to get her out of the Void. She couldn't believe that Lexi would risk her own sanity entering the Void for her.

Susannah could not remember ever feeling that much love before today. It was like she had an infinite source of love and light flowing out of her, powered by all the gratitude and gratefulness she had for these people. The light that shone out of her was pure joy—the brightest of lights that any soul could shine. The light was so bright that the beams were like fire, and anything that was not of love-light energy was incinerated if it dared to come near.

The path was clear, and Phantachus had no trouble flying to his destination, Earth.

Chapter 43

Lexi stirred, wiggling her toes, creating the intent for her spirit to come back into her body. At the moment that Tamara had seen Lexi's body flinch, she stopped ringing the bell.

As the sound stopped, Edward looked up to see why and noticed the smile on Tamara's face. He followed her gaze to Alexandra's body, awakening from a deep sleep. Getting up off the floor, he sat beside Alexandra's head, stroking her hair, smiling as she opened her eyes.

"Lexi, are you alright?" Tamara asked.

"Um, yep, I think so."

"Do you have Susannah and Marcus with you?"

"Yes, they are still on Phantachus."

"Perfect." Tamara had tears coming from her eyes from the joy she felt, knowing that they had succeeded. She looked at Edward and smiled. "Lexi, I need you now to grab hold of the lamb."

Lexi took the lamb from Tamara. Looking at the old stuffed animal brought back a memory of all the times when she was scared and crawled into Susannah's bed. Susannah would move over and make room for her and place the little lamb between the two of them to share its protection and love.

"Lexi, tell Susannah to climb off Phantachus and come over to the couch. I need to attach her Aka cord to the stuffed animal. Please tell me as soon as she does."

Lexi thought about what Tamara had requested, and instantly Susannah was lying beside her with the lamb between them.

"She is here beside me."

"Thank you. I am going to say goodbye to Marcus and Phantachus now, thanking them for a job well done. You can say goodbye to your father now too."

At the same time, both daughters said goodbye to their father and to the beautiful horse that flew them safely through the Void. Sending the two spirits love-light energy, together they said, *"Thank you to both of you, and Dad, we love you!"*

Closing her eyes, Tamara went inside her mind and said, *Thank you, Marcus and Phantachus, for saving Susannah's soul. Thank you, God, all the spirits and angels that helped us today. What an incredible journey.*

As Tamara opened her eyes, she said, "Edward, I need you to perform the ritual of the washing of the body. Please, use the lamb as if it were Susannah, for, at this moment, it is."

Chapter 44

Edward took the lamb from Lexi and just stared at it. *Is it possible that Susannah's soul could be attached to this toy? God give me the strength to accept the things that I do not understand. I know logically, the probability that a soul attached itself to a stuffed animal is more than ridiculous. It's ludicrous. I know as a child, I had many unexplainable experiences sensing ghosts. As an adult, the science behind the phenomenon became zero.*

I know that science has declared Darwinian theory of how man was created to be the truth. Still, there are so many unanswered questions and breaks in the timeline. I know Christianity has the Creationism theory.

Being a man of faith, I believe this theory to be the truth. I believe in a higher power, whom I call God. I think that this higher power created the Earth and everything living on it. I also know that this belief is not scientifically provable.

I set out tonight to help bring a soul into the light, not to transport a soul into a stuffed toy. I want to help, for Lexi's sake and her sanity. If she believes this to be true, then who am I to question her belief? I will do this to help a grieving sister. God, help me.

Edward picked up the glass pitcher from the table containing the holy water. He slowly started to pour its contents over the head and body of the stuffed lamb. "In the power invested through me, I proclaim this stuffed lamb to hold the soul connection of Susannah Grace Constantine. With this holy water, I thee cleanse and purify her body and soul for the ritual of the naming ceremony."

Edward put down the pitcher. "From this day forward, let it be known to all that are here that Susannah's new holy name will be Susanna. After Saint Susanna, the virgin and martyr. Martyrdom is the suffering of death on account of adherence to a cause and especially to one's religious faith. I call upon Saint Susanna to protect our Susannah and teach her the ways of belief in a higher power. So that her soul may one day return to the light."

Picking up the blessed oil, Edward poured a small amount onto the pad of his middle finger, then put the pitcher back down. Touching the lamb's forehead, he made the sign of the cross.

"Making this sign of the cross invokes God's protection. Susannah, may you always have the protection and strength of God and Saint Susanna with you. Knowing you will never have to journey through this earthly world alone again."

At that moment, the flame on the candle flickered wildly. Pointing to the candle that helped guide the group back into this room, Edward continued, "This candle represents your faith in a power greater than you. It will burn for twenty-four hours, honoring you while you are in transition."

Edward placed the stuffed lamb into Lexi's hands. "Lexi, your sister's soul needs to go into the light. You need to find peace in your heart to let her go."

Edward finished by saying a silent prayer. *God, if there is a possibility that Susannah's soul is attached to this lamb, please help Alexandra find a way to let her go and have her sister's soul ascend into Heaven for everlasting life. Amen.*

Chapter 45

xhausted from the night's ordeal, Lexi thanked Edward and Tamara for their part in helping her retrieve her sister's soul from the Void. Upon arriving home, she laid her head on her pillow. That was the moment when this evening's soul retrieval hit her. All the feelings came flooding in, being in her father's arms and the moment when Susannah's soul was safe from the anguish of being in the Void. *It sure felt real.* *"Susannah, are you there?"* Lexi picked up the stuffed animal that was lying in her bed beside her.

"Yes."

"Oh my God, I can't believe what I have done since your death. Who would have thought that I would go to see a psychic medium? Beg a Reverend to stop a funeral, go to lectures about the dead, be chased by the mob, and best yet agree to go into a meditative state and imagine

saving your soul from eternal torment? And guess what? I would do it all over again to save your soul, Susannah. . . You do know that I have to help you ascend into the light?"

"Yes."

"Susannah, what was the car accident like? What happened?"

"I was driving home from a dinner party at a friend's house. You remember Billy Randazzo, the boy I had a crush on in high school? I met up with him again, and I had been dating him for a few months. That night he had invited a few good friends over to his place to join us."

"I didn't know you were seeing anyone."

"Yeah, I know. I am sorry, Lexi, that I kept our relationship a secret for so long. He was a far cry from that wannabe jock you remember back in high school. But I remembered how you felt about him back then, and I didn't want you to influence my decisions. He was so sweet to me, handsome, and such a great kisser. Billy had grown up so much. It was great having him back in my life. We had just talked about me moving in with him the night before the party."

"So, how did the accident happen?"

"I left his house around ten-thirty, and I only had a couple of drinks that night. I was feeling pretty good about spending more time with Billy and getting more serious about trying the live-in wife thing. I remember smiling at what he whispered in my ear that night—Mrs. Randazzo.

I was waiting in line at an intersection when out of nowhere, a truck speeding through a side alley hit me, T-boned my side of the car. The last thing I remember was the sound of broken glass and the crunching of metal."

"Oh, my God. That is terrifying. Mom wouldn't tell me how you died. And at the time, all the police would say was that it was a horrific and tragic drunk driving accident. I remembered something interesting that Tamara told me about death. She said when a soul dies while under the influence of any mind-altering substance, be that recreational or medicinal, the soul does not have enough clarity to go into the light when it leaves its body.

"The body not being sober causes the soul to be disoriented and not able to focus on the source of light. The soul usually falls into a swirling tunnel of energy far away from the light, disappearing into the abyss. She also said that if no one is there to pray for a disoriented soul, he or she may be lost forever. Susannah, is that what happened to your soul?"

"I don't think so. I didn't have anything to drink for about three hours before I left Billy's. The other guy must have been the drunk driver. I remember seeing mom crying. Then I was at these beautiful gates, but they were locked, and the man said I couldn't come in because I didn't believe in God and Heaven. Then I was back at our childhood home, and I didn't know that I had died. I thought Mom had."

"Susannah, how did you get stuck in the Void?"

"After I realized I was the one who died, my soul was pulled by a force like a vacuum. It sucked me up, and as I was swirling through the celestial world. Dark entities started to chase me as if I was a fox. The entities and spirits were so demonic. I remember praying to God as I did as a kid. Asking for protection. The next thing I knew, I was stuck where you found me."

"What about the demons?" Lexi asked.

"They couldn't touch me because I was solidified in the Void. They tormented me for a bit but gave up quickly once they figured out they couldn't devour me."

"That was brilliant sending me the dream."

"Lexi, I never sent you a dream."

"Yes, you did. That's how I knew you were in trouble."

"No, Lexi, I didn't."

"Well, then you have a guardian angel looking after you, because how else would I have known you were in trouble?"

"That is a good question. Well, no matter what, thank you for believing in me and trusting your heart that I was innocent."

"About that. What the heck was after me? It couldn't have just been the mob. It was so supernatural."

"I don't know anything after I got stuck in the Void. Are you okay?"

"I am now. Thanks for sending me the letter. It is what cleared your name."

"What letter?"

"The letter you mailed me."

"Lexi, I didn't mail you a letter."

"What? Yes, you did. It was in your handwriting."

"Lexi, I swear I never sent you a letter."

"Susannah, maybe you just don't remember doing it."

"I can remember everything right up to when you and Dad came and took me to that place with you on the couch."

"Well, then who sent the letter?"

"Good question. I guess I do have a guardian angel."

"Susannah, do you know that you are a ghost now?"

"That's a silly question. I am here talking with you. Everyone knows there are no such things as ghosts."

"No, Susannah, we are dreaming that we are talking to each other."

"That's crazy. Lexi, stop kidding around."

"I'm telling you the truth, Susannah. Where is your body then? Look, is it here beside me in the bed?"

"No."

"So, where is your body if you aren't a ghost?"

"If I am a ghost, then why am I here?"

"Tamara said, for many different reasons, some souls can't move into the light. Instead, they will attach themselves to something tangible on Earth, be it a person, a place, or an object. Your soul had to be bound to something you could relate to. Susannah, we attached your soul to your favorite animal. See? Here is Lambie.

"Tamara said as a ghost, the soul loses its freedom and can't go anywhere that the person, place, or thing can't go. If it is attached to a building, the soul can't leave the building. If it is a person, it goes everywhere that person goes, even if it doesn't want to. If it is a thing, it is wherever the object is. The soul could even be left in the attic or sold to a stranger in an antique shop. No matter which attachment it chooses, the soul is never at rest and does not have peace."

"That is terrible. Then why have you attached me to Lambie?"

"Yes, I agree. It is terrible. But it was better than leaving you in the Void. That, to me, was much worse. Don't worry, though, Tamara said that now that you are back here on Earth, she can help you get to Heaven.

"All I have to do is make sure you are ready and that you believe. Is there any unfinished business that you have here on Earth, Susannah?"

"I have forgiven and made my peace with our father. He apologized to me in the Void. I remember now the stupidity of some of the decisions I made in my life. How my stubborn emotions made me make terrible mistakes that cost me my happiness.

"Yes. Lexi, I do have unfinished business that I need to do before I can rest. I need two things to happen. First, I need to see Mom and have her forgive me and tell her that I am okay now. And second, I need to make sure Billy is okay."

"Right. I am not sure how we are going to accomplish these two requests, but I will try my best. Anything else that you need?"

"No."

"Alright then, in the morning, we better get up and at 'em."

Being so grateful that she was able to save Susannah, Lexi said a prayer, *God, thank you for all your help in allowing me to save Susannah's soul. I know that it was you sending me the power to hold the love-light energy and test my grandmother. She looked so real; I could even smell her favorite perfume.*

As Lexi was praying, Archangel Azrael appeared. He is known to be the Angel of Death. His name means "Angel of God," and he is the angel of spiritual counseling where he assists ministers and spiritual teachers. He helps newly crossed-over souls adjust. Lexi could not see him, but he was there to bless her.

And Lord, please thank all the angels that came to help me today. Amen.

With that said, Archangel Azrael softly touched Lexi's head and blessed her soul. From this point on, she would be an advocate for lost souls. Her soul was protected from the dark, and her light would be forever enlightened.

Lexi made the sign of the cross over her heart, then turned on to her side and fell asleep.

Chapter 46

As Lexi slept, Susannah had nothing but time on her hands, lying there beside her younger sister. She started to remember how she and Billy had reunited.

She was at the Port of New York Container Terminal, which is a public berth where ships load and unload their cargo. She was waiting for a shipment to come in from Sweden. Her employer, Aryeh Kofman, had landed a large estate contract, and the items were being shipped to the United States to be auctioned in a private sale for his influential clients. The remainder of the items not sold would be auctioned off at a public sale. She was to meet a man named Lenny. He was a new guy who recently took over his family's business of import and export.

As she waited, she looked at the time on her phone. He was fifteen minutes late.

"Miss Constantine?" A tall Italian man held out his hand for her to shake.

Perturbed by his lateness, she didn't notice whom she was talking to for a moment. "Yes, I am. But you are late, Mr. Valentino."

"Oh, I am not Mr. Valentino."

"What? Then who are you?" Susannah looked at the man's face.

"Susannah Constantine?" Billy, all of a sudden, recognized her from fifteen years ago.

"Yes."

"It's me. Billy Randazzo. From high school."

"Billy? But why are you here? I'm supposed to meet a Lenny Valentino."

"He's my brother-in-law. He couldn't make the meeting with yuh and begged me to come. Lucky me," he said, giving her a wink.

"I see you are still the smooth-talking jock from high school."

"The new and improved version."

"Uh-huh."

"Let me prove it to yuh dah-lin. Let me take yuh out for dinner tonight."

"That is quick, Billy, very smooth."

"Yuh know yuh want to."

"Let's get down to the business at hand, shall we? You have a shipment for me?" Susannah smiled.

"Right. That is why yuh are here. A shipment." Billy pulled out some documents and had Susannah sign the release form.

As the shipment was being transferred into the one-ton truck that Susannah would follow back to Kofman's Staten Island warehouse, Billy made small talk. "Susannah, what have yuh been up to all these years? Married?"

"No, Billy, I am not married. I've been having too much fun adventuring around the world looking for treasures." Susannah pointed to the shipment being loaded into her company's truck. "How about you, are you married?"

"No. I haven't found Mrs. Randazzo yet. But." Eyeing up Susannah, he winked again.

"Funny. Billy, you're still the same as you were in high school."

"You never gave me a chance in high school."

"I was not the type to wait in line, and as I recall, Billy Randazzo, the lineup you had was a mile long."

"Hey, it was not my fault I was born this way," he joked as he raised his hands up and down his body to show it off.

Susannah laughed.

"So, what do yuh say? Dinner tonight?"

"How many are in line ahead of me?"

"Miss Constantine, you flatter me. For you, I would roll out the red carpet, and you would be number one and number one forever." And he meant it.

Chapter 47

The morning after the soul retrieval, Tamara was putting away the items she had brought with her to Reverend Hawthorne's.

Talking to her spirit guides, she said, *Amazing, just amazing! I am always amazed at the feeling one gets being near an omnipresence supernatural spirit—when you are in the grace of pure love and light. Where time seems to stand still, and nothing matters on Earth. All the cares of the world, money, fame, success, or as simple as what to make for dinner. . . disappears.*

A sacred moment when you are in the presence of a higher power and the belief in the spirit world becomes your truth.

I wish everyone could feel what I feel. Know what I know. See and hear what I do. How privileged it is to be a part of another person's life journey, a journey that can lead down a specific course of action just because of a dream. A dream that was so real that it could change a person's life, creating a paradigm shift in what that person believes.

So many times, I ask myself why, why me? As in, why did Lexi have a dream that her sister's soul was not in Heaven and was being tormented? Why did she call me? Coincidence? I think not.

At that moment, she remembered a passage in the Bible: Matthew 7:7.

Ask, and it will be given to you; search, and you will find; knock, and the door will be opened to you. Everyone who asks receives; everyone who searches finds; everyone who knocks will have the door opened. Is there anyone among you who would give his son a stone when he asked for bread? Or would hand him a snake when he asked for a fish? If you, then, evil as you are, know how to give your children what is good, how much more will your Father in Heaven give things to those that ask him!

My angels and guides, it makes so much sense to me now—the journey of a soul.

As an empath, I feel a tenth of the anguishing pain that a client is feeling. It doesn't matter if it is their pain or the pain they are feeling due to a loved one.

I can feel the frustration and anger my client may have toward God and the world, especially when they cannot do anything about the anguish.

I find it hard to explain to my clients that when they are praying for someone other than themselves, that no matter how hard they pray, the person they are praying for has all the control over their own life. It is always a person's life path. The choices they make while learning their life lessons and accomplishing their purpose do not always have a one-hundred-year contract attached to them. It is that person's contract with God.

Thank you for teaching me that it is far better to pray for God's will to be done for the benefit of that soul's journey through life and death. And that every person's life has a butterfly effect. Every action he or she does triggers the response of those around them.

Thank you for teaching me that it is considered selfish to pray for a specific outcome for another soul.

Thank you for teaching me that there is nothing our prayers should do for another soul other than to enhance their journey.

Thank you for teaching me that I am creating a negative energy force for a person or soul if I pray for a specific outcome and it is not what they are wishing, wanting, desiring, or dreaming of. And if I do, I am creating their manifestation energy to be pulled into two different directions, creating disharmony for both of us.

Thank you for giving me this example. That when I am asked to pray for someone, that I can say something like this. God, please help __________, for whatever is best for them. Allowing your love-light energy to emanate to them so that they can use it for the beneficial purpose of fulfilling their life lessons and life purpose. Thank you and Amen.

Thank you for teaching me to use the word Amen as an ending word. Explaining to me that it is needed to let the spirit know that I have completed my prayer. A way to say good-bye, thank you, or something of that nature. That unless I use an ending word, the spirit is still listening and waiting to do what I requested. It is reminding me that the language of spirit is literal. And, without using an ending word, I did not end the conversation I started.

Thank you for teaching me that it is only my outcome that I can pray for. I know this to be true because when a client asks me about one of their loved ones, I can only answer if they have permission from the other person. BUT even then, it is very limited to what I can get. It is nothing like when the person is right in front of me.

I love how in the Bible it says, "Ask, and you shall receive," without limiting me for what I can ask for. And if I pray at the same time with another person, then the power of two is amplified. We are creating the outcome that much quicker.

Tamara sat quietly for a moment, and prayed up to God, and asked, *"What is my next step in helping Lexi?"*

The answer that came back was, *"Give her time. In a few days, she will call you."*

With that answer, Tamara gave thanks and went about her day, for other souls needed her help.

Chapter 48

Edward entered the room that he usually used for counseling the loved ones of the recently deceased, the same room he used last night for Susannah's soul retrieval.

He noticed that the candle had died out overnight. After tidying up, he took the candle, walked over to his office, and placed it on his desk. Pulling out a lighter from the desk drawer, he relit the candle as he said a prayer that he had memorized from the internet.

In your hands, O Lord,
We humbly entrust our brothers and sisters. In
this life, you embraced them with your tender
love; deliver them now from every evil and bid
them eternal rest.
The old order has passed away:
welcome them into paradise, where there will be
no sorrow, no weeping or pain, but the fullness

of peace and joy with your Son and the Holy Spirit forever and ever. Amen.

Deciding that this whole situation had gotten a bit out of hand, he decided to say a second prayer as well.

Father, we stand before you today in confidence because we know that death has nothing on us who believe in you. Have compassion for those who have departed this world recently. Show them tender mercies, for they have sinned in one way or another before their sudden demise. We may have questioned and said things that are not pleasing to you. Lord, show us compassion and help us to accept what has happened so that we can heal. Amen.

Staring at the dancing candle flame, Edward was still thinking about Susannah's soul tethered and bonded to the stuffed lamb. *What have I done? Could it be possible, dear Lord, that Susannah is now a ghost?*

Lord, I know that there are no coincidences, that you have a perfect plan set out for all of us. I am grateful that you chose a lamb for her soul to be attached to. Very symbolic. A lamb to symbolize innocence, purity, gentleness, and representing Christ as both suffering and triumphant. They say God works in mysterious ways, and I would say that last night was one of those moments.

Still frustrated with how he felt, Edward picked up the phone and dialed.

Lexi was daydreaming in the shower about last night's events when the ringing of her cell phone brought her attention back to the present moment. Quickly getting out of the shower, she answered, a bit out of breath. "Hello."

"Hi, Alexandra, I am calling to make sure you are okay from last night's ordeal. How are you doing?" Reverend Hawthorne asked. He had to remember to be more professional and not let his personal feelings of desire for her cloud his judgment. *Thank God I am not a priest.*

"Great. I feel so at peace, knowing that Susannah's soul is out of the Void."

"About that. Alexandra, I do not feel right about what happened last night. I feel that you and Tamara tricked me. I thought we were saving your sister's soul and bringing her to Heaven. Not attaching her to a doll."

"Stuffed lamb, to be exact." Lexi felt hurt. She thought Edward was on her side. She thought he understood the amount of pain she was in, knowing that her sister's soul was in trouble.

"Sorry, toy lamb. I do not agree with what we did last night. A soul should not be attached to anything. I believe all souls must be free and go into the light. All souls need to ascend into Heaven so the soul can live in eternal bliss. In the Bible, Ecclesiastes 12:7, it says, the dust returns to the ground it came from, and the spirit returns to God who gave it. I blame myself. I had no proof that there was even a problem with

Susannah's soul. I took it on your word that there was. I did a terrible dishonor to the memory of your sister. Your sister is not supposed to be attached to a stuffed toy. Alexandra, I believe that this is your bizarre way of grieving, and you need help. I think it is time that you went to see a professional over this obsession."

Dumbfounded from what she just heard, she replied, "Thank you, Reverend, for your concern. I will not need your services again." And with that, she hung up the phone on him.

Staring at the candle, Edward hung up the phone, knowing that all he could do now and before it was too late was pray for both Alexandra's and Susannah's souls to be saved.

Chapter 49

Looking at Lambie on her bed, Lexi wondered if what Edward said had any truth to it. Was she losing her mind?

Deciding this was not the time, she lovingly placed the toy in her bag and left the apartment to go for a drive.

Lexi had to pull over to get gas and decided to call her mom. "Mom, is it okay if I come over right now?"

"Sure, what's up? Is everything okay?" Having a mother's intuition, Olivia could sense with the tone of her youngest daughter's voice that something was a bit off.

Not answering her mother's questions, she said, "I will be over in a few minutes."

Lexi knew her mother didn't need to work even after her father died because she could live off the substantial inheritance she'd received.

Six years after her mother was born, her grandmother became very sick. By the time her grandmother had gone in to see about it, it was too late. She had stage four colon cancer, and it had spread to her liver and lymph nodes. After her grandmother's death, the family's fortune went to her mother when she turned twenty-one.

The story was that her grandfather hadn't noticed his wife's ailments. Truth be told, he had fallen out of love with his wife a few years after their second child was stillborn. Not being able to deal with the grief, he made himself so busy as a surgeon that he didn't spend a lot of time at home. Lexi knew Olivia grew up in a very lonely world.

Driving into her mother's driveway, Lexi turned to the passenger seat and stroked the lamb's head. *"Susannah, you better know what you are doing because, at this moment, I am starting to believe that Reverend Hawthorne might be correct that I do need professional help."*

Getting out of the car, Lexi took a deep breath and went into her mom's house. "Hi, Mom. What room are you in?" Lexi called out as she took off her boots and her heavy coat. Winter was definitely on its way.

"I am in the kitchen, making your favorite cookies, chocolate chip." Olivia knew that her job as a mother didn't end when her children moved out of the house. She believed it was still her responsibility to help them in any way she could, no matter their age.

Walking into the kitchen and taking a seat on the barstool, Lexi smiled at her mom. Her parents had remodeled the kitchen a few years back when her dad was still alive. She loved seeing her here in the kitchen. It reminded her of all the good times they shared in this house, and chocolate-chip cookies were one of them.

"Hey, baby girl, what's up? Your tone of voice on the phone told me that something is off."

"Mom, I think you are psychic. You always know when I am not happy. Susannah could do that too. She must have inherited that from you."

"It is my job as a mother to be in tune with my children. Here. Lick the spoon." Olivia passed Lexi the spoon and placed the cookie sheets into the oven, shutting the oven door. "Fifteen minutes, and you can have milk and warm cookies."

"Mom, I am not a baby."

"You will always be my baby." Smiling at Lexi, Olivia came over and hugged her. Sitting down on the stool beside her, she said, "So what's up?'

"Nothing," she lied. "I just missed you. I have been thinking about Susannah and Dad. It made me think about how lucky I am that I still have you. How are you doing, Mom?"

"Reverend Hawthorne called me this morning and asked me the same thing."

"Really?" Lexi took a sip of the coffee her mom had just poured her. "What did he say?"

"He asked me how we both were doing. Lexi, is there something going on romantically between you two?"

"Mom. No. What makes you think that?" It had not even crossed her mind. He wasn't her type.

"Just a mother's intuition, I guess. So, what is the real reason you are here today?"

Lexi took another sip of her coffee and contemplated telling her mother the truth. She decided against it. Her mother would never believe such a crazy story about her sister's soul and would worry herself sick about the mob. "I just needed to be around family, that's all. I'm okay. How are you holding up, Mom?"

Once the cookies were done, Olivia went and busied herself with taking them out of the oven. "Mmm, freshly baked cookies—smell that." Using a plastic flipper, she moved the cookies onto a big plate to let them cool. Taking out a small plate from the cupboard, she put a couple of cookies on it and passed it to her daughter.

Lexi moved the plate closer and said, "Mom, you didn't answer my question. How are you doing?"

"It hasn't even been a couple of months, Lexi. I am still numb. I have a hard time believing that Susannah is gone. The fact that I will never be able to give her another hug, hear her laugh, or be at any of her future events." Olivia had tears in her eyes as she looked at Lexi.

Getting up to hug her mom, Lexi said, "Me too. Hey, Mom, did you know Susannah was dating a guy named Billy?"

"Yes. Susannah had come by the morning she died and told me she was thinking of moving in with him. Why?"

"I didn't know she was dating anyone. You wouldn't have Billy's phone number, would you? I would like to see if he is okay."

"I do. Susannah gave it to me that morning. That would be nice of you to check in on him. Here, I'll write it down for you." Handing her the paper with his number written on it, she said, "Hold on, can you give him this too, please?" Opening a drawer in the kitchen where she kept her knick-knacks, she pulled out a small sealed paper bag and passed it to Lexi.

"Ya, for sure. What's in the bag?"

"It is something that Susannah would have wanted Billy to have." Leaving it at that, Olivia changed the topic.

They talked about happier things for about another hour, and then Lexi got up and said, "Thanks, Mom. I always feel better when I am around you. It might be the cookies, though." Getting up to leave, she gave her mom a hug. "See you in a few days."

"Love you, hon, drive safe."

Driving home, she wondered what would happen when her mom found Lambie. *It is all up to you now, Susannah.*

Chapter 50

$\mathcal{L}$ooking at the clock on her side table, Olivia could see it was only one-thirty in the morning. Getting up to go to the bathroom, she could still smell the fresh scent of chocolate in the air and decided to go downstairs to get a glass of water and a cookie. Just before turning to go toward the kitchen, something that she hadn't seen in decades caught her attention.

Walking over to the front entrance, sitting happily between her boots, was Lambie. *How did you get there?* Picking the stuffed animal up, she hugged it to her breasts. *Oh, Susannah, how I miss the days when you were little.* Looking at the lamb, she kissed it, saying, "I love you." Tucking the lamb under her arm securely, she went into the kitchen for that cookie before she went back to bed.

"Susannah, is that you? I thought you were dead." There, playing on the swings, was her

little angel, Susannah. She was about five and would start kindergarten that September. Olivia enjoyed watching Susannah play with the other kids in the park. There was something about the sound of innocent children's laughter that made a person smile.

"Mom, it is me, Susannah. I just needed to make sure that you were okay. I am sorry for the pain I have caused you, any pain throughout this lifetime. I never meant to hurt you. I was so mad at dad for freaking out on me. I just couldn't let go of the pain and anger. I wanted to punish him. But I am so sorry that it punished you as well. Will you please forgive me?"

"Susannah, don't be silly. All little girls do stupid things. Of course, I forgive you." Olivia went over to the swings, picked her daughter up, and gave her a big hug and kiss. *"What a funny thing to say to me."*

"Mom, are you okay? I need to know you are okay."

"Susannah, you are so sweet to worry about me, but I will be okay. I miss you dearly when you are not with me, but I know we will be together again one day." Turning over, Olivia woke up from the dream. Lying there in her bed, she said a prayer for Susannah.

God, please look after my little angel, she had wandered off the righteous path, but I trust that she has found her way back to you. Please, take her under your wing and protect her. Bring her into your glory of eternal bliss, grant me the knowledge that she is safe and well cared for in the light of your glory.

Thank you for forgiving her analytical mind and her stubbornness for not always seeing what she can't see, touch, hear, or know to be the truth. I pray that my belief in you is enough to guide her into the light and that her soul is safe and sound, home with you.

And God, thank you for all the good times and love that I was able to share with her while she was on Earth. Amen.

The last thing Olivia remembered was kissing Lambie, and saying, "I love you, Susannah, go into the light."

Chapter 51

Staring at her mom lying there asleep in her bed, Susannah couldn't help but wonder what would happen now. *I was so wrong. I wish I knew then what I know now. I wish I could go back in time and fix what I did. I would have spent more time with you, Mom. I would have. . .*

The next thing Susannah knew, she was back in time. It was as if she was floating above herself, watching; she could see and hear everything. She was ten and went to a private Catholic school. As she was coming down the narrow stairway from her music class that was just let out, she innocently called out to her teacher, who was leading the way, "How do you know God exists?" Almost banging into her classmate in front of her due to everyone stopping because her teacher had stopped abruptly and turned around.

"You just do!" replied the teacher with the expression on her face as to "never ask that question again or you will be in trouble," kind of look.

Floating above her ten-year-old self, Susannah could see the shocked and disappointed look on her younger self's face. Wondering why an adult just wouldn't tell her the truth. All she wanted to know was how to tell that God existed. It seemed like a logical question to ask. So, why did she feel like she was in trouble for asking a simple question?

Instantly, she could hear the thoughts of her teacher. *Dear God, how could I tell a child that I don't know the answer to that question? Some days I hate being a teacher with all this responsibility. These children look up to me, and all I could answer was, "You just do." The look on her young face broke my heart.*

What! She didn't know the answer. How is that possible? She is teaching in a Catholic school, a school of God? And here I thought I had done something wrong. I stopped asking questions because of that incident. She doesn't even know that she was the start of my disbelief in God.

Susannah could not believe what she'd just witnessed and was instantly back in the bedroom with her sleeping mom.

Life is so unfair. Here I am with my mom, and I can't even talk to her. I can't hug her. Tears started to travel down Susannah's cheeks as she wished she could be alive again. Susannah jumped as the alarm clock on her mom's bedside table rang.

Watching her mom stir and fumble with shutting off the alarm, Susannah sent a thought to her mom. *Mom, it's me, Susannah. I am here with you.*

Oblivious to Susannah's soul being in the room, Olivia went about making her bed. Moving the toy lamb to have its head peek out of the covers. Saying, "I love you, Susannah," as she left the room.

Running after her mom, Susannah was jolted back into the room when she tried to go through the doorway. *What? I was able to roam through the house last time I was here. Why can't I this time?* She tried again to leave the room, and again she was jolted back inside. Susannah cursed as she figured out that being dead and bound to a stuffed toy was not all that she thought it would be. *This is not fair! Am I being punished for not believing in God?* Looking up to the ceiling, Susannah yelled, *Well, if you want all of us to believe in you, then why don't you show yourself?*

Susannah was instantly floating above herself again. This time, she was eleven. She was watching herself watching a caterpillar cocoon start to open. And within moments, a beautiful butterfly emerged from its constraints. Fluttering its wings, it flew onto her hand and rested there a moment before it flew away.

What! I am supposed to believe just because of the miracle of a worm-like insect becoming a butterfly? What child, let alone an adult, would believe in you just because of a butterfly? You are going to have to do better than that.

Susannah's memory shifted now to a family vacation when she was twelve, and they were in Hawaii sitting on the beach at a Luau. The sun was setting, and the magnificent red and orange hues of the sunset were being reflected on the soft ocean waves. She remembered being mesmerized by the music, food, beauty, and pleasure of being in her family's presence.

What are you trying to show me? I don't understand. In church, catechism class, school, and at home listening to bible stories, you are described as a father, the father of Jesus, someone that a child knows to be made of flesh and blood. Show yourself!

Susannah was back in her mom's bedroom. Frustrated with being stuck in the room, as if she was being punished, she screamed, *I hate you!*

Chapter 52

Night came, and Olivia went to bed. She pulled the covers aside, hopped in, picked up the little lamb, and kissed it on the forehead. *How I miss you, Susannah.*

Mom, I am right here!

Olivia closed her eyes and went to sleep.

If I believed in hell, this would be hell, being here so close to her yet having no connection. I am being punished! If there is a God, why would you do this to me?

Susannah was floating above her body again. This time, she was eight. She was in church kneeling on the little cushion that flips down. She was supposed to be praying. Instead, she was looking at the fur coat on the lady sitting in front of her, wishing for the lady to finish her prayer so that when she sat back, Susannah could secretly pet the soft and plush fur. *I am *being punished because I was a curious kid. All I wanted to do was feel the softness. Why would you put such a temptation in front of me if I was not supposed to touch it? How cruel you are to tease a small child like that.*

Susannah was now floating above herself. She was kneeling in front of a priest to give her confession. She was nine. She heard herself say, "I confess to Almighty God and to you, Father, that I have sinned. My last confession was a few months ago." Quickly thinking of what to say, not having sinned, she lied, "Father, forgive me for fighting with my sister." *He would believe that one.* "Also, forgive me for lying." *He would believe that one too, and now that I have lied to a priest, I can be forgiven for doing it.*

Waiting for the priest to tell her what prayers to say, the floating Susannah yelled, *This is what I am talking about, I am forced to go to confession, and I am in trouble if I don't confess something, and so I tell a lie to not be in trouble. What sense does that make? Any logical person can see that this belief makes no sense.*

Susannah's soul floated over to a private confessional box where she could hear the confession of a young woman. "I confess to Almighty God and to you, Father, that I have sinned. My last confession was two days ago. Father, forgive me for fighting with my husband. For fighting back when he hit me. I tried to be a dutiful, honorable, and obedient wife. I try so hard to have the house clean, and his supper made when he gets home. I try to keep the children quiet so that he can rest with his beer and watch TV. Please, forgive me for my sin of hate."

Susannah could not believe what she was hearing. *How could this young woman blame herself for sinning?*

Susannah could hear the priest reply back to the young mother, "Child of God, pray that you have the power to protect your children and when the time is right that you have the power to do what is needed. When you go home tonight, say ten 'Hail Marys.'"

"Thank you, father," the young woman said as she left the confessional.

Susannah could hear the priest's thoughts as the young woman left. *Dear God, please give me the strength to understand your reasoning in allowing this type of abuse. Give me the strength in not wanting to go and punish this man for abusing his wife. Give me the words to help her.* Bowing his head, he said a silent prayer as the next devotee came in to confess his sins.

Susannah floated to the home of the young woman who had just confessed. It was a couple of hours after she had visited the church and confessed her sins. A knock at her door was heard, and a lady was standing on the other side. As the lady from the confessional opened the door, the lady on the other side said, "Hi, I am here to offer you safety for you and your children. Please, pack up a few things and come with me."

Susannah could see the young woman was scared and didn't know what to do.

"Please, I know my visit is unexpected, but you have been praying for a miracle, and here it is. I have been sent to help you and your children. Please, come with me. I can help you."

Susannah could see the tears coming from the young woman's eyes as she dashed around the house, getting together some belongings quickly before her husband came home. Once the family was safely in the social worker's car was when Susannah started to understand.

I get it. The priest heard her confess and knew that the number of times that she had been coming to confess her sins was a cry for help. You are trying to tell me that being allowed to confess is one way that a person can ask for help.

Susannah was back in her mom's bedroom. *God, I still don't understand why you can't show yourself.*

Chapter 53

*A*gain, night came, and Olivia was back in bed. Pulling the covers aside, she hopped in and picked up the little lamb and kissed it on the forehead, just as she had done the night before.

Susannah was floating above herself again. This time, she was nineteen. Her family had taken a trip to Rome and were visiting Vatican City. Susannah was kneeling and praying in a pew. The room was incredible. There was gold everywhere; the altar looked like it was made from solid gold, the crosses on the walls had gold. Behind a screen wall, she could see nuns kneeling and praying, silently getting up and leaving as others came in and took their seats.

I remember this moment. This was the moment I decided I was never going to church again. All the years of hearing that there were starving children in the world, all the years of knowing that there were children needing clothes, food, and shelter, and here in front of me was enough gold to feed them all. This was the moment that I didn't believe in God. My belief shifted when I had the thought of how there could be so much money right here in this very room, let alone the art throughout the Sistine Chapel. It blew my belief to smithereens.

Susannah was now floating above herself again. It was the night she and her father had that life-changing fight. The night that she had an ultimatum of either going to church or moving out. And she chose to move out.

If I only knew then what I know now. How was I to know that money was power, and without money, you have no power? No way to play the necessary game of life. Without the money, the church would have no power, and then where would they be? I get it now, but all I thought about back then was starving children. I wasted so many years being mad at my dad that I couldn't see past the chaos.

Thinking about all the time she missed not spending time with her family brought her back to the moment. Looking at her mom sleeping, Susannah said a silent prayer, *Dear God, I still wish you would show yourself and prove to me that you exist, but I do forgive you for my feeling of being betrayed. Betrayed because all I asked for was proof, and no one could provide it for me. I felt betrayed and lied to by my dad, mom, teachers, and even the priest at church. All I wanted was proof.*

A bright light appeared as a large glowing hand, palm side up, came into her vision. A thought was sent to Susannah to get into the hand. Susannah clumsily climbed into the outstretched palm. Sitting with her knees tucked into her chest and her arms wrapped around her knees, she was the equivalent size of a Werther's caramel candy. The palm closed slightly to make sure she was safe as it moved through the air. God was holding Susannah in his hand and moved her up closer to his chest. Susannah knew what was happening but could not see his face. He was far too big for that.

No wonder I have never seen you. You are far too big for the human brain to conceive. Here I am looking for the size of a man, and yet you are bigger than the universe. You cannot fit onto Earth, but I understand now. When you take a breath, we can feel it in the wind. You fear moving so as not to disrupt our world. You send the angels to do your bidding, for they are smaller and capable without demolishing us. Fascinating that it has to take me to die to understand the truth. Thank you for not letting me into Heaven the first time. For I would not have learned what I so desperately was seeking on Earth—proof that you exist.

Chapter 54

Lexi loved this time of year. Christmas time in New York City is where the best NYC attractions transform into a festive winter extravaganza! There were open-air holiday markets to hit, family-friendly shows, such as the Radio City Christmas Spectacular, and other iconic traditions like the all-out-madness holiday displays on Fifth Avenue and the famous neighborhood of Dyker Heights. She had read that homeowners had spent up to twenty thousand dollars on custom decorations to resemble Santa's fortress up in the North Pole.

Day or night, as you drove or walked through the neighborhood, it was easy to believe that you were in a Christmas wonderland. Everywhere you looked, you could see the razzle-dazzle of breathtaking sparkling lights, Christmas trees, snowmen, life-size reindeer, horse-drawn sleighs filled with gift-wrapped presents, mounds of real snow that people paid someone to make for their display, and, of course, Jesus in his manger. You could even hear Christmas music playing throughout the community.

As she was driving through the picturesque streets to her mom's house, Lexi remembered back when she was younger. Some nights, her family would dress up in vintage outfits and sing Christmas carols outside their home for the people to enjoy as they walked by.

Each Christmas season, she was always impressed with the new theme and decorations the events company created for her mom. This year was especially impressive. As she pulled up to the house, there in her mom's front yard, was a carousel of horses manned by a man to safely allow the children to come and take a ride.

Walking over to the man, she said, "Detective, what are you doing here?"

"Miss Constantine, what a coincidence."

"A coincidence, my fanny."

"How are you doing, Alexandra?"

"Good, thank you. Is there a problem that I should know about? Are you on a stakeout?"

"No. Every year our unit donates time to help out. This year I offered to help out in Dyker Heights. The coincidence is that it is your mother's house that I was sent to. The coincidence is that you showed up while I was here."

"That is a coincidence, too crazy of one if you ask me."

"Alexandra, since you are here, I would like to inform you that because of your help in Susannah's case, I have been able to arrest all of Marko's gang. The court hearing was just the other day, and all of them were sentenced to life in prison. You did well."

"We did good," she said as she looked up to the night sky and winked.

"Well, it is a good thing to know that you haven't run to the convent to join the nunnery."

"That is a funny thing to say, Detective."

"After the ordeal you have been through, one might think that you would want the protection of God himself."

"I had the protection of God long before this ordeal, Detective," she said as she entered the house.

"Take care, Alexandra."

"You too, Detective."

As she closed the door, Lexi yelled, "Mom, have you seen Susannah's old stuffed lamb?" It had been a few days since she dropped it off at her mom's house, and she still needed to fulfill her sister's final request. Which was to make sure Billy was okay, and to do that, she required the lamb.

"Hi, nice to see you too. Yes, it is in my bed. Why?"

Going into her mom's bedroom, she retrieved the lamb from under the covers. It had been covered up so cozy in her mom's bed. Coming downstairs with it, Lexi put it by her boots at the front door as she went into the kitchen to join her mom to help with dinner. "I need to borrow it for a few days."

"That is odd. Why?"

"Mom, you wouldn't believe me if I told you, so just believe me that it is important and that it was one of Susannah's last requests."

"Sure, Lexi, it's not a problem to borrow it if it makes you feel better." Olivia knew that her daughter was grieving Susannah's death. If she needed the toy lamb to help her through the grieving process, then who was she to stop her? Sometimes the only thing a mother could do was give up her will and allow for divine intervention, trusting in God's love that he knew best.

"Your life was a blessing your memory a treasure. You are loved beyond words and missed beyond measure."
Unknown

Chapter 55

*I*t took a couple of days for Lexi to get her courage up. *Oh my God, who knew this would be so hard? What do I say?*

Billy answered his cell phone. "Buongiorno."

"Hi, Billy. I am Susannah's sister, Lexi." There was a pause on the line. "I know you probably don't remember me from high school. And to be honest, I didn't even know you were dating my sister until a few days ago. I forgot she had a crush on you back then."

In his thick Bronx accent, Billy replied, "Dahlin, how can I help yuh?" *What is she doing calling me? Susannah's death is hard enough, let alone having to deal with her family.*

She was smiling at the thought that her sister would date someone her father would have hated for his slur on the English language. At least her father would have been happy that he was

Italian. "Billy, I know this may seem odd, but may I come over to your place and talk?"

"Lexi, not tuh be rude, but I doan see the point."

"Please, Billy, it would mean the world to me if I could just meet you today." Lexi wasn't sure what she would do if he said no. "I promise it will be a quick, one-time thing. If it is easier, I can meet you for coffee somewhere."

"No, we don't need tuh go for coffee. Lucky for you, it's not Ferragosto, and I will be here for about de next two hours. Here's the address."

"Thanks, Billy. I am on my way." Getting her coat and boots on, Lexi put the toy lamb into her purse and rushed out the door. Smiling to herself at the thought of Ferragosto. She knew the Italian community shut down everything to celebrate the holiday. *Susannah, this better be worth it.*

Billy hung up his cell phone and went into the bakery to get a piece of pizza. Eating seemed to calm his nerves. *Bettuh make it two pieces.*

Hearing Lexi's voice brought him back to high school. He had just finished football practice and was walking off the field when one of the cheerleaders came over and started flirting with him. She flirtatiously tugged on his uniform, pulling him under the bleachers. They were making out when Lexi walked by. And he remembered her saying, "Oh, my God, get a room, you two."

When the girl he was kissing looked up, Lexi had given him a look of such disgust. It was a look as if he was cheating on her sister.

Billy, to this day, couldn't understand why she looked at him that way. Who was she to judge him? He wasn't dating her sister!

Chapter 56

$\mathscr{B}$illy worked in the "Real Little Italy" in the community of Belmont, to be more accurate. It felt better to give Lexi the bakery's address to meet him instead of her coming to his place in Skyville. He knew no one would care if he and Lexi went upstairs to talk in a more private setting.

His great grandfather was a Sicilian immigrant who moved over from Italy in the early 1900s. He had used all his savings to open an Italian forno and market on Arthur Avenue, here in the Bronx. His grandfather had died a few years back, and up until just a few months ago, Billy had lived with his folks and his grandmother above the same bakery. They were a close-knit family, and even though Billy had only been dating Susannah for less than a year, they had loved her as if she was one of their own.

The smell of fresh-baked bread filled the air as Lexi entered the bakery. To her delight, the décor was authentic. It looked like an Italian street scene—a cobbled courtyard with crumbling walls and peeling vintage posters.

With just a few days before Christmas, the bakery was full of people getting ready and ordering the goods they needed for the traditional evening meal.

There were shelves upon shelves of freshly baked bread that you could buy by the weight instead of just a full loaf. There were all kinds of noodles for sale, like the typical kind you find in a grocery store: spaghetti, lasagna, and fettucine. There were also many others that she had never heard of before: bigoli, capellini, mafalda, and pici.

In a glass counter, she could see cornetti and flat Margherita pizza, which you could buy by the slice. Then she spotted the pastries. Oh, the pastries. Lexi's favorite was the foot-long cannoli. So many ricotta cream fillings to choose from: chocolate, vanilla, pistachio, espresso, lemon, strawberry, peanut butter. The list went on. And, if that wasn't good enough, you could add all kinds of other goodies on top. Lexi felt like she had died and gone to Heaven.

"Buongiorno," said the most authentic-looking Italian grandma that Lexi had ever laid eyes upon, apron and all. In a very thick Italian accent, the old lady called out, "Don't fawhget tuh pull a ticket." She was pointing to a take-a-number ticket dispenser by the door.

Lexi turned her head away from the mouth-watering cannoli to answer. "Oh. No, thank you, I am here to speak with Billy."

Waving a hand implying for Lexi to come her way, she yelled out, "Billy, your lady friend's *la sorella* is here."

Understanding a little Italian, she knew *la sorella* meant sister. Lexi's face went red as everyone in the bakery looked toward the person whom the old lady was referring to, her.

"Nanna, how many times do I have tuh tell yuh, not tuh yell?" Billy said as he came out from the back kitchen into the front retail area. Not remembering what Lexi looked like, he looked around for a girl who looked like Susannah.

Lexi put up her hand for Billy to look her way.

He was surprised to find that Lexi didn't look anything like Susannah. She was so skinny, with dark hair. *It must have been de mailman*, he thought to himself. Seeing her, he waved just like his grandmother and said, "Make way fawh, Lexi." People seemed to part like the Red Sea, and she walked right on through the crowded room.

He greeted her by kissing her on both cheeks. Then quickly ushered her in through the kitchen to the private quarters upstairs where his family lived.

When she entered the suite, it brought back memories of when she had visited Italy. Her parents had bought her the trip as a gift to celebrate graduating from university. Being in this suite made her feel like she never left. The room's furnishings were very traditional, with the dinner table as the main focal point. You could tell their Catholic religion was very important to them, for there was a very large cross mounted on the one wall, with a rosary hanging over it. On the other wall hung an incredible amount of family photos, generations of Billy's family telling a story if one cared to examine them.

A lady in her late fifties came out of an adjoining room and greeted her. "My Billy tells me dat yuh are his sweet Susannah's sister?"

"Yes, I am." Trying to break the tension in the room, Lexi added, "Great business you guys have."

Ignoring the compliment that Lexi just made, his mother responded in broken English, "What is so impawhtant dat yuh had tuh come here and upset my Billy?"

"Ma, doan be rude. Go. Go downstairs." Billy almost pushed his mother out the door. "Overprotective mudder. Come, have a seat over here." He gestured, pointing to a sofa covered with an Italian textured Strato throw.

Lexi remembered seeing a similar blanket in Italy. Its texture was wave-like on one side and had stripes on the reverse. "I understand how you feel. This meeting is awkward for me as well," Lexi said as she pulled the bag her mom had given her out of her purse. As she did, the lamb fell out unnoticed and landed on the floor.

Billy took the bag from Lexi's outstretched hand. Opening it, he said, "What de hell, is dis some sick joke?" Inside was the box with the engagement ring that he had given Susannah the night she died. Tears filled his eyes and ran down his cheeks. Slamming the box closed, he yelled, "Get out! Get out of here, and nevuh come back."

Startled, Lexi stammered, "My mother thought it was best if you had it."

"I doan care. Get out." Billy got up and opened the door to the downstairs.

His mother was rushing up as Lexi started to descend. "What have yuh done?"

Lexi dashed out of there as fast as she could, trembling from the unexpected reaction. Getting into her car, she drove away.

Chapter 57

Sitting down, he put his elbows on his knees and his hands over his face.

Susannah had watched Billy freak out when he looked inside the bag that Lexi had given him. He was sitting so close to her that she could almost touch him. Tears were streaming down his cheeks when his mother, Maria, rushed in. "Oh, my poor baby, what has dat aweful woman done tuh yuh? I'll kill her." Maria knelt beside him, taking his head into her hands and kissing it.

A moment later, Billy's older sister, Katarina, came in with her daughter, Rosalina. Noticing her mother coddling her brother, Katarina said, "What is goin' on in here and who was dat running out of here like she was on fire?"

"Come over here and give your brudder a hug, Katarina. Yuh too, Nina, your uncle Billy needs some love."

Rosalina, whom the family called Nina, a nickname meaning "little one," came over to the couch. Her grandma's legs and big bum were in the way, and she was too little at the age of five to step over her. So, she went around the couch the other way. As she came around the other side, she spotted the cutest little stuffed dog. After hugging the knees of her uncle, she bent down and picked it up.

Katarina felt a bit awkward and said, "Okay, I see yuh two need some time. I will be back tomorrow for de family dinner." She quickly picked up Rosalina, and as they left, she said to her bambina, "Bella, we will come back for dinner, and yuh can see Nonna, Nonno, and all your uncles and aunties, 'kay?"

Rosalina nodded and hugged her new dog tightly.

Susannah's soul, attached to the lamb, went floating down the stairs with Rosalina.

Katarina put Rosalina into a booster seat in the back seat of her new BMW. She took the toy out of Rosalina's hands so she could do up her seat belt, saying, "Where d'ja get this, Nina?"

"It's my dog. It was lost, and so I am gonna take care of it." She grabbed the stuffed lamb back and hugged it tightly.

"Is that so?" Katarina sarcastically asked as she got into the driver's side of the car and drove away.

Sitting beside Rosalina's car seat, Susannah looked outside the car window as they drove away from the bakery.

Chapter 58

After a few minutes of driving, Lexi started to calm down. *Susannah, I did what you asked and brought you to see Billy. He is still a pig in my eyes. Whatever you saw in him, I don't understand. He is not okay with your death. I hope that satisfies your request because I'm not going back.* Looking at her purse, she noticed she was talking to nobody, for the lamb was not there.

Oh, my God! Susannah! She couldn't go back. Billy's mother would never let her step a foot through the front door. *Susannah, I am so sorry. How could I have left you? How on Earth am I going to get you into Heaven now?* Devastated, Lexi drove over to her mom's.

Frantically opening her mom's front door and running into the house, Lexi started to panic. "Mom! Oh, my God, Mom!"

Olivia came out of the kitchen and almost ran right into Lexi. "Dear God, child! What is the matter?"

Waving her hands in the air, Lexi hysterically cried, "Oh, my God! Mom, I've lost Susannah!"

"Lexi, you are not making any sense. Susannah is dead. She died weeks ago. Sit down. You're scaring me." Olivia carefully maneuvered her youngest daughter into the living room and onto the sofa.

"Mom, I went to see Billy."

"Yes, you said you were going to do that. Did you give Billy back his ring?"

"Is that what was in the bag? Yes, and he freaked out. He told me it was some sick joke and that I had to leave."

"Oh, I am so sorry, Lexi. Sometimes people under extreme stress do bizarre things," she said, in a tone that also implied Lexi.

"No, Mom, you don't understand. I lost Susannah."

"Lexi, you are not making any sense."

"Mom, Susannah was attached to the lamb I borrowed. She wanted to see how Billy was doing. It was one of her last requests."

"Have you lost your mind? Lexi, you sound like you need to be in one of those white suits. You know, the ones where they tie your arms? What is going on?"

"I think they call them straight-jackets. Mom, you have to believe me. Susannah did not make it into Heaven. She got lost in the Void. Reverend Hawthorne and Tamara helped me get her out. But to do that, Tamara had to bind her to something on Earth that Susannah loved. So, I chose Lambie, her favorite stuffed toy."

"That is ludicrous, Lexi." Olivia was getting very worried about her daughter's sanity.

"Mom, I didn't believe it at first, either. But Susannah is a ghost. Magically attached to her lamb, which is now misplaced at Billy's."

Lexi stared at her mom. Hardly taking a breath, she said, "This is why I didn't tell you in the first place. I thought you could help me, but I see now that you can't. I guess Susannah was right. You and Dad are so stuck in your Catholic ways that there is no other spiritual possibility."

Lexi could see the look on her mother's face and knew she would not get any help here. "I am sorry, Mom. I made a mistake in coming here. You can't help me." Lexi ran out of the house faster than she went in.

"Lexi, come back here! You are not in the state of mind to be driving," Olivia said as she ran out the door without her coat and boots on. "Watch out for the—"

Lexi almost hit someone as she speedily drove away.

Freezing, Olivia came back in. Shutting the door, she said a silent prayer for Lexi. Without hesitation, she went over to the phone and dialed.

Picking up his cell phone, Edward could see the name on the call display. "Hello, Mrs. Constantine, how may I help you?"

As soon as she heard him say hello, Olivia blurted out, "Reverend Hawthorne, we need to talk." Olivia had known Edward's father, Randell, for a few years before his death. Her husband, Marcus, was a golf buddy of his.

"I have been informed that you and Lexi participated in some voodoo exorcism thing with a witch named Tamara. And now Lexi is— I do not even know what she is. She is not herself, that is for sure. She is rambling on about Susannah's soul being attached to her childhood toy lamb, and now it is lost. I think the stress of her sister's death has finally pushed her over the edge, and she is going insane. Now, what do you have to say for yourself, young man? And it better be good."

"Mrs. Constantine, I assure you that my only part was to save a soul. The rest of what happened was a surprise to me. But what did you say? Lexi lost the lamb?"

"So, you did have a part in this voodoo stuff? You are supposed to be a man of God. How could you? What would people think if they found out you played with the occult? Dear God, what is this world coming to? Reverend Hawthorne, you better fix this problem you got my Lexi into."

"Mrs. Constantine, I—" But it was too late. She had already hung up. Edward stopped everything he was doing. This problem had to be fixed and pronto!

Chapter 59

Glancing at the Saint Christopher pendant swaying from a chain secured to the rear-view mirror of his SUV, Edward thanked the patron saint for his safe travel that day. In his haste to redeem himself to Mrs. Constantine, he forgot it was rush hour in Brooklyn. Maybe it was a full moon because it seemed that everyone was driving as if the devil was chasing them.

Fifteen minutes later, he pulled into Olivia's driveway and sat there for a moment. Edward had been over to Mrs. Constantine's home a few times over the years. Years ago, he would be invited every once and a while to go golfing with his father, and they would pick Marcus up along the way.

Thinking about golf brought back the memory of that horrible day. The three of them, plus another friend of Marcus's, had been playing at his dad's favorite country club. He loved playing at that golf course, with its championship reputation, hundred-year-old history, and perfectly manicured fairways.

He remembered it vividly. It was a beautiful day to be getting some exercise, fresh air, and some good laughs. Marcus was not only an excellent surgeon and above-average golfer, he also had a great sense of humor. They were on the seventh hole, and Marcus was about to tee off. He took a couple of practice shots and then set his stance as if he was aiming for a hole-in-one. With his club still in the air, Marcus silently crippled over to the ground, clawing at the left side of his chest.

After that, everything was a bit of a blur. He remembered his dad giving Marcus CPR while all the people stood around watching. He remembered the ambulance taking Marcus away. And he remembered Olivia screaming hysterically at the hospital when she found out that he had suffered a fatal heart attack, *"No, this can't be happening! He was perfectly healthy."*

The last two times he had been at this address, someone had died. Marcus, and then four years later, Susannah. Taking a breath to compose himself, he got out of his vehicle, walked up to the front door, and knocked.

Olivia opened the door with a shocked look on her face. "Edward, what are you doing here?

I thought for sure I would never see you again after the hocus-pocus stuff I accused you of."

Trying to keep his cool and not be offended by Olivia's accusations, he said, "Please, allow me to come in and explain myself." He stepped forward through the door without her invite.

Olivia stepped aside and followed Edward into the living room. Sitting down on the couch across from the chair he had sat down in, she said, "Edward, I don't think there is anything that you could say that could change my mind. It's like Lexi is possessed or something. Whatever cult you are in now, I don't want you to ever go near my daughter again."

"Whoa, slow down there, Mrs. Constantine. You have known me for many years, and I have never given you a reason to think about these things you are saying. I know that there is something a bit crazy going on with Alexandra, but I assure you that I have not joined any cult and do not practice voodoo.

"It is true that Alexandra and her friend Tamara came over to my place, and I did participate in saving Susannah's soul so it could ascend into Heaven. I did not have any idea they were going to attach her soul to a stuffed toy."

"Edward, everyone knows that ghosts aren't real. Are you trying to make me believe that Susannah is a ghost stuck in our world and not in Heaven?" Astounded at the thought, Olivia slumped back into the couch, saying, "The thought is ludicrous."

"Mrs. Constantine, your daughter believes that her sister's soul never made it into Heaven, and I was trying to help. In seminary school, we are taught how to do exorcisms, but this was new to me. Alexandra's friend, Tamara, made the thought of dying and being in the Void equivalent to being in outer space.

"With no one around, in the dark, stuck, and not being able to move, floating there for eternity. It was such a horrible thought that I just had to help in case there was any truth to it. You would never have forgiven me if I had left your daughter's soul in that condition." Edward was beside himself, imagining the anguish of a soul not being in Heaven.

Shaking her head from side to side, Olivia said, "Goodness me, Edward. This is all too crazy. How could all this be happening? It is hard enough trying to function day to day with losing one daughter, let alone having to deal with a second daughter who has lost her mind."

He sat straighter in the chair as he said, "Speaking of losing something, you said on the phone that Alexandra had lost the toy lamb."

"Yes. Lexi came over here earlier, saying frantically, that she had somehow left the lamb at Billy's when he so rudely kicked her out of his place. And here I thought Susannah had found herself a nice Catholic boy and all."

"What? Who is Billy, and why would she be kicked out?"

"Susannah's fiancé. And I had given Lexi the engagement ring to give back to him."

"She was engaged?'

"I know. Ever since Susannah moved out of our house, everything seemed to be hush-hush and secretive. She had just told me that she was going to move in with him the morning before she died."

"Did Alexandra know about it?"

"It didn't seem like it. Lexi was as surprised as you are."

"Did she know she was giving back the engagement ring?"

"No, I guess not. I had put it in a brown paper bag and stapled it shut after the police returned all of Susannah's possessions."

"I wonder why she took the lamb there in the first place."

"I am not sure. She said something about Susannah's last request. Lexi was pretty fixated on finding the lamb that day. That is why she came by in the first place, to get the lamb.

"Thinking back on it now, that lamb showed up in the most unusual place. I had come downstairs, and I noticed it by my boots at the front entrance. I decided to take the lamb back up with me to bed. I had the craziest dream."

Thinking about the dream she had, Olivia began to cry. "Susannah was quite young, and we were playing in the park. Lexi was in school, which was odd because they had reversed roles. In the dream, Lexi was the older child. Dreams are so weird. I remember Susannah asking me to forgive her."

Edward got up and went over to sit beside Olivia, putting his arm around her shoulder. As she put her head on his shoulder, all her pent-up emotions came pouring out. In his line of business, he was used to the emotional roller coaster of grief.

Edward just let her cry. Pulling out a clean tissue from his coat pocket, he passed it to her. Not being able to think of anything to say that would help her. Instead, he said a prayer. "God of love and mercy, embrace all those whose hearts today overflow with grief, unanswered questions, and such a sense of loss. Grant them space to express their tears. Hold them close through the coming days. Amen."

Chapter 60

What am I going to do?

Ah, what the heck. Lexi dialed Billy's number. It went to his answering machine. "Hi, you've reached Billy. Yuh knows what tuh do. Ya' dig? *Beep.*"

"Hi Billy, it's Lexi. Please don't erase this message without hearing what I need to ask. By accident, I left a toy lamb at your place. It must have fallen out of my purse in all the commotion. I need it back ASAP. I know—"

"Lexi, I do not know what kind of crazy yuh are. I am at my mom's, and dere is no stuffed lamb here. Ya' dig? Don't evuh call me again, or I will have tuh put a restrainin' orduh out on yuh." He hung up.

What nerve. Lexi was shocked that Billy would pretend to be an answering machine. *I must get that lamb back.* She was now tipping to the side of being dangerously close to hysterical. *Oh, my God, oh my God, what do I do now? If Billy is telling the truth and he does not have the lamb, then where is it?*

Putting on her shoes and grabbing her car keys, Lexi rushed out of her apartment and pushed the down button in the elevator.

Even at a time like this, she never seemed to get bored with the blissful garden view of Central Park from the elevator's glass window. A hidden piece of paradise even at Christmas. A place one could escape into from the hustle and bustle of their workday to relax, rejuvenate, and recharge, even for a few moments. A little smile escaped her mouth as she looked down at the miniature-sized people strolling through the grand park. She could see that the pathways were full of the local artisans displaying their wares of tantalizing fresh baked goods and crafts for the holiday season. Her body started to sway as she imagined hearing the soothing sounds of jazz music playing.

Exiting the elevator, she walked over to her favorite valet attendant and gave him her car keys, "Hi Sam. All I need you to do is check to see if there is a toy lamb inside the car."

"Right away, Miss Constantine," he replied as he dashed off.

"Check everywhere!" she yelled after him.

Looking around the well-designed entrance and admiring all the incredible pieces of art hanging on the walls, Lexi decided to go and have a seat as she waited and watched the other residents coming in and out. Her apartment building had a fabulous heated swimming pool with a lifeguard, an on-site health center with a fitness lounge, an entertainment lounge, a screening room, 24-hour valet parking, and security. She was even greeted by a doorman when she came in or out of the building.

Right at that moment, Nick, a guy whom she had met a few times in the gym, came over to her from the communal mail slots. Not only was he sexy and built like a Greek Adonis, but he seemed smart too.

"Lexi, will I be seeing you up at the Christmas party tonight?" he asked as he walked up to her.

The owners of the apartment believed in the community. They hosted a variety of in-building events throughout the year, like holiday parties and summer barbecues, allowing the residents to connect with their neighbors.

"Oh, right. That's tonight. No, sorry, I have more pressing commitments that I have to deal with." Lexi had forgotten all about Christmas. She was so caught up in saving Susannah's soul that Santa and all that merry cheer was the last thing on her mind.

"Too bad, I was hoping to get you under the mistletoe," he said with a smirk and a wink.

Seeing Sam coming to her rescue, she smiled back at Nick, saying, "Well, have a good night. See you in the gym," and walked toward Sam.

The young valet came back a bit out of breath and said, "Miss Constantine, I checked everywhere in your car. I could not find a toy lamb."

She was disappointed that the toy was not there. Lexi passed a ten-dollar bill as a tip for his effort. It was not his fault the lamb was not there. "Thank you anyways, Sam. Have a Merry Christmas."

Taking the tip, he said, "Thank you, and I hope you have yourself a Merry Christmas, as well."

Lexi walked over to the elevator and pushed the up button. *Susannah, where are you? I hate that this will be our first Christmas Eve that we have not spent together.*

Lexi and Susannah started the tradition after the latter had moved out of the house so they could connect at Christmas and celebrate, just the two of them. *I miss you so much. And now I don't even know where you will be spending the holiday.*

Christmas was in two days. She needed to find that lamb.

Chapter 61

Phoning her mom and without saying hi, Lexi said, "Mom, I am so sorry that I lost it. I need you to call Billy and ask him to give me back the lamb. I have to get it back. I need it to save Susannah's soul." She was so exhausted from all this crazy searching and soul rescue stuff that all she could do now was cry.

"Oh, my dear Lexi, you poor child. Don't cry. Should I come over? You know how much I hate to drive in this weather."

"No, Mom. All I need you to do is call Billy and get Lambie back. Can you do that?"

"I can try, but I don't know why you need that toy. Really, Lexi, this is getting out of hand. Are you sure you don't want me to come over?"

Still sobbing, Lexi said, "No, I just need you to call Billy."

"Reverend Hawthorne was just over. He is worried about you too, dear. We think that you are taking Susannah's death too hard. Maybe you need a holiday?"

"Mom, I am fine. Really. I need the lamb back, and then all this will be over. I promise. Please, can you promise me that you will phone Billy?"

"Fine, I promise that I will phone Billy, but on one condition. That you come over here tomorrow night for supper."

"All right, I promise. See you tomorrow night."

"Lexi, I love you."

"I love you too, Mom. Night."

As Olivia hung up the phone, she decided to call Billy right away. "Hi, Billy. I'm Mrs. Constantine, Susannah's mom. I am sorry for the pain I have caused you. I am the one who gave Lexi the package to give to you. It was not her fault. She didn't even know what was in it. Will you forgive me?"

"Mrs. Constantine, I was in shock. Dat was all. It just brought back all de memories in one big punch tuh the face, yuh know what I mean? A hard blow. Yuh is a fellow Catholic, yuh wouldn't do something like dat on purpose, now would you?"

"Oh, my goodness, no. I just thought that the ring looked like it cost so much that you deserved it back."

"I loved your daughter so much. She was my angel. I miss huh so much."

"I know. The reason I am calling you is that Lexi accidentally left a toy lamb at your place. Can you be so kind and look around for it?"

"Not dat again. I already told Lexi dat there is no toy lamb at my mom's. Okay? What is it with dat toy? Why is it so important?"

"As crazy as this will sound, Lexi believes that Susannah's soul is attached to the toy. She insists that she needs the toy so that she can help Susannah's soul get into Heaven."

Billy made the sign of the cross. "Did I hear yuh right?"

"I know. It seems ridiculous to me too. But Lexi is going nuts over this lost toy lamb. Please, help me find it."

"Alright, Mrs. Constantine. Just for yuh, because I loved your daughter so much and I wouldn't wanna disrespect my elders. I will have another look around my mom's place for yuh. I will call yuh if I find it."

"Thank you, Billy." Olivia hung up the phone. All she could do now was pray that her life would get back to some sort of normal.

Chapter 62

"Rosalina, supper's ready!"

"Okay, Mama, I'm coming." Rosalina picked up her new toy dog, saying to it, "I am going to call yuh Susie." Walking into the dining room, Rosalina pulled out a chair and placed the stuffed animal on it. Then she sat on the chair beside it.

Katarina put a plate down on the table in front of her daughter and said, "Yuh eat all your dinner. We have a big day tomorrow."

"Mama, Susie's hungry too. She needs a plate."

"Yuh don't say." Katarina got a small plate and put a little bit of dinner on it, and placed it on the table in front of the toy. "Here, Susie, eat all your vegetables."

Rosalina laughed. "Mama, Susie doesn't like vegetables eithuh."

"How do yuh know?"

"'Cause she's not eating them." Rosalina started laughing so hard, some milk came out of her nose. "Susie, yuh are funny."

"Nina, stop dat now and eat your vegetables," Katarina said, scolding her daughter.

"Okay, but Susie is makin' funny faces, and it is makin' me laugh. Stop dat, Susie. Yuh are getting me in trouble."

The front door opened, and Katarina's husband, Lenny, walked in. To her, it was evident that he was good at his job because he made lots of dough. She was living the lifestyle of the rich and famous.

He owned his father's international trading business after his dad died suddenly. The coppers said it was an accident, but he wasn't so sure. He had only been running the company for a few months now, and Marko Calponi's gang seemed to be around the docks a lot, especially when his shipments were coming in for Mr. Kofman. But he was paid so well by Kofman that he put the coincidence out of his mind.

"Yay, Daddy's home!" Rosalina got up to go and hug her dad. Holding his hand, they both walked back into the dining room.

"Smells good, dah-lin," Lenny said as he kissed his wife. "Nina, what d'j and your mama do today?" Sitting down beside his daughter, he almost sat on her new toy.

Jumping up to save her dog, she pushed her dad away. "No, Daddy, dat's Susie's chair. Yuh sits ovuh dere. Okay?"

Lenny pulled out an empty chair and sat down. "Oh, excuse me. I see now we have a new guest in de house. And how long will she be visitin' us, Nina?"

"Forever, Daddy, yuh silly dilly."

After eating dinner, Katarina said to her daughter, "Nina, get ready for bed. It's been a long day, and it is bedtime. Yuh with me?"

Picking up her new dog, Rosalina went to her bedroom. It was decked out in the latest cartoon craze, with princess stuff everywhere. She got into her nightie that, of course, had a princess decal on it and climbed into her canopy bed. Her mom came in a few moments later to tuck her in and say a bedtime prayer. Katarina said good night by kissing her on both cheeks.

"Mama, Susie needs a kiss."

Katarina picked up the dog and made big kissing noises on both checks and then tucked it into bed with Rosalina.

"That is funny, Mama. Susie made a face."

"That is nonsense. All dogs like kisses," Katarina said as she shut off the light and left the room.

Rosalina pulled the covers up over her new toy. "Aunt Susie, does it hurt being dead?"

Startled that Rosalina was talking to her, Susannah answered, *"No."* She had seen

Rosalina quite a few times over the last six months and had come to love the child.

"I can hear you in my head, Aunty Susie, and I can see you. Why are you always so close to my new dog?"

"I think it is because my soul is attached to it. It used to be my stuffed lamb when I was young."

"Oh, dat is funny. It looks like a dog to me. Night, Aunty Susie." Rosalina kissed the toy and tucked it under her arm.

"Night," Susannah said back to her, lightly rubbing her cheek.

Rosalina twitched at the touch.

"Interesting a child can see, hear, and feel me." Being in the dark, in somebody else's house, all Susannah could do now was wait.

Chapter 63

It was Christmas Eve, and Billy had been in a bad mood all morning. Tonight was the night that Susannah was supposed to move in with him. How could he pretend to be happy when all he wanted to do was buddy up with a good old brewski, put his feet up to watch the telly, and forget Christmas altogether.

He was just about to call his mom and cancel dinner with the family when his cell phone rang. Answering by sliding the "yes" button, he put the phone to his ear. "Ya?"

"Billy, it is your mama. Don't forget to bring your surprise Santa gift. Oh ya, and wear something nice."

Putting the phone down, Billy sarcastically said, "Love you too, Ma."

Soberly sauntering into his bedroom with his shoulders rolled forward, he decided to get changed, knowing his mother would not be happy with what he was wearing now.

As he walked into his bedroom, he picked up a shirt that was on the floor, hidden by his dresser. It was the one Susannah had bought him. He had worn it to dinner the night she died. Bringing it up to his nose, he could still smell her perfume.

Inhaling even deeper, an image of her flashed before his eyes. She was kneeling on top of him teasingly. Her tousled hair was flowing down to her shoulders, wearing his shirt with the top three buttons undone, revealing the outline of her breasts. His heart felt like it was being pulled out of his chest. The pain of remembering her was too much to bear.

Tears started to form. He missed her so much. Tossing the shirt into the laundry bin, he grabbed some dress clothes from the closet. *When is this pain going to stop*?

Billy walked over to the front closet and brought out all the gifts. Luckily, he and Susannah had been buying Christmas presents since September. He remembered her saying that it was never too early to buy a gift. Especially when she worked for an antique dealer and found one-of-a-kind, remarkable pieces.

There, at the bottom of the pile of gifts, was a small box that he had wrapped up for Susannah. It was an old antique key he had custom-made to fit the door to his apartment. She would have treasured it forever. With more tears clouding his vision, he tucked it back into the closet and left.

Driving over to his parents' place, he got out and quickly unlocked the front door to the bakery, locking it behind him. As he rushed up the stairs to his parents' suite, he forced a smile. Coming into the room, he went over to his mom and gave her a kiss on the cheek. As he patted his dad's shoulder, he said, "Merry Christmas, everyone."

The aroma of turkey dinner and all the trimmings lingered in the air. Billy took a seat beside Daniella, his younger sister, at the dinner table. His mom had transformed the old table into a beautifully decorated festive sight to behold. It was covered with a hand-crafted tablecloth printed with sparkling gold snowflakes and two tall white candles with their flames flickering and dancing. His mother's best Italian china was placed perfectly for each guest.

About to pour her brother a glass of Chardonnay, she changed her mind to the Pinot Noir, remembering he liked red wine. "So, big bro, what is all de commoshun about a lamb, I hear? Mama was just tellin' us all about it."

"It is all just some kind of weird joke. I think God is punishing me." Billy made the sign of the cross.

"Billy, don't say that. God loves yuh. Daniella, it is just crazy how Susannah's family is treating him. I think they are stupido." Maria kissed the top of Billy's head as she placed a bowl toppling over with mashed potatoes onto the table.

There was quite a commotion as Katarina, Lenny, and Rosalina came into the apartment. Katarina interrupted their conversation by saying, "Merry Christmas, everyone," as she came around and gave her Mama, Papa, Nonna, Uncle Vinny, Aunt Clara, Billy and her sister, Daniella, a big hug. A smile came to everyone's faces as Rosalina copied her mama, trying to hug everyone.

"Billy, don't yuh a worry about no lamb. Yuh said there is no lamb, so there is no lamb. We believe yuh," said his Aunt Clara.

"What are yuh guys talking about?" Katarina asked as she sat down.

"It's nutting. Guys, I don't wanna talk about it," Billy said as he took the bowl of stuffing from his mom and placed it on the table.

Billy's dad, Antonio, boomed over all the other voices, "Nuttin', dis lamb has everybody in an uproar. Nuttin'. Can Jesus turn watuh into wine? Nuttin' my—"

"Mama, Mama." Rosalina was tugging at Katarina's skirt. "Mama."

"Not now, Nina, de adults are talking."

"Uncle Billy, Uncle Billy," Rosalina said as she tugged at his elbow.

"Nina, don't budder Uncle Billy, can't yuh see he is unhappy?" Katarina said.

Rosalina went over and started pulling an empty chair to the table. Seeing his niece struggling, Billy got up to help her. He placed the empty chair between his and Rosalina's chair.

Katarina looked over at her daughter and Billy as she said, "What are yuh doin', Nina? Yuh has a chair here already?"

Placing her dog on the empty chair, Rosalina said, "Mama, Susie needs a chair."

Shaking his head and sitting back down, Billy said to everyone, "I don't even know what Lexi was talking about. A toy lamb and some crazy noshun about Susannah's soul being attached to it."

"Uncle Billy, Susie is with us."

"That is nice dah-lin." He patted her toy.

While making the sign of the cross, his uncle Vinny said, "How can anyone believe a person can be a ghost?"

"Susie's a ghost," Rosalina said to everyone.

"That's nice, dear," Maria said as she took the plate of turkey from Antonio, who had just finished carving and placed it on the table.

"Let's say grace." Maria took her seat at the table, as they all held hands and bowed their heads.

Billy reached for the little girl's hand. "Nina, give me your hand. Nonno is gonna say grace. Okay?"

"No, yuh have tuh hold de dog's paw. Okay?"

"Nina, stop bein' silly and hold your Uncle Billy's hand. Yuh with me?" Katarina said very sternly.

"No," Rosalina defiantly said.

"Little lady, he is not gonna hold a toy's paw. Now take his hand." All eyes were on Katarina and her daughter.

"Mama, Uncle Billy has tuh hold Susie's hand. She wants him to." Rosalina started to cry. "She still loves and misses him. Okay?"

"What are you talking about, Rosalina? Who still loves him?"

With big tears running down her tiny face, Rosalina responded, "Aunty Susie. She is right here." She pointed to her dog.

There was not a sound to be heard as everyone looked at Rosalina and then at the toy.

Shivers ran down her arms and legs as Maria asked her granddaughter, "Rosalina, where d'ja get your dog from?"

"By the couch." She pointed to the couch in the living room.

Making the sign of the cross, she said, "When?"

"The other day."

All eyes went from Maria to Billy.

Billy picked up the dog and looked at it. *I guess it could pass as a lamb.* Time stood still. The last few days of events went zooming through his mind. Lexi. The ring. Her calling and asking for the lamb. Olivia, calling and asking for the lamb. By the grace of God, he was holding the lamb. Tears started to form in his eyes as he hugged the lamb to his heart and said, "I love you, Susannah."

Antonio broke the silence. With a voice that sounded like thunder, he grumbled, "What in God's name is goin' on here?

"Mama, I gotta go. I need to find Lexi. Right now." Billy shoved a piece of turkey into his mouth, grabbed his coat, and took the toy with him before anyone could say another word.

Chapter 64

Jumping into his restored 1956 Ford F100, he buckled up the lamb in the passenger's seat. There was no way he was letting that lamb get hurt. He thought to himself, *What if I had tuh slam on de brakes or somethin' and de toy went flying? What would happen to Susannah's soul?*

Pulling away from the curb, he set out to find Lexi. *Lexi, where would yuh be right now?* An image of her sitting at a table popped into his head. *Right, it's Christmas Eve, you'll be with your mom.*

Looking over at Billy, Susannah smiled to herself. *Even though he doesn't believe I am really here and does not know how to communicate with me, at least he is open enough to get my messages.* She turned her head abruptly to see why the car pulled over to the side of the road.

He pulled out his cell phone to search. *Damn it. I don't know where Susannah's mom lives. Where did Susannah say they lived? Was it Manhattan? Constantine—Crap, dere are a lot of people with the last name Constantine.*

He put his head on the steering wheel to think. *You're gonna have to help me, Susannah. Where is Lexi?* Looking up to the stars, Billy said a prayer. *Lord, I know I am not your best follower, but I do need your help tonight. Please, God, help me find Lexi.*

A memory popped into his head of him and Susannah holding hands as they walked along the East River in DUMBO near her apartment. DUMBO, an acronym for Down Under the Manhattan Bridge Overpass.

It was some time ago, and she was telling him about the night she and her father had that awful fight. The night she had moved out of the house and hadn't stepped foot in it ever since, even for the holidays.

Brooklyn, dat's it. Susannah's mom lives in Brooklyn. Frantically, Billy looked up Constantine in Brooklyn. Scanning down the list, he found Marcus Constantine's name. Hard to forget the name when that was whom she referred to instead of calling him dad. He looked for an address, *Sydney Place, in Dyker Heights. Whoa, fancy part of town.*

Traffic was pretty good, considering it was Christmas Eve, and fewer people were driving on the road tonight. As Billy entered the neighborhood, he slowed down to see the house addresses. Since the driveway was full already, he pulled up along the curb to park. *Nice digs, Susannah.*

As he walked up to the front doors, he could see three people sitting at the dining room table: a man in his mid to late thirties and two ladies, one older lady with similar colored hair as Susannah's, and one that looked like it could be Lexi. She had the right color of hair. Trembling for the first time in his life, he knocked at the door.

Getting up to answer it, Olivia said, "Who could that be on Christmas Eve?" She opened the door to a good-looking young man.

"Mrs. Constantine?"

"Yes."

"I am Billy. Susannah's Billy."

"Billy, what are you doing here on Christmas Eve? Shouldn't you be at home with your family?"

Lexi got up to see who was at the door. Seeing it was Billy, she said, "Mom, invite him in."

"Yes, of course. Please come in."

"Wait. I have tuh get somethin' first." Billy ran back to his truck and unbuckled the lamb, tucking it under his coat to protect it from the weather.

"Hurry, Billy. It is cold out here," Olivia said as she hurried him into the house. "Come and sit down. We were just about to say grace." She went into the kitchen to get another dinner plate and silverware.

Lexi introduced Reverend Hawthorne to Billy. "Nice to meet you, Billy. Call me Edward. What brings you here?"

Placing the plate and silverware in front of Billy, Olivia interrupted them, saying, "That can wait. The food is getting cold." Going back to her seat, she said, "Everyone, hold hands. Reverend, please say grace."

Edward bowed his head and said grace. "In a world where so many are hungry, may we eat this food with humble hearts; In a world where so many are lonely, may we share this friendship with joyful hearts. Amen."

Billy, Olivia, and Lexi all said, "Amen," together.

Olivia passed the peas to Billy and said, "Let's eat. Lexi, be a dear and pass the plate of turkey to Edward."

After following her mother's orders, she poured everyone a glass of red wine. Holding up her wineglass, she said, "Cheers," and took a drink.

Still holding the lamb, Billy took it out of his coat and placed it lovingly on the empty chair beside him. "I think this is whatcha all were looking for."

Lexi, almost spitting her wine out, swallowed quickly as she screamed, "Oh, my God! Yes,

Lambie!" as she got up to hug the lamb. "Susannah!"

"I came over as soon as I figured out dat my five-year-old niece, Rosalina, had taken the toy. She had called it her new dog, Susie." He decided he didn't need to tell them the whole story.

Olivia put her hands on her heart and said, "It's a Christmas miracle."

Edward stood up and shook Billy's hand. "Thank you. You don't know how much this means to Alexandra."

"Who is Alexandra?"

"Oh, right." He pointed to Lexi. "She is. That is her full first name. The first time we met, she insisted I call her by her full name, and so I have ever since."

Joyfully, Olivia said, "A toast to our sweet angel, Susannah." Everyone clinked glasses.

Too excited to take a drink, Lexi quickly picked up her cell phone and texted Tamara. *I HAVE GREAT NEWS! WE FOUND SUSANNAH. I WILL BRING HER OVER TO YOU THE DAY AFTER BOXING DAY. MERRY CHRISTMAS! :)*

Chapter 65

As Lexi dropped off the toy lamb to Tamara, she said, "Hi, Tamara. I'm so happy that I could fulfill Susannah's last two requests. What a crazy few days I have had. I will have to tell you one day about the drama with her fiancé, Billy." Passing the toy lamb to Tamara, Lexi continued, "I have a deadline at work, so I hope you don't need me right now." Hugging Tamara, Lexi turned around and left.

Tamara said goodbye as she closed the door and went into her office. She set the toy lamb on a chair across from her. *Little lamb, it sounds to me that you have caused quite a stir in our world.*

Talking to a stuffed animal seemed silly, but believing that Susannah's soul was listening to every word she was saying made it feel more lifelike.

Tamara took a moment to set her intention and focus on the importance of today's goal, which was to give Susannah the best description she could of Heaven.

Closing her eyes and taking a breath, Tamara went into a meditative state to talk to Susannah.

"My usual role as a medium is for communication. I am connecting a human being with a ghost or spirit. My gift of "distinguishing spirits" can also be used to help a ghost move on and separate themselves from the earthly attachment keeping them from going into the light. Unfortunately, being a ghost is like being locked away in jail with minimal freedom, and you can't get out unless you have help or have completed your sentence. As crazy as this may sound, some of the souls I have helped have been attached to a specific place or object for centuries, and some of the souls have been attached to the same person for many lifetimes.

"To get to my point, here is an excellent reason, Susannah, why I am adamant that you go through the pearly gates and enter the level I call Heaven. Heaven is the real reality, and your experience on Earth is just a dream that your soul is having and believes to be real.

"In a moment, I am going to call down Archangel Michael to help me explain Heaven to you."

Tamara took a deep breath and shifted her vibration so that she could communicate with Archangel Michael.

"Archangel Michael, please come and explain Heaven to Susannah."

Tamara heard in her head Archangel Michael's reply, *"Dear one, it is not my job to explain Heaven. Let me get you someone who can."*

A new spirit introduced himself as Maximillian and started to speak.

"Hello, and welcome to the realm of Heaven, a magical place to most humans. A place like nothing on Earth. There are two reasons a soul comes down to Earth.

"First, it reminds them of being back at home in Heaven compared to anywhere else a soul has a choice of going, and second, it is the only place a soul can develop new abilities and evolve.

"The closest I can compare Heaven to is a tropical island. No, that won't explain it. Trying to explain Heaven to a human is like trying to explain Disneyland to an aboriginal who has never left his village and has no idea that a modern world even exists.

"Try explaining to him a place where he can go with themed rides, rollercoasters, and people dressed up in costumes. A place that he can go to play and have fun.

"Try to explain a place to someone who doesn't even know what electricity is, let alone a cartoon or movie character.

"Where do you start?

"The best description I can give is this. Heaven is a level of energy—if you could mix love and light energy, you would have Heaven.

"Heaven is just one locality in the realm that it exists in, as Earth is to the Universe. On Earth, a human soul lives in a home in a district of a village or city. The city is located in a province or state—one of many that make up a country. There are many different countries located on planet Earth.

"Each human, each house, each district, each city, each state, each country has a different vibe, and the joined consciousness creates a very distinctive vibration.

"You can tell the difference between a person from Europe and a person from the United States of America, even though most original families came from Europe and moved to the USA.

"You can tell the difference between someone who lives in New York City and someone who lives in Los Angeles, even though the people live in the same country. You can tell the difference between a person born and raised in Manhattan to a person born and raised in the Bronx.

"Heaven is just like that. There are fifteen different countries called levels, and each level has a different energy or vibration.

"On each level, the souls that reside there have a different perspective of reality and a different purpose. The laws of Heaven are much stricter than Earth's. When a soul passes through the portal of the pearly gates and lands in the first level of Heaven, a soul can only advance to the next levels if they have successfully completed their life lessons. Meaning, they only have access, let's call it a security pass, to travel or reside in their level of evolution. However, the soul can create any version of Heaven, but it must do that before it gets back to Heaven.

"That soul cannot ascend into any of the higher energy levels unless it has evolved.

"To gain access to the higher levels, a soul must come down to Earth and live a life where it can gain knowledge and the skills needed for the next level. The only luggage a soul can bring through the portal is its memories from Earth.

Tamara thanked Archangel Michael and Maximillian for the description of Heaven.

"Susannah, that was way better than what I was going to try to explain. I would have tried making a case about atoms making up molecules, which create a substance of matter such as a human body. Blah, blah, blah.

"Then probably something about science proving that when a human body dies, the

original matter can all be accounted for except for a minuscule amount of weight. The discrepancy is believed to be the soul that leaves the body.

"Good thing I didn't blabber on because I am sure I would have mucked it all up and caused you to be more confused.

"I do agree with the spirit who just told us his version of Heaven. Earth is the closest example of this love-light energy called Heaven that a soul can visit.

"To me, it is a place that is more spectacular than any Macy's Fourth of July fireworks display, a place that is better than any dream you have ever dreamed of.

"Heaven is a place where there is a community, a place you can belong to. A place of freedom and choice. But to me, Heaven is so much better than Earth because there is no judgment, poverty, crime, sickness, pain, or grief. Only bliss.

"What I want you to remember is that Earth is where a soul must come to gain the experiences needed for advancement and to access the higher levels of Heaven.

"Susannah, I know you missed the first attempt of getting into Heaven, and you can't have a 'Beam me up, Scotty' experience again. Unfortunately, that is a once-in-a-lifetime travel option. I need you to trust that I have another way for you to get back to the gates of Heaven.

"Before I do, I first want you to remember the best experience you've ever had on Earth. And while you are doing that, I am going to get your sister. I need her for this next part. So, enjoy your memories. I will be back soon."

Tamara called Lexi to set up a time that was convenient for her to come over and help her. As she dialed Lexi's number, all she could think about was how this next part was essential for the success of Susannah's journey home.

Susannah heard every word that Tamara had said and stayed invisible so the other spirits in the room would not notice her.

Chapter 66

Tamara opened the door to let Lexi in. "I am so glad you could come over so quickly. I have been meditating on how to get your sister's soul into Heaven, and I can't do it without your help.

"Silly me, I was hoping I could get out of this part," Lexi said as she got herself settled on the couch next to the lamb.

"Lexi, I need to ask your sister some questions, and since you seem to be the only person she talks to, I will need you to tell me her answers."

"Whatever you need to save Susannah's soul. I am here for you."

Tamara smiled in acknowledgment. "In a few moments, I am going to have you go into a meditative state again to talk to your sister. I'll tell you when I am ready. As you both know, part one of ascension into Heaven is believing.

Part two is determining if they are good enough to get into Heaven using the evaluation of a person's virtues versus sins. I am going to have Susannah take a pretest. That way, we will know ahead of time what her chances are for getting through the gates."

"Oh, this should be interesting. I would like to know that for myself."

Tamara made herself comfortable on the chair across from Lexi and the toy lamb. "Susannah, I need you to listen very carefully to me. This is all about the second part of getting through the pearly gates. In the last few days of researching on how to get you into Heaven, I found that over eighty percent of religions on Earth believe in an afterlife, and of those, almost all of them believe that you must be a good and virtuous person to pass through the gates of Heaven. The frequency of good versus the frequency of evil is the key to entering. I am going to try to explain virtues and sins with science first."

Lexi adjusted her posture on the couch to get a bit more comfortable, saying, "This sounds like it might take a few moments."

"The best example I can give you is by Dr. Masaru Emoto. In 2004, he published his results in a book titled 'The Hidden Messages in Water.' One of his most astonishing discoveries was experimenting with frozen water. He used a controlled experiment, using the same water, temperature, the time allotted, etcetera.

"Dr. Emoto would look under a microscope at the distinctive crystalized snowflake pattern that frozen water would form. Testing his theory, he stuck a piece of tape with a specific word written on it to the container before he froze the water. Once frozen, he would examine the results of the water crystal formation. His scientific breakthrough proved that words in any language have a positive or negative energy frequency, and the proof was in the water crystal formation when frozen. A good or positive word written down resulted in a beautiful snowflake pattern. A bad or negative word written down resulted in a deformed and many times discolored snowflake formation.

"Why does this matter? To me, he verified the significance of being virtuous or sinful, all depending on the words we choose to use."

Lexi again shifted in her seat, but this time she picked up the lamb and put it onto her lap. "Tamara, I don't understand."

"Lexi, I would like you to imagine an ocean. Do you agree that the external and internal energy controls the degree of turmoil?"

"Yes, I guess so."

"And that there are days at sea when the water is smooth as glass and other days where the waves are enormously dangerous and every degree in between?"

"Yes, that makes sense."

"Lexi, water is considered one of the most powerful conductors of energy. And since your body is seventy-five percent water, it is also a powerful conductor of energy. Meaning that, like an ocean, your body changes when the internal and external environment shifts around it, making you happier or sadder. And in a human's case, it is specifically your emotions that control the degree of turmoil. Good thoughts and feelings—smooth sailing. Evil thoughts and feelings—rough sailing. As your emotions shift, so does your pH level, and when your pH level shifts, it dramatically affects your health and well-being."

Lexi interrupted Tamara by saying, "What does this have to do with Susannah?"

"I am telling you this because negative or sinful energy has a unique vibration and cannot get through the pearly gates of Heaven. In contrast, positive or virtuous energy can easily pass through the gates. And in the metaphysical world of science, there is a belief that a unique high-frequency energy field is protecting and guarding the port of Heaven called the 'pearly gates.' These gates are a vibration of energy like a deflector shield, a barrier. A soul carrying the memory of too much negative energy CANNOT pass through the shield of the pearly gates."

Tamara shifted in her seat. "Lexi, for Susannah to get through the gates of Heaven, we have to ask the question, 'Does she believe that she was a good person? And if so, to what degree?' Lexi, the only person who can answer that is you."

"How are we going to find that out?" Lexi asked, afraid of the answer.

"A person's belief system determines if he or she was a good or bad person. If a person thinks they are virtuous, then they are. If they think they are evil, then they are. Lexi, this is where you come in. I need you to connect now with Susannah. You are going to take the 'Virtue and Sin Evaluation' pretest."

"How exciting." That was not the scary part she was expecting to hear. Leaning back on the couch, she shut her eyes and took a deep, relaxing breath. Nodding, she said, "Okay, I am ready. I have connected with Susannah."

"Perfect. Susannah, this test is based on your life on Earth. All you need is fifty-one percent to pass through the gates. Your soul carries with you the memories of your virtues and sins that you accumulated while on Earth. The importance of this pretest is for you to know if you will make it through the gates. I want you to remember that you have no brain when you die, so your energy has no way to lie when asked a direct question. Let's go over the meaning of each virtue and opposing sin. There are seven of each.

"First is the virtue of Charity or Generosity, which means kind, compassionate, and generous giving without expectation of anything in return.

"The opposite of Charity or Generosity is the deadly sin of Greed, which is described as insatiability, materialism, ravenousness, and voracity.

"Second is the virtue of Chastity. Which usually refers to refraining from any sexual conduct or romantic relationships, abstinence, and restraint.

"The opposite of Chastity is the deadly sin of Lust. Lust is described as an intensely powerful desire, craving, or yearning for a person, place, object, or circumstance.

"The third is the virtue of Kindness, which means having compassion, sympathy, thoughtfulness, or helpfulness toward someone in need.

"The opposite of Kindness is the deadly sin of Envy. Envy is described as wanting what another has with malice intent, resentment, ill will, or rivalry.

"Next is the virtue of Patience. The state of endurance, tolerance, and persistence that one can endure before negativity.

"The opposite of Patience is the deadly sin of Wrath or Anger. Wrath, rage, fury, madness is an emotional response to a perceived provocation, hurt, or threat.

"The fifth is the virtue of Temperance, which is typically described as self-restraint, self-control, abstinence, or sobriety.

"The opposite of Temperance is the deadly sin of Gluttony, which means excess, piggishness, or over-indulgence in food, drink, or wealthy items without having any control.

"Next is the virtue of Humility. It is defined as being humble, obedient, modest, or unpretentious.

"The opposite of Humility is the deadly sin of Pride, which refers to gratification, arrogance, conceit, egotism, superiority, or any absurdly corrupt sense of one's vanity, value, status, or accomplishments.

"Last is the virtue of Diligence. Diligent behavior is indicative of a hardworking, industrious, and conscientious work ethic.

"The opposite of Diligence is the deadly sin of Sloth. Sloth is defined as being lethargic, lazy, and reluctant to exertion."

Tamara shifted her focus back to Lexi, saying, "Lexi, now that I have gone over the seven Virtues and Sins, tell me when Susannah is ready to take the test."

"She's ready."

"Susannah, I want you to focus on the virtue of Charity and compare it to Greed. Scanning back on your life from birth to today, what number from zero to one hundred do you think your virtue of charity is?"

"Seventy," Lexi answered for Susannah.

Tamara wrote down the number Lexi had said on a piece of paper she had on a clipboard.

"I want you to focus on the virtue of Chastity and compare it to Lust. Scanning back on your life from birth to today, what number from zero to one hundred do you think your virtue of chastity is?"

"Sixty-five."

"I want you to focus on the virtue of Kindness and compare it to Envy. Scanning back on your life from birth to today, what number from zero to one hundred do you think your virtue of kindness is?"

"Seventy-five."

"I want you to focus on the virtue of Patience and compare it to Wrath. Scanning back on your life from birth to today, what number from zero to one hundred do you think your virtue of patience is?"

"Seventy."

"I want you to focus on the virtue of Temperance and compare it to Gluttony. Scanning back on your life from birth to today, what number from zero to one hundred do you think your virtue of temperance is?"

"Eighty."

"I want you to focus on the virtue of Humility and compare it to Pride. Scanning back on your life from birth to today, what number from zero to one hundred do you think your virtue of humility is?"

There was a long pause from Lexi.

Susannah remembered the fight she and her dad had the night she moved out of the house. Her feelings were hurt, and her pride cost her from ever stepping foot into her childhood home again, spending quality time with her family during any special event, the comfort of being home, the relationship she could have had with her dad, and closure of not saying goodbye before he passed.

"Forty."

"I want you to focus on the virtue of Diligence and compare it to Sloth. Scanning back on your life from birth to today, what number from zero to one hundred do you think your virtue of diligence is?"

"Seventy."

"Great. Let me tally these up and tell you what mark you have." Tamara added the numbers of the total virtues that Lexi said were Susannah's answers.

"Excellent, you passed with sixty-seven percent. Good enough to get through the gates of Heaven." Tamara showed Lexi the paper she was writing on. It was the test she had for her clients to take.

Virtue & Sin Evaluation Test

Name: _Susannah_

Focusing on Virtues: on a scale of 0% to 100%, write down the number that first comes to your mind with reference to the opposing Sin.

0% Bad ————————————— 100% Good

Sin	Virtue	
Greed	Generosity/Charity	70
Lust	Chastity	65
Envy	Kindness	75
Wrath/Anger	Patience	70
Gluttony	Temperance	80
Pride	Humility	40
Sloth	Diligence	70
	Add All Virtues = Total	470

(Pass is 50% or better—add the total of all seven virtues and divide by 7) Mark _67.14_ %

Lexi looked at the paper and asked Tamara, "What if a person gets to the gates, and they believe, but they take the test and fail it? What happens to the soul then?"

"Great question. If a soul believes and takes the test, but he or she fails, that soul will be able to redeem themselves by being reincarnated to live another life on Earth.

"The new life is chosen by a random spin of the wheel, who, what, where, when, why, and how. That soul does not get to choose the life experience needed this time around. Instead, the higher power, or God, decides for them. Then, at the end of that new lifetime, the soul gets to try again and retake the test.

"If they fail again, back down they come. They keep learning new lessons on how to gain more virtue each lifetime, eventually gaining entrance to Heaven."

"Interesting. May I take the test?" Lexi asked, wondering how she would do on it.

"Sure. Take one home and do it for yourself." Tamara handed a pretest to Lexi. "Lexi, we are ready to take Susannah home. Are you ready?"

Chapter 67

"*I* want to say thank you to the spirit world for providing me with this opportunity to find another way for your soul to travel back to the pearly gates. Susannah, you have already passed the pretest, so we don't have to worry about that part. And because of your recent experience in the Void, Lexi and I know that you believe in Heaven. I am confident with the help of Spirit, along with today's meditation, your sister and I will be able to help you get back to the gates of Heaven. I know you will pass through the gates this time.

"Okay, Lexi, do you need anything before we start?"

"Yes. I need to go to the restroom first," Lexi said.

Tamara showed her to the washroom and then went back to the living room.

With a bit of sorrow in her voice, Lexi said as she came back into the room, "I know it is for Susannah's highest good that her soul goes to Heaven, and it would be selfish of me to hold her back." Getting settled again on the couch, she said, "I am good now, thanks. I am ready to let her go now."

"Great. Let's begin." Tamara pulled out a sheet of paper with a drawing on it.

It was titled "Destination Map." She was showing it to Lexi so that she could get an idea before the meditation of where they were going to travel.

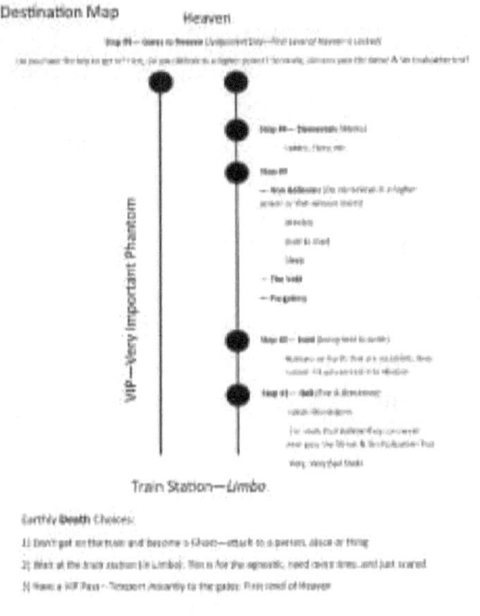

Looking at the paper, Lexi instantly saw the 3rd destination, titled the Void. She knew that stop well. *Definitely not visiting that location again.* The route to the gates looked simple enough to her.

"Lexi, you've done this before. Get yourself comfortable and take a few deep breaths. This time though, your role is to help me get Susannah to the train station and make sure she gets on. Imagine the same one you were at before, Penn Station. Lexi, I want you to take a couple of deep breaths and relax. I will talk to you again in a few moments."

Tamara continued, "Susannah, when it is time, your job will be to get on the train. Don't worry, I will be right beside you the whole way, right up until you get off at the Pearly Gates Train Station.

"All right, now that everything has been explained and everyone is ready, let's explore this journey of a soul as far as it will lead us. Lexi, I would like you to imagine the train station now. Imagine that Susannah and I are with you. Susannah has luggage that she will be bringing with her. It contains all her memories that she has decided to keep from this last lifetime's journey.

"Imagine that I am going over to the ticket kiosk to purchase mine and Susannah's train tickets.

"At the kiosk, I have several choices for the journey. The first stop's destination is Hell. The description reads, 'For Satan worshipers, and for the sinful souls that believe that they deserve to be punished.'

"The second stop is Held. The description reads, 'For souls that are held and bound to Earth by a human who is so selfish that they cannot let the soul ascend into Heaven.'

"The third stop's destination is Non-Believers. The description reads, 'For atheists, souls that do not believe in a higher power or that Heaven exists. For souls that believe they're just dust-to-dust or will go to sleep.' This third destination is also for souls going to the Void and Purgatory. I want to mention that there is a special note that reads, 'With help from a human medium or minister, a soul may have a chance for atonement.'

"The next destination is Elementals. That description reads, 'For mythical souls, such as fairies, elves, mermaids, etcetera.'

"The fifth destination is the Pearly Gates. The description reads, 'Express train for souls ready to take the Virtue and Sin Evaluation Test.'

"The sixth stop and final destination is Heaven. The description reads, 'For VIP— Very Important Phantom ticket holders. Instant access through the Pearly Gates, no test required. While on Earth, the VIP soul or apparition must meet both entrance requirements. One, believe in a higher power of energy and two, lived a virtuous life.'

"Okay, here we go. I'll tell the ticket conductor that I will have one ticket for the Pearly Gates and one round trip ticket. I give the Pearly Gates ticket to Susannah and keep the other ticket for myself.

"Lexi, this is where you can hug your sister and wish her farewell for now. Tell her that once she is in Heaven, you both will have the ability to contact each other as often as you would have on Earth. If you talked daily, then you can still speak daily to her in the afterlife. If it was weekly, then that is the same agreement. Once a year, then that is the agreement of contacting each other. Whatever the amount of communication you had with her on Earth, you will have when she is in Heaven."

Tamara made herself a little more comfortable in her chair. "Susannah, have your ticket ready. As I promised, I have the special pass that lets me travel with you on the train, but I can't get off the train. I will be coming back to this same train station here in *Limbo,* where I will meet back up with Lexi. Then I will come back to my own body and continue on my own soul's journey."

Tamara took a breath. "Now, the two of us get on the train and find our seats. As I have told your sister Lexi before, on the train, you can sit in either direction, facing me or beside me. You choose.

"The train conductor comes and checks our tickets, punching a special hole in a corner, marking that we have used it.

"We can hear the engine starting and the ringing of the bell. With the conductor yelling the last call, 'All aboard.' The doors close, and the train slowly starts to move out of the station.

"We will be stopping briefly at all the destinations since we do not have a VIP pass," was the last thing Tamara said.

The phantom train picked up speed, lifted off the tracks, and started to fly through the sky, rocketing into outer space. Everyone inside had a choice to watch a movie, read, chat, or look out their window. The scenery at first resembled Earth's atmosphere. Next, you could see the moon, and then from the moon, you could look back and see Earth. The train's speed increased again, and all you could see now was a blur of stars as the train moved through the Milky Way.

There was a shift in energy, and the lights on the train blinked on and off a couple of times. It felt like being scanned at an airport. Every molecule of your being went through a scan. Some of the passengers triggered an alarm. The conductor came over to their seat and turned off the overhead light that was blinking and put a special bracelet on their wrist.

Over the intercom, you could hear a voice yell, "Next stop, Hell."

The bracelets all lit up and glowed bright blood red. As the train pulled into the station, it slowed down and stopped. As the train doors opened, there was no sound. Then the creepiest of mists entered the train, swishing to-and-fro through the passengers, whispering demonic incantations. And then, the most unnerving sound pierced the passengers' ears. The sound of misery, suffering, and agony from the souls being tortured in Hell for their sins could be heard as Satan himself entered the train. He was in the form that most humans imagine him as, the entity of a hideous half-man, half-goat with horns that grew from his head and a tail split at the tip.

As he walked through the train, he stopped at Susannah, and his eyes glowed a fiery red. He went to touch her bracelet, but none was to be found. He threw his head back and roared. The train shook from the sound of thunder that escaped his lips.

Susannah's soul quivered and held on to Tamara for dear life.

Tamara started to pray, and light emanated from her soul.

Satan, within seconds, moved on through the train, and when he touched the last soul wearing a red bracelet, his tail shimmered and became a tongue. The rest of his body transformed into a snake and slithered away.

The doors of the train closed, and a shower of orange light shone on all the remaining passengers, cleansing the energy of Hell off their souls. The train started to move.

The train barely picked up speed before there was a shift in energy again, and the lights on the train blinked on and off a couple more times. Again, it felt like being scanned at an airport. With the trigger of the alarm, the conductor came over to these souls' seats and turned off the overhead light that was blinking and put a special bracelet on their wrist.

These bracelets also lit up, but this time they glowed orange. The voice over the intercom said, "Next stop, Held."

As the train pulled into the station, it slowed down and stopped. As the doors opened, the passengers with orange bracelets started to weep, cry, and beg not to be taken off the train. Archangel Azrael entered the train with his amazing but stern energy. As he passed through, he held each section of the train captive. Only the orange bracelet souls were taken against their wishes. Azrael, the Angel of Death, had no choice but to follow the celestial laws. Any passenger being tethered by an Aka cord from a loved one on Earth had no choice but to stay on this level of energy until the human released their soul and allowed it to ascend higher.

The doors of the train closed, and a shower of yellow light shone on all the remaining passengers, cleansing the energy of Held off their souls. The train started to move.

The train's speed increased again, and all you could see was pitch black out the windows.

A few moments later, the lights on the train blinked on and off a couple of times as the energy shifted again. The alarm triggered again. The conductor came over to these seats, turned off the overhead light that was blinking, and put yellow bracelets on the passengers' wrists.

This time the voice over the intercom said, "Next stop, Non-Believers."

The doors opened. Nothing happened. The doors of the train closed, and a shower of pink light shone on all the remaining passengers, cleansing the energy of Non-Believers off their souls. The train started to move, but if anybody looked around wondering what just happened, they would have noticed missing souls.

The train's speed increased again, and the windows disappeared. Moments later, the lights on the train blinked on and off a couple of times. The alarm could be heard as the conductor came over to the appropriate seats, turned off the overhead light, and put green bracelets on their wrists.

The voice over the intercom said something incomprehensible, but the sign above the door read, "Next stop, Elementals."

The doors opened. Merrily, the fairies, pixies, elves, gnomes, leprechauns, dwarves, sprites, nymphs, goblins, brownies, mermaids, and dryads got off. You could feel the train sway as the trolls, ogres, and giants got off.

The doors of the train closed, and a shower of violet light shone on all the remaining passengers, cleansing the energy of Elementals off their souls. The train started to move.

The train warped with light-speed through the celestial realm, and within seconds, the lights on the train blinked on and off a couple of times. The alarm triggered again. The conductor came over to Susannah's seat and turned off the overhead light that was blinking and put a violet bracelet on her wrist, then carried on to the other passengers.

The words "Pearly Gates" were sung as if by angels. Then the voice said, "After this stop, we will be heading back to Limbo."

Tamara piped up, "Susannah, this is where you will be getting off. Let me quickly recap for you. The key to unlocking the gates is that you must believe in a higher power, which you do. Then, you must pass the Virtue & Sin Evaluation Test to gain entrance, which you will.

"Once through the gates, a brochure of all your choices will magically appear in your hands. Any questions?"

Susannah didn't answer, so Tamara took that as a no.

"Susannah, thank you so very much for the gift of knowledge that your journey has granted me. Here is a big hug. Enjoy the rest of your afterlife." At that exact moment, Tamara felt it. The instantaneous sensation of poof, gone. Susannah's soul had ascended into the light.

Tamara knew Susannah had passed the Virtue & Sin Evaluation Test because if she hadn't, she would have been back on the train.

The doors of the train closed, and a shower of silver light shone on all the remaining passengers, cleansing the energy of the Pearly Gates off their souls. The train started to move.

Taking a breath, Tamara imagined coming back to Limbo and getting off the train. Opening her eyes, Tamara walked over to Lexi and, taking her hand, said, "Lexi, please wiggle your toes and come back perfectly into your body. Sense your spirit bringing back with you a sparkle of that love-light energy. As your senses return, notice that you feel even better than before you started this meditation."

Tamara said a closing prayer, "I would like to thank all the angels and guides for helping with this incredible journey, Lexi for being so courageous and trusting her intuition, and a special thank you to Susannah, bless her angelic soul for gifting me this opportunity for my soul to grow and evolve. Amen."

Chapter 68

Susannah knew this time that she had the keys to unlocking the gates. She believed, and she knew she passed the Virtue & Sin Evaluation Test because she crossed right through the Pearly Gates portal, granting her the freedom of Heaven.

Magnificent, just magnificent. I heard Heaven was beautiful, but this is exceptional. No words can describe the beauty.

I can hear my favorite music being played in the background. I can feel the heat of a warm summer breeze soothing my skin. The temperature is absolutely perfect.

The most incredible scent is lingering in the heavenly air, it reminds me of a fresh spring day, and the taste on my tongue reminds me of the most decadent chocolate with a hint of rose petals. Oh, and the colors in front of me are more vibrant than anything I have ever seen on Earth.

After lingering a little longer in the essence of energy she felt at the Pearly Gates, Susannah started to walk forward into her oasis. As she crossed over, the next step she took was her favorite place on Earth. She was lying on a beach with a tropical breeze flowing over her body, listening to the waves as they softly crashed onto the shore. She could smell the salted sea air and hear the seagulls flying above.

As she bathed in the glorious sunlight, a brochure magically appeared in her hands. *Tamara said I would get one when I enter through the gates, and here it is.*

Lying there in the sand, she opened the pamphlet and read the first sentence. "There are over forty-three hundred known religious beliefs." *Ya, I'm not ready to move on.* She put the pamphlet aside.

She lay there for what seemed an eternity. Nothing changed. It all stayed just as the first moment she set foot on the beach.

Deciding that she was now bored of a tropical paradise, she got up and started to walk along the shore. As she walked, her dad, Marcus, appeared.

"Hey, kiddo, how you doing?"

"Hi, Dad!" She gave him the longest hug. *"Thank you for getting me out of the Void."*

"If I could have done it on my own, I would have, Susannah. You have always been in my heart."

"What should I do now, Dad?"

"Anything that you want to," Marcus replied.

"I would love to see Grand-mère."

Marcus took Susannah's hand and led her down a path that magically appeared. As they came through an opening, all of Susannah's family that had passed on over the years was there to greet her. Both sides of her family from Earth: grandparents, great aunts, and uncles. The reunion was fabulous. She talked for hours with each and every one of them.

When she was finished, Marcus took her down another path, and in this clearing was her soul tribe. Souls that were part of her history from this lifetime and past lifetimes. Thousands of souls came to greet her. It was like in the movies; souls were dressed up in their character from all different eras of her past. She visited for eons, catching up with everyone.

Eventually, she got bored. *I wonder what else I can do in Heaven.*

The brochure magically appeared in her hands. This time she read it. She could see that there was an alphabetical list of all forty-three hundred known religious beliefs.

The pamphlet read, "You have two choices. Mark the box beside the one you believe in or tick this READ MORE box if you would like to find out more about each option you have."

At the perfect moment, a pen magically appeared in her hand. Susannah check-marked the "READ MORE" box.

She was instantly teleported into a classroom. It resembled an amphitheater-style layout. It was located just inside the gates within the gardens. The stage below was a beautiful serene pool of crystal-clear water, with an exquisite waterfall cascading down into it. There was an array of the most luscious tropical plants she had ever dreamed of as the backdrop.

An iPad magically appeared in her lap, with instructions printed on the screen.

"First, scan the list and choose twenty of the forty-three hundred beliefs of the afterlife that you would like to know more about.

"At any time, you can click the 'Go-To Now' button, and you will instantly teleport to that location.

"To start, click on the first of your twenty choices. By clicking on the individual religious belief, you can READ MORE."

Susannah's first twenty choices came up on the screen. Each showed the average of how many people living on Earth will choose that destination to go to when they die. It also had a quick reference to each religion.

Christianity (2.1 billion) - Virtue & Sin Test, all believe in an afterlife, and some believe in reincarnation.

Islam (1.3 billion) - Virtue & Sin Test, believe sleep or reincarnate, all believe in an afterlife.

Nonreligious (Secular/Agnostic/Atheist) (1.1 billion) - Virtue & Sin Test for memories only and have no belief in an afterlife.

Hinduism (900 million) / KARMA - Virtue & Sin Test, all believe in reincarnation, and all believe in an afterlife.

Chinese traditional religion (394 million) - Virtue & Sin Test, all believe in an afterlife of immortality.

Buddhism (376 million) - Virtue & Sin Test, all believe in reincarnation, all believe in an afterlife and Nirvana.

Primal-indigenous (300 million) - Virtue & Sin Test, all believe in an afterlife and a Great Spirit.

African traditional and Diasporic (100 million) – believe in a Supreme Creator.

Sikhism (23 million) - Virtue & Sin Test, all believe in reincarnation, but believe there is no afterlife.

Juche – North Korean (19 million) – believe man is the master of his destiny.

Spiritism (15 million) - Virtue & Sin Test, all believe in an afterlife and that the soul can evolve.

Judaism (14 million) - Virtue & Sin Test, all believe in reincarnation, and all believe in an afterlife.

Bahai (7 million) - Virtue & Sin Test, all believe in an afterlife.

Jainism (4.2 million) - Virtue & Sin Test, all believe in an afterlife and enlightenment.

Shinto (4 million) - Virtue & Sin Test

Cao Dai (4 million) - Virtue & Sin Test, all believe in reincarnation, all believe in an afterlife and Nirvana.

Zoroastrianism (2.6 million) - Virtue & Sin BRIDGE Test; fall off, you go to purgatory for a re-test. Cross, and you get an afterlife.

Tenrikyo (2 million) - Virtue & Sin Test

Neo-Paganism (1 million) AKA Wiccan - believe in an afterlife – also called Eternal Summer.

Unitarian-Universalism (800,000) – Science & Spiritual based, all blessings, and open to the idea Heaven might exist.

After reading each religion in more detail, Susannah figured her choices were:

To be reincarnated and live another life experience on Earth.

To live in bliss and stay in Heaven for eternity.

To live in bliss for as long as she wished to, and when her soul was ready, be reincarnated to live another life experience on Earth.

To live in bliss, and when her soul had accumulated enough life experiences, evolve to on one of the seven levels of Heaven, or choose one of the remaining eight levels in this realm, such as becoming an angel and helping humanity—knowing that at any time, she had a choice of reincarnation and living the life she needed to experience on Earth.

To ascend to Nirvana – The only requirement is that she must have passed the enlightenment evaluation examination.

Susannah didn't need to read about any other religion. She had made her decision.

I believe my choice is going to be. . .

Chapter 69

Lexi came out of the meditation, wondering what was happening to her sister in Heaven. Still groggy from being put into a semi-sleep state, she could hear Tamara talking to her as she was coming back to the moment.

"Lexi, please wiggle your toes and come back perfectly into your body. Sense your spirit bringing back with you a sparkle of that love-light energy. As your senses return, notice that you feel even better than before you started this meditation."

Tamara was used to bringing herself out of meditation and loved the exhilarating and refreshing feeling of coming out of a trance state. "How are you feeling? Any questions?" Tamara asked as Lexi was opening her eyes.

"Tamara, that was amazing! I could sense you guys getting onto the train at the station. So, what happened once you were on the train? She made it through the gates, right?"

"Lexi, I have to tell you that it is the most incredible feeling to be in the presence of a spiritual encounter. My whole body tingles with glee as a soul ascends into the light. It's just magical!" Tamara said as she was still soaking in the remnants of that radiant energy.

"Yes, your sister made it to the level of love-light energy that you and I call Heaven."

"That's a blessing. Tamara, what do you think Susannah is doing in Heaven?"

"Well, I guess she gets to choose her next path. To stay there in bliss or be reincarnated and come back down to Earth to live another lifetime so she can evolve her soul and reach Nirvana."

"I'm not sure if I believe in reincarnation, Tamara. Why would I want to leave Heaven?"

Tamara gave a little giggle. "Lexi, you left Heaven at least once. You've incarnated and are talking with me right now. To be honest, it's not my belief that matters. It's only the faith of the person dying that matters. For whatever they believe will happen, it will happen."

Lexi thought about what Tamara had just said. *I guess she is right that it only matters what that person believes, and it does say in the Bible that everyone has the right to free will.* "I hope Susannah is happy."

"She is in Heaven. Of course, she's happy."

"Hey, Tamara, what is Nirvana again?"

"Think about Nirvana as a final resting place for the people living in Heaven. Just as on Earth, we are reaching for Heaven. The souls living in Heaven are reaching for Nirvana. Hence, the reason to come back down to Earth and live another lifetime. To evolve our soul so we can pass the Nirvana enlightenment evaluation test."

"Wow, I guess there is more I need to learn. When do you start your lectures again?"

"Soon, but they are not what you are expecting."

Chapter 70

*L*ucifer held another meeting with all the demons and dark energies in Hell. There was a rumble as the sound of his voice thundered over the crowd, *"There is going to be hell to pay, Satan!"*

"Father, she did not have the bracelet on. And she had an Earth angel traveling with her. There was nothing I could do," Satan boomed back from his section.

"We need to prepare for the war that is coming. The war between Heaven, Earth, and Hell."

"Why Earth?" Satan yelled back.

Lucifer looked at his son. Lilith put a hand on his shoulder to tame his temper. He looked away from Satan. *"Humans are becoming overconfident. They think they are privileged and deserve everything and anything. Most of them don't even remember how to pray and give thanks. Many say that they are 'Christians' because they believe and they even pray, BUT they are hypocrites. They commit sinful acts every day! My Heavenly Father is getting to the point where he will do to them as he did to me. Toss them out of his home. He created the Earth in seven days, yet they do not understand that he can demolish it in seconds.*"

"*How do you know this?*" Satan challenged his father.

Again, Lilith put a hand on his shoulder to tame his temper. "*He warns them with disasters, wars, famine, but they do not listen.*"

"*What do you care if my grandfather punishes all the human souls? You should be happy. Then we will have all their light,*" Satan replied.

"*Satan, do you actually think that if God could kick me out of Heaven, his favorite son, that he is going to let any of you have them? And, even if he did, how are we going to feed? There will be no humans left.*"

Mammon snickered and said, "*I guess that is why Lucifer is Ruler of Hell.*"

Satan slapped his son on the back of the head for being a smart ass.

"*What is your plan then?*" Satan asked.

"*We are going to have to go to war with Heaven.*"

You could hear the snarls, growls, and rumble of the other archdemons, kings, and dark entities throughout the cave they had met in. Fights broke out. The darkness was furious with the prospect of having to fight Heaven.

"*STOP!!!*" Lucifer boomed.

The other Archdemons sent their troops away and stood council with Lucifer.

Asmodeus spoke first, "*Lucifer, there must be another way. I desire the sweet souls of Earth just as much as the next demon, but going to war with Heaven?*"

Beelzebub interrupted by patting his big belly and saying, "*I can't survive long without the human soul's excessiveness of wanting more. The last few decades have been my best feast ever. These souls can't get enough. If they start to use temperance, I will starve.*"

Archdemon Belphegor lazily said, "*Lucifer, darling, I do not have the energy for a war with Heaven.*"

"*I command that you are all ready when the time is upon us,*" Lucifer demanded. The fires in Hell intensified with his power. Flames shot up everywhere.

Leviathan sarcastically put his two bits in, "*Lucifer, I am jealous of how calm you can stay. By this time, I would be fuming at the mouth.*"

Even though Mammon was the most avaricious of them all, he knew that the time was not now to let his greedy side show. He would wait until his perfect moment came and scoop all the succulent sinful morsels on Earth.

"*Fine, let's say that we are ready. What is your plan?*" Satan questioned.

All the archdemons slithered in so they could hear better.

"My plan is to tempt the humans one hundred times more than we are now. Get the humans to anger my Father so much that he blows a gasket. The humans on Earth have no idea how harsh a punishment he grants. Even though they know my story, all they see is his glory. As I have said before, they forget or are blind to the fact that he cast me out of Heaven. They are in for a surprise! He has a temper."

"That is your plan, to provoke God?" Satan said. He was the only Archdemon that wasn't afraid of Lucifer.

"No. It is to save the Humans from God."

"What? I don't understand," Mammon said to his grandfather.

"Mammon, I know you are still a young demon, but God doesn't need humans. They are how he watches TV. If he incinerates Earth, most souls just go back to Heaven. It is only our demons who will have a problem. Again, without humans, we cannot feed. We are the ones that will suffer. The time will come when we must protect the Earth."

Chapter 71

Susannah made her decision. She decided that she wanted to become Lexi's Guardian Angel. She wanted to protect her from the dark energies that were lurking around and never go through what she did with the mob again. Susannah felt responsible for what happened to Lexi and wanted to repay her by protecting her.

Deciding this was what she wanted to do as a spirit, she went to find out what all this involved. Susannah was not used to her spirit form and was surprised that she could still use many of the human abilities that she had while on Earth, like typing. She imagined that she was typing into her iPad. . . "Becoming a Guardian Angel."

The first thing she read was,

"Guardian Angels can give comfort, offer guidance, and bring people and opportunities into the human's life.

"If you choose to become a Guardian Angel, you are committing one hundred percent of your time to the human soul that you decide to guard. There is no going back. You cannot change your mind. Once you click 'yes,' you will be committed to this contract. Your contract will become void at the time of the human's death.

"As every human is born with a Guardian Angel, you will be assisting the original Guardian Angel. If your human asks for you by name, you will be in control of aiding in whatever it is that they are asking for help with.

"If you were related by blood to the human in the lifetime they are still living, then you will be asked to assist in most situations."

Susannah was excited to read the last paragraph. This was what she wanted the most, to be connected with Lexi. She clicked the "yes" button.

She was instantly teleported to another classroom. Sitting in her seat, she could see that it was a smaller room that could fit about one hundred spirits. To her immediate left and right were other spirits. The room was packed.

The instructor was a Teacher Spirit. At first, it was hard to look at him; the illuminating light from his wings was blinding. Susannah winced.

In his thick accent, the spirit to her right said, *"If you take a breath with the intent that you can see him, your eyesight will shift."*

"Thanks."

Taking a breath, Susannah's eyes adjusted. *Interesting. So, taking a deep breath works here too. I noticed Lexi practicing the technique of breathing.*

The instructor stopped what he was saying and looked directly at Susannah. *"Do you have something to share?"*

Susannah looked around, not understanding. *Is he referring to me?*

The spirit beside her said, *"Yes. He is talking to you."*

"What, can you guys hear my thoughts?"

The instructor said, *"Yes. Now, will you please be quiet while I am talking!"*

"Yes," Susannah said. *This will take a bit of getting used to it.*

The spirit beside her whispered, *"You'll get used to it."*

The instructor continued. *"When your human, also known as your charge, asks you to intervene and help them with something specific, it gives you more leeway to assist them. It is your job to almost always honor their free-will choices—unless you know their free-will choice will be very detrimental to them or others or be a major detour away from their highest good.*

"The human must ask you exactly what they want assistance with: romance, finances, health, career. Then you can send them your messages!"

Susannah was taking notes.

"But this is where it gets interesting. You are going to have to be creative. Most humans can't tell that we are around, and most have no idea how to ask for help.

"That will end today's lecture. I will continue tomorrow."

"What? No!" Susannah had so many questions.

The spirit beside her said, *"You can always look up an answer on your iPad."*

"Oh. Thanks. I am Susannah, by the way."

"I am Raadhak. Nice to meet you," he said.

"Where were you from on Earth?" Susannah was curious to know.

"India. Mawlynnong, Meghalaya. It is a remote and small village located in the East Khasi Hills district of Meghalaya, Asia. My village is referred to as 'God's own garden.'"

Susannah was fascinated that an East Indian would become a Guardian Angel.

"Anyone can become a Guardian Angel," he replied to her thought.

"Oh. I am not good at this not thinking thing. Can everyone hear my thoughts?"

"Yes. But each spirit can tune them out when they are not in direct contact with you or your intent is not on that spirit."

"Oh. Good to know. How long have you been here, Raadhak?"

"Not long. In Earth years, about one thousand years."

"Really? Wow!"

"Time goes by fast up here, Susannah."

"Oh. Another good thing to know."

"I have to go now, Susannah, but I will save you a seat for tomorrow's lecture."

"Okay. Thanks. Nice to have met you."

"You too," he said as he disappeared.

Susannah looked around, and all the other students had left. She was the only one in the classroom. *Now, what do I do?*

Chapter 72

Since spirits don't sleep, Susannah decided to take a walk through the gardens. The gardens reminded her of a trip her family took when she was a teenager. They had flown all the way across the country to this small place called Vancouver Island. The garden was located off the Pacific coast in the city of Victoria, British Columbia, Canada.

One of her favorite memories was when they visited the Butchart Gardens. As she recalled the memory, the garden transformed into her thoughts. Mesmerized by the miracles that one could experience in Heaven, she marveled at the wonder of "thought into action," as she touched a rock that metamorphosed into a beautiful pink flower right in front of her eyes.

Deciding to take the stone path directly in front of her, she walked among the lush plants that grew there. Along both sides of the path was a one-foot stone wall with pink and white hyacinths cascading over the edge. Behind grew six feet tall rhododendrons which had the most vivid hues of pink.

Susannah stopped to admire a hummingbird as it fed off the nectar of one of the flowers. Continuing along her way, the day shifted to night, and the elegant lamp posts that were about three feet high lit the path, illuminating the flowers, so they shimmered their light. It was breathtaking.

One path led into another, and the scenery changed. This time, she walked into a daylit Japanese garden. There were water features everywhere, with red bridges and bright-colored koi swimming in the ponds. Set randomly throughout the garden were stone statues of little buildings with slanted roofs, rocks cast strategically amongst sand that was raked in marvelous patterns. Completing the magical effect were magnificent cherry and plum blossoms.

Walking further down the path, it changed again, and the most incredible aroma of cedar tickled your nose. This path led down a forest of trees with trunks so big it would have taken five people holding hands around it to touch each other. Ferns grew among the trees, creating the illusion of a soft green carpet.

The next path was pretty, but it was intended to entice the sense of smell and sound. You could hear the wind chimes musically dancing in the breeze and the tall ornamental grasses that were rustling in the wind. Waterfalls were cascading down the rocks and spilling into a pond below. Growing between the rocks were herbs such as rosemary and thyme, producing a wonderful fragrance. Scented geraniums, roses, violets, and jasmines were not only pretty to look at, but the fragrance was incredible.

Susannah walked into her favorite part of the garden. It was adorned with hedges that were trimmed into patterns throughout the area. It resembled a labyrinth if you looked from above, but the borders were only a foot and a half high. In some areas, there was a blanket of grass with low-lying shrubs and ground cover planted to create magnificent patterns. It made you want to take your shoes off and walk on the grass.

Finishing her walk in the garden, she enjoyed the birds' songs that were so tranquil.

Marcus appeared and took hold of her hand as she finished her walk.

"Hi, Dad, what brings you here?" Susannah squeezed her dad's hand lovingly.

"Just checking up on you. How are you doing?"

"Isn't it lovely?" she said as she looked behind her in the garden.

"It was a great trip we had that year."

"Do you ever miss those days?"

"No. Once you are up here, the human emotions of Earth disappear. They are replaced with bliss."

"I decided to become Lexi's Guardian Angel."

"That is wonderful. I am so happy that you made your decision. That is the toughest part of dying, deciding what to do next. Once a soul makes their decision, then the rest is heavenly."

"That's funny, heavenly. Nice pun."

Marcus smiled and gave his daughter a hug. *"I love you, Susannah, and I am sure we will meet again."*

"What do you mean? Are you leaving?"

"No. Susannah, once you are finished your training, you will be the one leaving."

"Oh. I never thought about that part."

"Susannah, you will make an excellent Guardian Angel. I am so proud of you." Then he kissed his daughter's forehead and vanished as quickly and quietly as he had come.

Chapter 73

*R*unning into the classroom, afraid that she was late, Susannah looked around for Raadhak. He was standing up and waving at her, pointing to the seat to his right.

Making her way up the stairs to her row in the classroom, she shuffled past the other spirits to the empty seat beside him.

"You know you can teleport, right?"

"Oh, no. Well, I do now. Thanks."

"Just think something, and it becomes your reality."

"Good to know for next time."

Archangel Gabriel was teaching today's lecture. *"Good day, everyone. Please, take your seats. Today, you will be learning about the four main aspects of your job as a Guardian Angel: Protection, Prayer, Guidance, and Record-keeping.*

"As you learned yesterday, each new human baby is granted a Guardian Angel for their entire life. Unfortunately, most humans have not been taught how to communicate with us properly. Maybe one day it will be taught in their schools.

"Your main job is to follow them around and keep them out of danger to the best of your ability. Humans are born with free will, and they can choose to do anything that they want to. The trick is not to intervene unless it is detrimental to their well-being or conflicts with their life purpose."

Susannah thought to herself, *How will I know?*

Archangel Gabriel looked up at her and said out loud to everyone, *"You will know at the time of need. It will be programmed into you when you are granted your wings."*

We get wings! Susannah was so excited she couldn't control her thoughts.

Raadhak said, *"Shh."*

Archangel Gabriel continued, *"What you can do is protect them by sending them messages via dreams, thoughts, and signs. As an example, let's say that your charge is a seamstress, and she is frustrated with a project she is working on. You notice that she keeps trying to fix it, but she is getting it all wrong, and it is going to cost her time and money. You are allowed to intervene and make the sewing machine's bobbin get all tangled up, stopping her from continuing. You can do this as many times as needed until she finds the real problem and fixes it.*

"Or, you can protect what they are working on by sending them a message. Let's say someone is working with important papers and their coffee is too close. You can send them a message to move their cup by showing them a thought of it spilling on the documents, wrecking the papers.

"Or, they are driving, and there is an accident up ahead, and they will be late to work if they continue in the direction they are headed. So, you send them a message to turn and take a different route.

"Or, they are planning to go cliff diving into a lake the next day, but you know it could mean death for them, so you send them a dream of them diving off and killing themselves that night, in hopes they will change their plans.

"Or leave them a dime. When humans find dimes that show up in unexpected places, it is a reminder that we angels are near.

"Sometimes to protect them, you can make it rain, or they get sick. There are many creative ways that you can use to protect them.

"The only thing is. . . they have free will, and you cannot make them listen to the warning. You cannot make them do anything; you can only pray that they do.

"You are the go-between with the other angel helpers because most humans cannot communicate with us. Your guardianship includes talking to us for them. It is your responsibility to not only talk to us by keeping a record of their day-to-day activities, and each day when they are asleep, transcribe the day to be recorded in the Akashic Records, which is located in the Level of Knowledge.

"It is the Guardian Angel's responsibility to keep detailed records of every moment of that human's life. So, each and every lifetime that soul reincarnates in, through meditation, he or she will have access and the opportunity to awaken to their true potential from the information you collected.

"For example, if your charge was an artist in a past life and wished to attain the knowledge collected in that past life and bring into this lifetime, all they would have to do is go back into the past life and bring the knowledge forward into this lifetime.

"Many humans find record-keeping a vital part of their existence; they like to journal their experiences, and some people turn their writings into history books. And even the Bible shares many pages of people's important record-keeping, some of which are the best metaphysical stories out there. The Old Testament tells stories that people today think are fantasy, even though they are based on real-life experiences. In the New Testament is where

you will find the stories explaining the 'Nine Spiritual Gifts' that all humans can learn: Wisdom, Knowledge, Faith, Miracles, Healing, Prophecy, Distinguishing Spirits, and both Tongues—Interpretation and Communication.

"To sum it up, you can communicate through thoughts, dreams, feelings, and images.

"Now for the lucky Guardian Angels whose charge actually learns how to communicate with you, here is what you are allowed to do. The Celestial Laws state that for any human who wishes for a specific person, place, or thing, it is your job to help them attain it. AS LONG AS it does not interfere with their life's purpose, cause them any harm, or is detrimental to others."

Susannah thought about Lexi. *How can I get her to notice me?*

"Good question," Archangel Gabriel said. *"How do you get your charge to comprehend your messages?"*

Susannah was embarrassed. She kept forgetting that all the other spirits could hear her thoughts.

"Not all angels can feel the emotion of love in Heaven. As Guardian Angels, you have a rare capacity for love. When you decided to become a Guardian Angel, you did it because you either respect your charge and their life purpose or because you share empathy with their soul. You will develop a strong sense of duty toward your

charge, and your devotion will be based on pure love for them. "

At that moment, Susannah had an overabundant amount of love pour out of her being. She was remembering why she was becoming a Guardian Angel—because she loved her younger sister so much that she would do anything for her.

Archangel Gabriel looked up and smiled at Susannah. *"If you think you feel love for your charge now, just wait a few earthly years, you will protect them as a mother does her baby."*

Susannah smiled back.

"As Guardian Angels, you will have very close contact with Spirit, so you will have access to all the destinations, experiences, and relationships Spirit planned out for your charge on Earth. You will know what they came down to earth to learn, and you will work with your charge's teacher spirits in fulfilling their life's purpose.

"You will be able to see straight into your charge's heart. So, you will be privy to their deepest desires and most troubling fears. They can ask for your help with anything that is weighing on their heart. You will become an expert on their well-being."

This time it was Raadhak that had a thought. *I pray that my charge can get my messages.*

Archangel Gabriel looked up at him, and winked, and said, *"That is why you are a*

*Guardian Angel in training, to learn the tricks of
the trade."*

Susannah said to Raadhak, *"I wish I had
learned how to pray better on Earth; then maybe
I would be a better Guardian Angel. I sure hope
I am cut out for this. I would hate to fail my
sister."*

"You and me both." Saying this, he was
thinking about himself failing his family.

Archangel Gabriel said to the class, *"You are
taking classes on how to become a Guardian
Angel; you don't have to think you need to know
everything on day two. With that said, see you in
the next class, everyone."*

Susannah got up and walked out of class with
Raadhak.

"Raadhak, what do you do after class?"

"I go and hang out with my soul tribe."

"Oh, I didn't know we could. Good to know."

*"Remember, choose your intent and, poof,
you will be there. You're in Heaven now.
Anything is possible."*

"Oh, right. Thanks." Susannah thought of her
soul tribe, and poof, she vanished.

Raadhak smiled. *"She's getting the hang of
it."*

Chapter 74

"Have any of you been a Guardian Angel
before?" Susannah asked her family in Heaven.
   Her great-great-grandfather on her Mom's
side said, *"Yes. I have."*
   *"Do you have any tips on how to be the best
Guardian Angel?"*
   "Be patient."
   "Can you expand on that, please?"
   He walked over to her. Even though he should
have been near one hundred and ten years old,
he didn't look a day over thirty. He was dressed
in a three-piece suit with a cravat as a necktie
and a top hat. The outfit resembled something
you would have seen in the first decade of the
20th century. They dressed so formally in those
days.
   Taking her hand and giving it a kiss, he said,
*"Nice to see you again, my dear. You don't
remember me right now because your soul has*

not fully adjusted to Heaven. But we have spent years together up here. Who are you going to be a Guardian for?"

"Lexi, my sister."

"Ah, our spirited Alexandra. How is she doing?"

"Granddad, I thought you guys knew everything about everyone?"

"No, that is a myth. Once you are up here for a while, unless the new generations ask for us or think of us specifically, we do not get to keep tabs on them. How it works is like this, you know me and think about me once in a while, but if you have children, they have never met me, and unless they think of me, I cannot look into their lives."

"Oh, I will remember that next time I reincarnate. I will look you up."

"It doesn't work like that either. You will be in a different body with a different family. In that life, I might be your brother or husband or a friend of a friend. I might be a woman or a small child. Unless you say, soul tribe, you will never contact me, and then it will be indirect."

"Okay then. Nice to see you here."

"You too, my dear."

"Do you have anything you can tell me that will help me with Lexi?"

"Yes. Above all else, you are entrusted with your charge's salvation. You need to do what you can to get them to Heaven; that is your *primary goal. Therefore, your foremost purpose is to protect them from harm. Make sure they come out unscathed. However, if some sort of illness will draw them closer to God, you will allow them to become sick."*

One of Susannah's soul tribe members came over and shook her hand, stealing her away from her great grandfather. *"Archibald, your granddaughter needs to visit with us before she leaves tomorrow."*

"Am I leaving as soon as tomorrow? I don't think I am ready."

"Don't you think about that right now. You will be ready. Come, join the celebration. There is music, wine, and food. Let's enjoy and celebrate your return."

"You guys eat food?" Susannah was stunned.

"No. But we like to pretend that we are. It reminds us of being on Earth."

Chapter 75

$\mathcal{S}$usannah saved Raadhak a seat in class.

"Hi Susannah, are you excited for today's graduation?"

"To be honest, no. I don't think I am ready for the job. I want to be perfect for Lexi."

"You're a natural, Susannah. You will know exactly what to do when needed."

Archangel Raphael was teaching the class today. The other two instructors from the previous days were sitting on the sideline.

"As a Guardian Angel, your energy and powers increase every time you are able to help your charge. You never have to worry that you are stealing their life-force energy because you feed off God's love-light energy.

"Today, I am going to teach you how to help through kinesthetic messages—the sensation of feelings. You can send your charge messages by

feelings of hot, cold, and tingles. You can also use sounds, music, and books. You can whisper into their ear."

Susannah was so honored to be in the presence of so many esteemed angels.

"The last thing that you need to know before we grant you the title of Guardian Angel is how to call for us in times of need. If your charge needs healing, call on me or my troops of healing angels to come to their aid, though the same spiritual laws apply. The charge still must ask for our help, and only then can we intervene. Your job is to inform us when we are needed, and we may be able to help send subtle messages in the hope that they will hear us and ask for help.

"Archangel Raziel is there to help when your charge is requesting more knowledge.

"Archangel Azrael is there to help when your charge dies and needs help ascending into Heaven."

"Wish I knew this when I died," Susannah said to Raadhak.

"As you have met Archangel Gabriel, you know to request help when your charge needs communication skills.

"Archangel Michael is there to help when your charge needs to get rid of dark or negative spirits.

"Archangel Cassiel is there to help when your charge needs to bring balance to their body, mind, or soul.

"*And Archangel Uriel is there to help when your charge needs to bring in more love and gratitude.*

"*Many charges know of Jesus. He is asked to assist in miracles, even though most people think of him as only a healer. Archangel Hamied can also assist your charge with a miracle.*

"*There are many, many angels that can come to help. Ask, and you shall receive. Meaning, if you do not know how to help your charge, ask us for help.*

"*Repeat after me,*

> *Angel of God*
> *My guardian dear*
> *To Whom His love*
> *Commits me here*
> *Ever this day*
> *Be at my side*
> *To light and guard*
> *To rule and guide. Amen.*

"*Memorize this prayer. Whisper it into your charges ear as they are growing up.*

Another older prayer,

> *O Holy Angel,*
> *attendant of my wretched soul*
> *and of mine afflicted life,*
> *forsake me not, a sinner,*
> *neither departs from me for my*
> *inconstancy.*
> *Give no place to the evil demon to*
> *subdue me*

with the oppression of this mortal body;
but take me by my wretched and
outstretched hand,
and lead me in the way of salvation.
Yea, O holy Angel of God,
the guardian and protector
of my hapless soul and body,
forgive me all things
whatsoever wherewith I have troubled
thee,
all the days of my life,
and if I have sinned in anything this day.
Shelter me in this present night,
and keep me from every affront of the
enemy,
lest I anger God by any sin;
and intercede with the Lord on my
behalf,
that He might strengthen me in the fear
of Him,
and make me a worthy servant of His
goodness. Amen."

As Susannah was listening, she remembered a prayer that she learned in catechism class.

O Angel of God, my blessed protector,
to whose care I have been committed by
my Creator from the moment of my
birth, unite with me in thanking the
Almighty for having given me a friend
and instructor, an advocate, and a
guardian in thee. Accept, O most
charitable guide, my fervent

thanksgiving for all thou hast done for me; particularly for the charity with which thou didst undertake to accompany me through life; for the joy with which thou were filled when I was purified in the waters of Baptism; and for thy anxious solicitude in watching over the treasure of my innocence. Thou knowest the numberless graces and favors which my Creator has bestowed on me through thee, and the many dangers, both spiritual and temporal, from which thou hast preserved me. Thou knowest how often thou didst deplore my sins, animate me to repentance, and intercede with God for my pardon. Ah! Why have I so little merited a continuance of thy zealous efforts for my salvation? Why have I so often stained my soul by sin and thereby rendered myself unworthy of the presence and protection of an angel, of so pure a spirit as thou art, who never sinned? But as my ingratitude and thoughtlessness have not lessened thy charitable interest for my salvation, so neither shall they diminish my confidence in thy goodness nor prevent me from abandoning myself to thy care, since God Himself has entrusted thee with the charge of my soul. Penetrated

with sorrow for the little progress I have
made in virtue, though blessed with such
a Master, and sincerely determined to
correspond in future with thy exertions
for my salvation, I most earnestly
entreat thee, O protecting spirit, to
continue thy zealous efforts for my
eternal interest; to fortify my weakness,
to shield me from innumerable dangers
of the world and to obtain by thy
powerful prayers that my life may rather
be shortened, than that I should live to
commit a mortal sin.

Remember, O most happy spirit, that it
was one act of profound humility, and
one transport of ardent love for thy
Creator, that caused God to establish
thee forever in glory; obtain that those
virtues may be implanted in my soul and
that I may seriously endeavor to acquire
docility, obedience, gentleness and
purity of heart. Conduct me safely
through this world of sin and misery;
watch over me at the awful hour of my
death; perform for my soul the last
charitable office of thy mission, by
strengthening, encouraging, and
supporting me in the agonies of
dissolution, and then, as the angel
Raphael conducted Tobias safely to his
father, do thou, my good angel and
blessed guide, return with me to Him

who sent thee, that we may mutually bless Him, and publish His wonderful works for a happy eternity. Amen.

I wonder if Lexi remembers this prayer, Susannah thought to herself, forgetting again that everybody could hear her thoughts.

"I would like to welcome you all into the ranks of Guardian Angel. Please, put your hand over your heart and repeat after me:

"From this day forward,

"I so declare my dedication, protection, guidance, and unconditional love to, say your charge's name."

"Alexandra Elizabeth Constantine," Susannah said out loud.

"I proclaim in the power of the almighty, go forth as Guardian Angels." As Archangel Raphael finished his speech, the other angels appeared beside him, and all sent good wishes to the students who graduated.

"Susannah, I would like to give you praise," Raadhak said as he bowed to her. *"Till we meet again. By the way, nice wings!"* And he disappeared.

Susannah bowed back even though he had already left, having to re-adjust her balance to accommodate the new wings as she stood back up. To her surprise, they were heavier than she thought they would be.

She could hear Raadhak's voice say, *"Intent them to be lighter."*

"Right. Thanks! Next stop, destination Earth." And with that, she teleported to Lexi's side.

Chapter 76

That night Lexi had a dream of her sister Susannah coming to her.

"Lexi, I am disappointed in Tamara's description of Heaven."

Scared that her sister was in trouble and needed her help, Lexi cautiously said, *"Why?"*

"Because it is even better!" As Susannah was about to disappear from the dream, she reappeared and said, *"Yeah, mom is praying that you and Reverend Hawthorne get together, is there a chance?"*

"Ah, I haven't thought about it."

"He's cute and into you. You might want to think about it."

"He's into me?"

"Sis, sometimes you are so naive. Yes, he is into you. Hey Lexi, have you found out what unfinished business Hans has?"

"Who's Hans?"

"The spirit who has been hanging out in your apartment."

With that said, Lexi instantly awoke from her dream. . . *Hans.*

Epilogue

It has been a blast creating my life's work into a novel. I had many days of writing, where I was even excited to know what would happen next. As you might have figured out, I am Tamara, in the series. But truth be told, I am a bit of all the characters. I pray that my message was understood.

- The importance of having a belief before you die
- How to test a Spirit
- And to connect with Spirit, you must go within—meditate.

For the ways of how to remove dark energy, read this novel's companion manual, *Archangel Michael's Soul Retrieval Guide*.

The Art of Teaching Is the Doorway to Discovery

Writing is using an object, let's say a pen filled with ink, to scribble marks of lines and curves, forming the letters of words. The ink has no power. It can't write on its own. The words have no power. They are only created by the person writing them. The brain has no power. We have already established it is just a bunch of vibrating atoms. So, that only leaves the human soul that has the power to give the intention of a word. Only the soul's intention has the power to change.

Shift happens... Create Magic!
Constance Santego

A Letter to My Gran,

Gran, thank you so much for all the things you have done for me on Earth, the hugs, the laughs, holding me tight at night, all the cakes you helped me decorate for Brownie's, the fort we made for science class, how to fold towels, dust, the extra special birthday parties *(all my favorite foods)*, how to cook, bake bread, all the Halloween costumes you sewed, the infamous shoes you bought for me. And lastly, for telling me that the worst thing my dad could do was kill me, but not to fear because I would be in Heaven *(Thank you so MUCH for this last one because as weird as it may sound to someone else, it gave me the strength to not fear him)*.

I am glad that I was able to help you over the years with your physical pain, with being able to bring your great great-grandson over to visit (I know how much joy you get from him), to listen to your stories, and I am so glad I am able to spend time with you and that you want to spend time with me.

Now it is time to ease your fear of dying. It may happen tonight, and it could happen in a few years from now. Just know that no matter when it happens that your soul is looked after, you will be in Heaven. You will have made it through the Pearly Gates. Through the power invested in me, from this day forward, no matter if I am there or not, when the time comes, your soul will be guided to Heaven. Spiritual Angels hear my prayer, and when the time comes of my grandmother's passing, you will guide her soul back home to God, her Heavenly Father. In the name of the Father, the Son, and the Holy Spirit, Amen.

For all the grandparents, parents and children out there, know that all you have to do is believe... believe in the light and live a virtuous life!

Sequel – Celestial Language of a Soul

The blue spotlight was on her. The color from the light inspired Isabella to take a breath and play her role.

She had beautiful regal eyes painted to look like a goddess. Her hair was as dark as night and reached her shoulders with bangs that accented those sexy eyes. Her head was adorned with a web of jewels that sparkled in the light as she moved. She wore a floor-length gown that seemed enchanted, so silky smooth with a sash around her slim waist. The softest leather sandals cradled her feet.

Many called her majesty, some braved "Queen," but very few ever called her by name, Cleopatra, Queen of the Nile. She was born into an era that required strength and hope.

"We desire riches, fame, and success, but in life, most of us desire love."

Isabella was the actress playing the part of Cleopatra and knew that to excel in this movie, the audience needed to believe she was Cleopatra.

Her confidence and inner beauty shone through in all that she said, how she moved, what she wore, but it was her inner knowing that guided her toward stardom.

After filming a few hours of the dailies, as the film business likes to call the unedited footage shots for the movie, Isabella went back to her dressing room. For the last few months, her living quarters had been in a very extravagant recreational vehicle with air conditioning. Not that Isabella these days even noticed the temperature in Egypt. *I don't think I can go on like this. . . not without him.*

She had met the man of her dreams while skiing in Aspen a couple of years ago. She knew she had fallen madly in love with him the first time she laid eyes on him. She couldn't believe the chemistry they had. . .

What celestial adventure are Lexi and her friends in for this time?

Acknowledgments

My deepest gratitude to my friends and family for beta reading this debut novel and inspiring me with your responses, Linda, Diane, Gran (Anne), Colena, Roselie, Jennifer, Lynda, Sonya, Kandus, Karen, Kimerly, and Silvana.

Nick, you are the love of my life, and I am sooo grateful for having you in my life. Thank you for sharing your tears, laughter, and input for this book. I love you!

Morgan, my heart is bursting with love for your start to the editing. I grew so much as a writer seeing your edits. Thank you for choosing my son. Colten, thank you for, Maximillian.

Kathy Ver Eecke and her "Path To Getting Published" course. Who knew you needed 80,000 plus words in a novel and 240 characters in a pitch? Thank you, Kathy, for your charismatic personality; you make learning fun!

A special thank you to my dear friend, since elementary school, Jennifer Louie, for the amazing

graphics of Archangel Michael Soul Retrieval Guide, the companion manual to this novel.

Many blessings to all my past students and clients for bringing these stories to life.

My most heartfelt gratitude is for Archangel Michael and all the Celestial Beings for their love and support throughout my life, even when I forget to say thank you.

I have created this **Companion Guide** to go with this novel, ***Archangel Michael's Soul Retrieval Guide.*** For those of you who need to get rid of dark energy or who need to help a loved one to move on, this manual is for you.

Learning Outcome

When you have completed this manual and studied the concepts and techniques, you will be able to perform basic soul retrievals.

- Learn who to ask for help
- Learn the different types of attachments
- Learn how not to become a ghost
- Be able to perform a "Soul Retrieval" for yourself, friends, or loved ones
- Learn how to get into Heaven
- Learn how to remove dark energy

Footnotes &

Bibliography

Aka Cord –
https://en.wikipedia.org/wiki/Max_Freedom_Long

Archangel Michael
https://en.wikipedia.org/wiki/Michael_(archangel)
https://www.biblestudytools.com/topical-verses/archangel-michael-in-the-bible/

Celestial Languages
In my book 'Your Persona… The Mask You Wear' I have written in more detail about the four channels of communication: audio, visual, knower and feeler.

Dark Energy
It took me several months to learn what he knew, and years to perfect it. Thank you for your teachings, Reverend Weston Bailey. The knowledge of the dark side has helped me and my clients immensely.

Some spiritual problems have a darker origin. Reverend Weston Bailey of FSSH, in Sacramento, CA, is often called upon as a "last resort" when those who are suffering from demonic possession or ritual abuse have tried every other type of "orthodox" treatment. With client permission, medical doctors and therapists who refer their patients to Weston are invited to observe this often dramatic spiritual healing process.

Rev. Weston D. Bailey
https://spiritscienceheal.wordpress.com/

Edgar Cayce
www.thesearchforlifeafterdeath.com/2016/04/23/sometimes-you-dont-see-the-light-the-void-a-place-of-nothingness-in-the-afterlife/

Prayers
https://www.catholic.org/prayers/popular.php
https://www.nursebuff.com/prayers-for-the-departed/
https://connectusfund.org/12-good-prayers-for-the-recently-deceased
https://www.sympathymessageideas.com/sympathy-prayers/
https://www.learnreligions.com/dinner-prayers-and-mealtime-blessings-701303
https://connectusfund.org/10-good-opening-prayers-for-funerals
https://elegantmemorials.com/funeral-prayers

Guardian Angels
https://www.beliefnet.com/inspiration/angels/galleries/7-things-you-should-know-about-guardian-angels.aspx

Religions
https://www.theregister.co.uk/2006/10/06/the_odd_body_religion/
Saints
https://www.beliefnet.com/faiths/catholic/saints/10-influential-saints-and-their-legends.aspx
https://en.wikipedia.org/wiki/St._Germain_(Theosophy)
Science
Angel particle - https://newatlas.com/angel-particle-own-antiparticle/50579/
Atom - https://en.wikipedia.org/wiki/Atom
https://www.livescience.com/37206-atom-definition.html
Dr. Masaru Emoto. (2004) The Hidden Messages in Water.

The Author

Constance Santego is a Master Educator, Author, and Holistic Spiritual Coach. She is known for bridging the body, mind, and soul consciousness to create your dreams into reality.

Her passion is teaching self-empowerment through the many ways of improving oneself: Emotionally, Spiritually, Mentally, and Physically.

MY GOAL
To provide healing, coaching, and training that motivates, inspires, transforms, and enlightens souls through the development Sof the nine Spiritual Gifts you were born with, namely, Knowledge, Wisdom, Faith, Healing, Miracles, Prophecy, Distinguishing Spirits, and Tongues.

Constance continually strives to advance her knowledge and is currently in the process of attaining her Ph.D. and DOCTORATE in Natural and Integrative Medicine.

Also Available

Play the IKONA game and test your
Virtues and Sins

SCAN TO READ MORE:

For additional information on
Constance Santego's wide range of Motivational
Products, Coaching Sessions, Spiritual Retreats,
Live Events and Educational Programs or
To book a speaking engagement
Go to www.ConstanceSantego.ca

Follow me on:

Instagram - Constance_Santego
Facebook - constancesantego
YouTube Channel - Constance Santego
Subscribe and receive free information &
Meditations